TAURUS

REVENGE AND RETRIBUTION

ZODIAC SERIES
BOOK 3

JOHN WEGENER

Taurus
Revenge and Retribution

Written by John Wegener.
Published by Prosolin.
© Copyright 2025. All rights reserved.
© Copyright 2025 Cover designed.

1

THE CHASE

Chooli Richards knew something would test her integrity and determination to the limit one day.

But it wouldn't be today.

Today, Chooli wove gracefully between the traffic in the express airways above Arbor, the largest city on the planet Caerus and capital of the Tau Ceti star system, chasing fleeing felons in her GIA flyer, with Nascha Powers, a senior agent of the Galactic Intelligence Agency, seated beside her. She risked a glance at Nascha, who stared straight ahead, her white-knuckled hands gripping the armrest, her aureole glowing a green-red color.

Aureoles were glands that absorbed carbon dioxide from the atmosphere and photosynthesized it to top up the oxygen in their bloodstreams, a feature genetically engineered for planets with low oxygen levels. Folklore suggested the function was added by an alien race in the dim past. However, this marvelous development had the unwelcome side-effect of producing a visual display of a Cetusean's emotions, a phenomenon they spent their whole life attempting to control.

Chooli displayed an amused smile. Usually, it was Nascha flying at aggressive speeds.

"They're getting away," Nascha said.

In response, Chooli pushed the throttle forward as far as it would go, sending the flyer rushing past commuters as if they were stationary. Nascha said nothing, but Chooli sensed her nervousness, which was odd. Nascha was the one who had taught her to fly to the limit. Chooli chuckled inwardly — she would tease Nascha later about growing timid in her old age.

Chooli gained on her prey.

The fleeing craft veered from the airway and darted toward the city skyscrapers in a maneuver common to fleeing criminals. Chooli sighed. They were so predictable. She looped her flyer and spiraled after them, gaining speed as she descended closer to the ground. Once in amongst the buildings, she darted and weaved around them in the chase, gaining ground on the felons, sometimes missing a skyscraper by inches but remaining focused on her target.

"You're crazy!" Nascha said.

Chooli hazarded another glance at her. "I learned from the best."

Just as she returned her concentration to the chase, she clipped a building, sending a chunk of plasti-crete flying into the air. "Oops!"

She kept up the pursuit, steadily gaining on the other flyer until she was within capturing distance of their drive shutdown override beam. Suddenly, the felons' vehicle turned a sharp right, but they misjudged their turning radius and slammed into the structure on the far side of the gap between the avenue of buildings they had tried to enter. The vehicle spun out of control and plunged to the ground.

Chooli instantly pulled back on her flyer's throttle and followed the wrecked craft slowly as she watched the broken vehicle smash into the surface, flipping and rotating, before coming to a noisy halt. Not wanting to chance fugitives escaping, she descended and landed nearby but outside the danger zone if the vehicle exploded, which it did.

She and Nascha disembarked and ran toward the heat, searching for survivors, although Chooli knew there would be none. The stench of smoke stung her nostrils. Machine parts lay sprawled across the ground. Screaming pedestrians rushed to safety. Once they confirmed the occupants were dead, the two agents moved to a safe distance as well.

"We'd better come up with a good excuse for the Chief," Nascha said.

Chooli stared at her, baffled by her comment. "It's not our fault they smashed into a building."

"But we were in pursuit in a built-up area — our speed prompted a crash that could have killed civilians, and as the senior officer, I should have warned you when it got risky."

"What did you expect me to do? Let them go?"

Nascha sighed. "Sometimes that's the better option. Results like this always attract unwelcome press, and you know his reaction to bad press."

After the exhilaration of the chase, Chooli's emotions deflated, despondent that her boss might reprimand her for trying to do her job. Nascha saw her dejection. "Cheer up. He'll only tell us off. We're not the first ones who've had a dressing down from him."

"Maybe. Let's call it in and wrap this up before our shift finishes. I want to be home to meet Alex."

Nascha laughed. "You've got no chance of that. There'll be mountains of paperwork when we return to the office."

Her words made Chooli even more dejected.

"You're reckless and foolhardy!" Chief Inspector Shilah shouted at Chooli. "You should have called off the pursuit and commed for backup."

Chooli stood at attention, staring straight ahead. Nausea threatened to migrate to her throat. She managed to contain it where it belonged, but she couldn't stop a bead of sweat from traveling down her cheek as she gulped. She hoped Shilah hadn't noticed it. He would certainly have noticed her ashen gray aureola.

He sighed and said more quietly, "You are better than that."

"I didn't want them to get away, sir."

"No one does. But there's a right way and a wrong way. As it stands, we have a massive bill for the damage caused. We're lucky innocent civilians weren't killed. Didn't Nascha warn you off?"

Fear gripped Chooli's chest tighter. The last thing she wanted was to drag Nascha into trouble. "I didn't listen, sir. I thought we could safely apprehend them."

"In that case, I have no choice but to suspend you for two weeks. I will note it in your personnel file, too."

Chooli stared at him in shock but said nothing. Not only would the incident blemish her record, but it would also dishonor her family. How would she tell her parents of her punishment? How would she face Alex? She hoped her dressing down was complete, allowing her to escape to somewhere private to mull over her misfortune.

"Dismissed. And reflect on your mistake. I don't want to see your face for two weeks."

Chooli saluted and marched from the Chief Inspector's office, relieved he had not fired her and glad the dressing down was over.

She headed for her desk, conscious of everybody's eyes on her as she passed them. Too embarrassed to raise her head, she endured the agony silently, quietly packing her belongings and readying herself to leave.

"Are you OK?" Nascha asked.

Chooli couldn't raise her eyes for fear of what might happen. She shook her head.

"What happened in there?"

"I have been suspended for two weeks."

"What? Why hasn't he called me? If anyone gets suspended, it should be me. Look, I'll go straighten this out."

Fear piled on top of her grief. Chooli was terrified of the Chief

Inspector's reaction if he discovered she had lied to him too. "No! Let it go. I deserve what I got. Just leave it."

"Why? Why should he punish you for my failure to stop you from continuing the pursuit?"

"I said, leave it go." Chooli ground the words from her mouth.

Nascha stepped back in shock. "If you insist. Tell me if you need anything in the meantime." She turned and headed to her office, but not before giving Chooli another uncertain glance.

Chooli watched her leave, castigating herself for her outburst. Nascha didn't deserve that. To prevent more contact with her colleagues, she hurried outside to her AGrav, where she sat and shook until she could regain control enough for the trip home.

———

S he was still frozen in shock when she opened the door to their apartment. Alex was already there and sitting in the living room. He looked up at her and smiled a welcome.

She felt her lips tremble and fought back tears before rushing to the bedroom and privacy, converting Alex's smile to confusion. Throwing herself onto the bed, face first, she released the pent-up tears and grief in one burst, unable to contain them any longer.

The door opened after a few minutes. Footsteps approached the bed, and it swayed as Alex sat. He stroked her hair. "What's wrong?"

"Leave me alone," Chooli blurted out between sobs.

"Why?" His tone crooned to her. "No point in keeping it to yourself. You'll have to tell me eventually, so save yourself all this heartache."

He was right, but Chooli couldn't find it within herself to tell him of her punishment. After several more sobs, however, she turned onto her side, wiped the tears from her cheeks, and said bluntly, "Shilah suspended me for two weeks."

A shocked expression passed across Alex's face, followed by a smirk of amusement. "Is that it?"

Chooli punched him. "Don't make fun of me — this is serious."

Alex's tone immediately became consoling. "I'm not making fun of you. It's nothing to make light of, but it's not as serious as you think. Do you know how often Commissioner Harris suspended me — and for even longer?"

"No, you haven't ever been suspended."

"Yes, I have. Just ask him."

Chooli sniffed. "Really?"

Alex nodded. "And it didn't taint my record. Not much, anyway. What made Shilah suspend you?"

Chooli explained the day's events.

"Nascha should take the wrap. She shouldn't have let you continue."

"No, it's my fault. And don't raise it with anyone."

Alex studied her, suspicious. "You didn't tell the Chief Inspector about Nascha, did you?"

Chooli shook her head. "And don't you say anything. It's terrible enough I'm in trouble."

"I'd give you two more weeks for lying."

Chooli started to protest.

"OK, I won't say anything. But this will get out, eventually. What if Nascha lets it slip one day? You're forcing her to lie, too, you know. One lesson you must learn is never to lie even for a seemingly good reason. It will catch up with you in the end."

A wan smile crossed Chooli's face. "Is that said from experience?"

He looked pensive for a moment before saying lightly, "Sure is." His expression changed. "Now, what can I do to distract you from your problems for five minutes?" he said as he drew closer to her.

"What will I do at home for two weeks?" Chooli got out before Alex swept her away with intent.

A REVELATION

Vito Riva surveyed his minions as they sat around the enormous conference table with him on Xi Boötis, the planet Vito had made his home. The high-backed uphol-stered chairs smelled of expensive leather. The oak table came from Earth itself and was French polished in the traditional fashion.

They sat pensive and patient, waiting for Vito to reveal his agenda for the meeting. Despite their outward passivity, Vito knew every one of them would slaughter him without remorse the first chance they got to make his throne their own. Hence, a small army of bodyguards followed him wherever he went.

He noticed his production manager, Carlos, was frowning heav-ily; his chubby, circular, acne-pocked face looked disturbed and uncertain.

"Carlos," Vito said in a gentle, soothing tone.

"Yes, sir?"

"Our chimera stardust production seems to have declined over the past month."

Carlos gulped. A bead of sweat appeared above his left eyebrow as he realized the spotlight was on him. "Crystal Boramide is scarce, sir. We struggle to get our feedstock on time from our supplier, even when we lean on him. The deposit is running out, and they supply the electronics equipment manufacturers before us. You know it has such tight regulation." Carlos stared at Vito, fearing his reaction.

"I see." Vito sat chewing his lip as he absorbed Carlos' words. Despite his annoyance, he knew Carlos could be correct — in which case, they needed to tread lightly. He paid enough people to maintain a semblance of legitimacy for their Crystal Boramide needs and couldn't afford to get their license revoked. Still, a warning was called for. "Poor performance disappoints me, Carlos. I'll give you another month to improve. Give me a reason not to replace you."

"Yes, sir. Thank you, sir."

Vito glanced at his chief enforcer towering next to him, his stolid expression giving no hint of what his boss had communicated to him with his eyes. But Vito knew he understood his meaning. One month was all Carlos would get.

"Sir," Carlos said.

He refocused on Carlos, surprised he had the nerve to speak out of turn. "Yes?" Vito smiled a thin-lipped smile when he saw how nervous Carlos was.

"I've heard a rumor about a new crystal boramide deposit. Maybe you could acquire it?"

The news surprised Vito and almost made him give an uncharacteristic start. He stared at Carlos. *He's not as dumb as he looks.* Recovering his usual poise, he asked, "Where?"

"On Sirius. The mine's owned by a Cetusian businessman called Ahiga Powers from Caerus."

He's surprising me more by the second. "I know that name well. He's the son of that murdered ambassador." Vito pondered the news before returning to the meeting. "Have you approached him on the matter?"

"No, sir, not without your approval. We should move fast, though, before he progresses too far in developing the mine. Once he has it operational, regulations will tie up the miners' options, like the rest of them."

Vito nodded. Carlos might have earned himself a longer reprieve than one month.

After considering whether to continue with the meeting, which was just routine business anyway, he decided against it. "That's all. Go make me more money."

His minions filed out of the room, but Vito's bodyguards stayed. Vito sat staring at the closed door. Contemplating. Scheming. He wondered how difficult it would be to buy the deposit from Ahiga. Owning it would certainly make his business dealings easier and remove the supply headache he constantly encountered.

He turned to his enforcer. "Find out everything you can about Ahiga. I want to know when he takes a shit; everything. ...And Carlos, give him a bit more slack."

The enforcer nodded.

Satisfied his instructions were understood, Vito stood and started for the door. The effort strained his obese frame, making him break into a pant. He reminded himself to start the reducing diet his physician was repeatedly urging him to do.

3

A CONFESSION

C hooli decided she should take advantage of the free time afforded by her suspension to visit her parents and confess her shameful misdemeanor before they heard of it from some other source. Alex did not accompany her because he had an important work meeting to attend in Arbor. Besides, she didn't want him there to witness her parents' reaction to her shame.

She smiled at the thought of Alex's strong features and gentle touch. His love soaked into her. The memory of their time on Franconia returned, causing her thoughts to sour momentarily. The physical and psychological wounds inflicted on her there by The Reaper were still healing, the scars slowly fading, but Alex's love was helping her cope with the worst of her depression and pain.

She cruised over the mountainous countryside in her AGrav vehicle until her childhood village came into view, admiring the utilitarian but valuable houses lined up along the streets like a ticker-tape crowd waiting for a special guest. Pity it was just her coming to scandalize her family. She sighed, the load of her news weighing on her as she descended to the familiar parking bay in front of her childhood home.

While still a distance from the house, the front door swung open, and her mother, Haseya, emerged smiling with arms outstretched and her aureole registering surprised delight.

"Chooli! What a wonderful surprise." She rushed to her daughter and hugged her, then looked past her, eyebrows raised, and asked, "No Alex?"

Chooli grinned, warmed by her mother's love and enthusiasm. "No. He's away working. I had spare time, so I came to visit. I haven't seen you both for ages."

Haseya stopped. Her expression became serious as she grabbed Chooli's arm. "You fought?"

The question made Chooli giggle. "No, we haven't fought."

"What then? Are you pregnant?" Haseya gripped Chooli's arm with more pressure and a hopeful smile.

Chooli shook her head. "No, I'm not pregnant either."

Her mother frowned, releasing her grip, her elation deflated. "What then?"

Chooli outwardly sighed, but her stomach tightened into knots. "Can't I just come and visit my parents? Anyway, are you going to invite me inside?"

"Of course. Come in, and I'll make tea for us."

"Yes, thanks. Where's Papa?"

"He's out somewhere. He never tells me where he's going. But he'll be back soon." Chooli smiled to herself. She knew her father would have mentioned where he was going, but her mother rarely listened to seemingly trivial details.

They strolled into the house and into the kitchen, where Haseya started preparing a brew of Caerus spice tea, Chooli's favorite. The aroma transported her back to her younger years when she would help her mother prepare the meals, the fragrance of the herbs and spices filling the entire house. Those were simpler days without worry and few responsibilities.

Once the tea began brewing, mother and daughter headed into the living room, where they sat on soft cloth-covered sofas and talked.

Chooli was careful to avoid her most pressing topic until her father was present. She didn't want to repeat herself. Nor did she want him receiving whispers of the news from any second-hand source, even if it was her mother.

The front door opened and closed.

"That smells good," Naalnish called, his voice carrying through from the hallway.

"We're in here," Haseya called back.

"What do you mean, w—," Naalnish said as he appeared in the living room doorway and stopped in his tracks at the sight of his daughter. "What are you doing here?"

Chooli grinned and stood. "Surprise!" She strode over to him and hugged him. He reciprocated, his aureole registering his delight at seeing his daughter so unexpectedly.

Once they parted, he held her at arm's length and studied her. "You look different. Are you pregnant?"

"That's what I asked," Haseya said.

Chooli huffed and raised her eyes to the heavens. "No, I'm not pregnant. Can't I come and see my Mama and Papa for no reason?"

"Of course you can. It's just … unusual."

"Tea?" Haseya asked Naalnish as she rose from her armchair.

"Yes, please."

Haseya left the room, much to Chooli's chagrin. She had just worked up the courage to tell them her news.

"So," Naalnish said as he headed toward his favorite armchair. "What's Alex up to?"

"He's tending to more business for Ahiga. He's always attending to business for Ahiga."

"Yes, that man certainly keeps Alex busy. I suppose your busy job means you don't notice it too much."

Chooli cringed inside. Trust him to bring work up with her so soon.

"Why aren't you working now?" her father continued. "Have they given you a few days off?"

She knew she couldn't delay her news any longer.

Just then, Haseya walked back with Naalnish's tea. She gave it to her husband and settled in her chair again, both their aureoles registering contentment at having their daughter home.

Relieved her mother had returned, Chooli decided she had to deliver her news then or never — and never wasn't an option. Doing what she could to stop her aureole from revealing her tumultuous feelings, she lowered her gaze and said, with as much casualness as she could muster, "I'm having some unscheduled time off work."

"That's unusual, isn't it?" Naalnish asked, a small smile accompanying the words. "Have the criminals gone on strike?"

Chooli shook her head. "I've shamed our family."

"What!" both parents exclaimed together. Their aureoles were now clouded, and Haseya spilled her cup of tea.

"How?" Naalnish wanted to know.

Chooli related the chain of events to them, not daring to raise her eyes to her father's face.

When she finished, Naalnish, his aureole now a dark shade of gray, said, "I see." He stood and left the room.

Chooli bit hard on her bottom lip, determined not to cry.

Her mother came to her side and rubbed her shoulder. "I'm sure you had good reason to do what you did." The sympathy only made it harder for Chooli not to give way to her feelings.

"But it was against procedure. I should have known better."

"We all make mistakes."

Chooli shook her head. "Good agents don't make mistakes."

"Nonsense!" said her mother.

"Chooli!" Naalnish shouted from the backyard.

Mother and daughter glanced at each other.

"You'd better go," Haseya advised.

Chooli's muscles wouldn't work. She couldn't raise herself from her chair. When she did, they wobbled until they found the means to walk again. She trudged toward the back door and to her father. He sat in a seat by the outdoor table they often used for meals when the weather was balmy. Papa stared at her, but not with the furious intensity she was expecting.

"Sit," he invited.

"I'm so sorry, Papa."

"Don't speak."

Chooli sat and remained silent, eyes lowered and waiting for her reprimand.

"What you said disappoints me," he began.

His words were disapproving, but his tone was affectionate — and not what she'd expected. It confused her, so she risked a glance at his face. Her confusion deepened. He wasn't displaying the reproachful glare he usually did in these situations, and his aureole reflected calm.

"But you haven't shamed yourself or us," he continued.

"But—"

Naalnish held his finger up to silence her. "Yes, you disappoint me, but not for the reason you think. You said Nascha was with you, didn't you?"

Chooli nodded.

"They didn't suspend her?"

She shook her head.

"Why not? She's the senior agent. Calling the chase off was her responsibility."

Heat radiated from Chooli's face, and she knew her aureole had lit up like a beacon. She could never discipline her aureole around her father. "I told the Chief Inspector that she did and that I didn't listen. I didn't want to get her into trouble. What was the point of us both being in trouble?"

"In other words, you lied."

She nodded, lowering her eyes again.

"As I thought. That's what disappoints me, not the incident."

Chooli shot her eyes back up, struggling to stop a tear from escaping her left tear duct.

Naalnish leaned toward her. "We all make mistakes. It shouldn't have happened, but it did. Ultimately, calling off the chase is as much to prevent unpleasant publicity as for public safety … in my opinion. But lying was wrong. It did nothing for your cause. I thought I had raised you better than that." He sighed. "You always had a propensity to protect your friends from sharing any blame for your mischief. I see you haven't learned your lesson yet. What did Alex say about it?"

"He said it was wrong, too. And if the Chief ever discovers it, I'll be in bigger trouble. We should never lie, he says, even for what we think is a good reason."

"That's good advice. I couldn't have said it better myself."

Before Chooli could react, Naalnish extended his hands and held hers, something he had never done before. He smiled at her. "You're too old to smack. And you can never shame our family. I know where your heart is, and it will never waver from what your mother and I taught you."

Chooli stared at her father, her chest tight with emotion. "Papa," she murmured and gave way to tears, but tears of relief rather than grief. Her father's love had overwhelmed her.

Naalnish stood and raised her, too. He pulled her close, so she cried on his chest; he was too tall for her to cry on his shoulder. After a minute, she pulled away and wiped her face as she sniffed. "Papa—"

He raised his finger to silence her. "I know."

Chooli gave a half-sobbing giggle. "Alex said I shouldn't worry about the suspension. It's no big deal. He's had plenty in his career."

"Has he, now?"

She nodded.

"I'll need to give him a talking to when I see him next."

She gave him a playful slap on the arm. "Don't."

He grinned. "Let's go inside. You can clean yourself up and tell us whatever else you've been doing."

Chooli nodded, and they entered the house to join Haseya, their hearts and minds united and their aureoles registering harmony.

She ended up staying overnight and returning to Arbor the next day. She wondered what she would do with herself for the rest of her suspension.

4

A TENSE MEETING

Alex Warner frowned as he entered the plush executive conference room in the Arbor office of Powers Enterprises on Caerus. He had little inclination to meet with the arriving guests despite his boss' curiosity about the purpose of the meeting. Alex was sure nothing good could come from talking with the likes of Vito Riva.

He found his favorite chair and sat, continuing to attend to the paperwork on his tablet while waiting for the others to arrive. Several minutes passed before Ahiga entered. Alex looked up and nodded. Ahiga reciprocated and sat next to him. As well as being employer–employee, the two men were friends.

"We shouldn't be meeting with these guys, Ahiga," Alex said.

Ahiga shrugged. "He's an entrepreneur, Alex, just like me."

"He's not."

The conference room door opened, and the secretary ushered Vito Riva inside, followed by his chief enforcer and two other body-guards. Both Alex and Ahiga stood and rounded the table, shaking hands with Vito and voicing a few pleasantries before returning to their seats. Vito found a seat opposite them, but his entourage remained standing behind him against the wall.

"Will you need any refreshments?" the secretary asked.

"No, thank you," Ahiga said to her. "I'll call you if we want anything."

The secretary nodded and left, closing the door behind her.

"It is good of you to see me at such short notice," Vito began, smiling urbanely.

"Not at all," Ahiga replied. "My secretary surprised me when she mentioned you wanted to meet with me, but I confess I'm intrigued. We don't move in the same circles."

Vito gave a thin smile. His eyes were alert and wary. "No, we don't."

"So, how may I help you?"

Vito placed his arms on the table and steepled his fingers. "I understand you've made a mineral discovery on Sirius."

Ahiga frowned. "I'm not sure where you received your information, but you seem to have an excellent source. It's not public knowledge yet — supposedly. We're still assessing the deposit's size and viability."

Alex looked on, suspicious. Ahiga was right. They had deliberately cloaked the finding in secrecy because of the type of mineral discovered. Only three people knew: Mine Manager Kansas Salter, Ahiga, and himself as Ahiga's Risk and Security Director. So, how had Vito received his information? Was there a leak in the organization?

Vito's thin smile broadened. "That is not important."

"So, you know what the deposit is?"

Vito nodded. "We also produce high-end electronics that use crystal boramide. Sourcing feedstock is proving difficult at present. This has led us to contemplate owning a source of the mineral ourselves. Cut out the middleman, so to speak."

"It's strictly regulated."

"Certainly."

Ahiga glanced at Alex before returning his attention to Vito. "I'm not in a position to sell the mining rights to anyone at present."

Vito's smile dimmed. "I don't understand."

"We are still assessing the deposit. It's registered with the authorities. So, any change of ownership would need excessive paperwork. Besides, until I confirm what I have and its profitability, I'm reluctant to rid myself of what could be a lucrative resource."

"I see." Vito turned and glanced at his enforcer. He faced Ahiga again. "I'm sure we could come to an arrangement that benefits both parties."

Alex sensed the conversation's direction and didn't like it. It was heading the wrong way, as he feared. He hadn't advised Ahiga why Vito might be so interested in the mineral before the meeting, but he needed to tell him now. Tapping Ahiga on the arm, he gestured for them to turn away from the others. He whispered. "This material is a precursor for chimera stardust. Rumor is Vito is the major supplier of the drug."

Ahiga stared at him and nodded before facing Vito again.

"There is no point at present. The mine is not for sale."

Vito's smile broadened again, although with a sinister undertone. "Everything has its price."

"Some things are priceless."

Vito's smile vanished, and his eyes focused on Alex. "Have we met before?"

"I doubt it," Alex said. "We move in different circles."

"We have met before. At least, I'm sure one of my associates has met you before. I don't take kindly to having my business interrupted."

"Is that a threat?"

"Just years of experience." Vito returned his attention to Ahiga. "Are you sure we can't negotiate?"

"I am sure."

"I have not wasted my time. We will meet again and discuss this further. In the meantime, I wish you both a healthy future."

Vito removed a napkin from his pocket and wiped his brow where perspiration had accumulated. Alex noticed a slight flush in his complexion and a frown of frustration. Obviously, Vito was unaccustomed to having someone refuse to give him what he wanted. He looked up at Vito's enforcer and wondered whether they would receive any problem from that quarter in the next few minutes. But before he could decide on a defensive strategy, Vito rose from his chair and tidied his suit, which barely fit his bulky frame. He turned to his enforcer and stared at him as if relaying a predetermined message.

Vito returned his attention to Ahiga. "Have a pleasant day. I am ready to leave."

Ahiga contacted his secretary, who came and escorted Vito and his entourage from the office. She closed the door behind Alex and Ahiga when they left.

"What was that about?" Ahiga asked Alex.

"I'm not sure. He definitely issued a veiled threat. He believes I am the source of your reluctance to sell."

"To be honest, I considered exploring avenues for negotiation before you mentioned chimera stardust. Too many maintenance mechanics on the crew servicing spaceships where I worked before inheriting my father's business were on it. Once you're hooked, you can't get off, and finding a supply becomes an obsession until it destroys you."

"We need to be careful. Vito is powerful. He's also ruthless. If he acts, he will come after me first."

"That's what he implied." Ahiga nodded in agreement.

"In the meantime, how did he discover the source on Sirius?"

"Yes. That was one of my most confidential pieces of information." Ahiga rubbed his chin and thought. He glanced at Alex. "It might be prudent for you to visit the mine and ask some questions. It's unacceptable to have intelligence leaked to the open market before I determine my options."

Alex nodded. He agreed with Ahiga. However, he wasn't happy

at having to travel off-world again after just returning home. His time away was increasing, preventing him from seeing Chooli as much as he wanted. He sighed. "If you insist."

"I know this encroaches on your time with Chooli, but it's important."

"That's what you pay me for. I'll just have to break the news to Chooli gently."

"It's not urgent. Spend a little time at home first."

"Are you sure?"

"I'm sure. An unhappy Chooli means an unhappy Mei, and I can't have that. She isn't pleasant when she's upset with me."

Alex laughed. "I understand."

5

ALEX VISITS THE SIRIUS MINE

Alex woke to the sound of his comm buzzing. He looked at the clock. Two thirty in the morning. Who would call him at that hour? He rubbed the sleep from his eyes and answered the call. "Yes?"

"Sorry to wake you," Ahiga said, his own voice sounding sleepy. "But there's been an explosion at the crystal boramide mine on Sirius."

The mention of the Sirius mine jarred Alex to instant awareness, a talent he had picked up in his years in law enforcement. "Oh. You thinking what I'm thinking?"

"What? Riva's behind this?"

"Could be a coincidence. Crystal boramide is volatile, isn't it?"

"Yeah, but we take special precautions to prevent any accidents."

And people can circumvent special precautions if they know what they're doing, Alex thought.

"You called me at 2:30 in the morning to tell me that?"

"No. I mean, yes. But I need you there now. We must identify the cause before we lose evidence in the clean-up. Was it an accident or

TAURUS 23

sabotage? And if there's a leak, which is looking likely, we need to know who's leaking."

"And it can't wait a few hours?"

Ahiga produced a cheeky grin over the video feed. "I thought since I'm up, I may as well wake you, too."

"Wait till I see you next. I might do a bit of sabotage myself. Better still, I'll get Chooli to sort you out."

Ahiga displayed a mock shocked expression. "Please don't. Anything but her wrath."

"I heard that," Chooli mumbled, half asleep beside Alex.

"So, will you go straight away?" Ahiga asked.

"Yeah, OK," Alex said. He didn't want to agree, but he had little choice.

After disconnecting the link, he turned to Chooli. "I presume you heard most of that."

"Explosion. Mine. You've got to go. Now get up and let me sleep." Chooli's tone was grumpy.

"Don't I get a cuddle first?" Alex said, implying she'd hurt his feelings.

"No." She rolled over.

Alex snuggled back into bed and attempted to cuddle her anyway. After unconvincing resistance, she rolled back over to surrender. "You're incorrigible."

"I know."

They were intimate for a time before Alex sighed and stumbled from the soft, warm bed, grumbling over Ahiga's unreasonable demands. Then again, if Riva was behind the explosion, perhaps they weren't unreasonable.

lex arrived at the Sirius mine two days later. The site was a mess, even discounting the destruction the explosion had caused. Given the mine's recent development, most struc-

tures were still temporary and of questionable stability. The wind could blow some buildings over, in Alex's opinion. Still, the workers had made progress in establishing a long-term presence. The makings of an administration block and mining storage sheds stood firmly in place. It showed a definite commitment to the mine, reflecting the knowledge of its profitability well into the future. He pushed the door into the site establishment office, which the workers still used as their base until the permanent buildings were ready for occupancy.

He peered into the dark interior. Compared to the blazing sunlight where he currently stood, it was pitch black, but lighting appeared suspended from the ceiling once his eyes adjusted. The place looked deserted.

"Hello? Anyone here?" Alex called.

A partition stood in the far corner. Without notice, a head popped out from behind it. The head belonged to a male Earth-human. "Oh. Didn't hear you enter. Alex Warner?"

"Yes."

"Welcome." The man stood and rounded the edge of the partition, striding toward him. He was tall and thin, with a receding black hairline. "Kansas Salter, Mine Manager." He extended his hand.

Alex shook it.

"Come. Take a seat — if you can find an unbroken one not covered in grime."

Alex scanned the office for a suitable chair, but after reviewing his choices, he remained standing. Instead, he pushed back bits and pieces littering a desk and brushed the surface before leaning against it. "I'm here to discuss the explosion."

"Yes, Ahiga told me he was sending you. There's nothing to add to my report, I'm afraid, but I'm happy to go through it with you."

"Good." Alex eyed him for several seconds before continuing. "How did it happen? What chain of events caused it?"

Kansas grabbed a chair, wiped it with a rag, and sat. He had to hold his head backward to meet Alex's eyes. "We were preparing to blast a sample of material from the seam. But the explosives expert over-packed the charge. When we detonated it, part of the ore exploded with it. It can happen, but rarely. The concentration is too low for the crystal boramide reaction to generate enough energy to sustain it. But this vein is exceptionally rich. You probably saw the result as you approached the site. The place is a mess."

"Didn't you sample the deposit first? Tailor the charge to prevent that?"

"Should have. The explosives expert made a mistake."

"Expensive mistake."

"Sure is. We'll take weeks to clean it up before we can continue."

Alex processed what Kansas had told him so far. "Where is this expert now?"

"Good question. He's either under the rubble or has done a runner for being a fool. He's a new guy. Only just arrived."

Alex's eyebrows rose when he heard the guy was new. "What happened to the last one?"

"He left suddenly. Said he had a better offer elsewhere." Kansas rubbed the back of his neck and rotated it as if it was sore from holding his head at an awkward angle. He stood and rested on a desk opposite Alex.

The circumstances of the previous expert leaving and a new one arriving soon after they met with Riva was suspicious. "Where did this new guy come from?"

"Dravo Chinko from Procyon recommended him. Don't know where he found him."

"But you checked his credentials?"

"Dravo recommended him, which was good enough for me. He wouldn't have suggested a guy he thought was incompetent, especially with crystal boramide. He knows its volatility."

Was Kansas negligent? Could he be the leak? Alex couldn't tell. He could understand him taking Dravo's word for it. Mining crystal boramide was a specialty. The people involved ran a tight fraternity with a busy network. He had heard nothing against Salter. Regardless, it wouldn't solve the mystery of the explosion now. "And you know nothing else about this guy?"

Kansas shook his head. "Sorry."

"Have you looked for him?"

"We did a head count and searched the rubble in reasonable detail. No scattered body parts anywhere. I'd say he ran. He wasn't saving his job here either way."

Alex sighed. He was hoping to return to Caerus, but fate had other ideas. "Looks like I'm off to Procyon, then."

"Lucky you. Wish I was joining you. Procyon might not be home, but it has a nightlife. Sirius is dull and lonely."

Alex knew Ahiga's workforce fell over each other for a placement to Procyon because it was an extensively settled planet compared to Sirius. But he got the impression Kansas might be more into the nightlife than some.

With a grin, Alex said, "Don't you enjoy the camp you have here?" The mine project team had established a camp on-site for its workers since the mine was so isolated. It removed the commuting time they would otherwise spend each day going to and from the city.

Kansas huffed. "Better than nothing, I guess, but not a patch on a proper nightlife."

"Surely, you get to the big smoke sometimes?"

"Sure — once every few weeks ... for a night. Can't do much in one night."

"You might get lucky with the next job."

Kansas gave him a dagger-eyed glare.

Alex laughed.

The conversation paused while Alex gathered his thoughts. "Anything else?"

Kansas rubbed his chin before answering. "No. That's all I can tell you."

"How long until you're running again?"

"Two, maybe three weeks."

Alex straightened his stance. "I'll let you get started."

"You don't want to give us a hand?"

"Not on your life. Too dirty for me."

"You office boys are all the same."

"You enjoy it."

Kansas tried to find something non-threatening to throw at him, but Alex made a quick exit while he could. Frustrated, he returned to the capital and booked immediate passage to Procyon. Dravo had questions to answer. He also needed to examine Salter more closely. He didn't think he had been bought, but he may have inadvertently let something slip to one of Riva's people on one of those coveted trips to the capital, sparking Riva's interest in the mine.

ENTER RAMIRA

Ramira Lopez sauntered into Vito's office on Xi Boötis as if she didn't have a care in the world, but inside she was seething. He had promised to let her retire in peace. Still, she knew better than to refuse a command to visit.

Vito sat in his usual high-backed leather seat of power, his ever-present bodyguards standing to attention nearby. When she glanced behind her, she noticed another thug at the door, preventing any premature departures. She was conscious of his eyes following her movement through the room. No chair stood in front of his desk — another power ploy — but one stood next to the wall by a window on her left. She moved to get it.

"Stay where you are!" Vito commanded.

Ramira froze for a moment, then turned and glared at him. She wanted to spit at him for daring to order her around like some worthless cur, but she could see he was in one of his dangerous moods. Her keen sense of self-preservation decided there was no choice but to play his game. Otherwise, he would pile more brutal burdens on her than she was about to bear anyway. She sighed and returned to the front of his desk, maintaining a disinterested posture.

"What do you want, Vito?"

Vito steepled his fingers as he studied her and tapped two forefingers on his chin. "I have a job for you, m'dear."

"You retired me, remember!"

"I'm bringing you out of retirement. It suits your specialty. Besides, you need to finish the job, so to speak."

Intrigued despite herself, Ramira asked, "Finish what job?"

"Alex Warner."

She stiffened at hearing that person's name. She had never wanted to hear it again, not after the suffering he had inflicted on her. Still, Vito was right: he had to pay.

"What about him?"

"He's become a pest. I need him distracted. And I can't think of a better person to distract him. You two get along so well."

"*Got. Got* along well — before he screwed me. I'll kill him if I ever see him again."

Vito looked amused. "You might get the opportunity, though I would prefer it if you didn't kill him immediately."

"What type of distraction are you looking for?" Ramira was starting to warm to Vito's request, although she didn't kid herself that it was anything less than a demand.

"No offense, but you can't use your looks. He may not be interested anymore — he's got some new bitch to sniff. A Cetusean at that. And he's married her, something you never managed. I suggest you play on his emotions and sense of chivalry instead. He was always a big softie. Say your child needs rescuing from bad, nasty Vito — or something like that."

The thought of Alex married infuriated her. He was hers, always. But the thought of herself with a child made her laugh. "Ha! That's a good one."

"One that should prove effective on someone as sentimental as Alex, don't you think?"

Ramira mused and then nodded. She could play the distraught

mother well enough. "OK, then. But I'm finished for good after that, promise?"

"Successfully fulfill your task, and you'll never hear from me again."

"That's what you said last time. What's your goal in all this, anyway?"

"A crystal boramide mine owned by that annoying, sanctimonious trillionaire Ahiga, and Alex is in the way. I can't just kill him to get it, though. I need him alive as a bargaining chip. Hence, your part. Play it well. You can toy with him if you like, provided you eventually bring him to me. After he has served his purpose, you can do whatever you like with him — and then get on with your life in peace."

"How do I find him?"

"He's about to arrive on Procyon to investigate a little event I orchestrated at Ahiga's mine recently. Use your brains. Now leave and get to work." Vito waved her away.

Ramira obediently turned and left, her head already overflowing with schemes of how to tackle her assignment.

ALEX VISITS PROCYON

A lex smelled the refined scent of Procyon as soon as he entered the spaceport terminal. Every surface was clean; anything metallic gleamed. The ambiance whispered: *You're welcome if you have money.* Anyone could get anything with money on Procyon — provided they were not Cetusean. *Chooli would hate it here,* he thought. Of all the star systems in the Confederation, Procyon displayed the most prejudice toward Cetuseans, even worse than on Delta Pavonis, now that it had amended its discriminatory laws.

He leased a vehicle and headed toward the metropolis in the distance, its towering skyscrapers emphasizing the wealth generated by the planet. After a half hour in the airway, he descended to his usual hotel, the Procyon Imperial. Being already late afternoon, there was no point in contacting Dravo before morning.

Once checked in and settled in his room, he grabbed a Franconian brandy from the bar, slumped into the soft cushioned armchair, rested his head backward, and closed his eyes. The exhausting day of travel drained from him before he opened his eyes again and sipped his drink. The potential connection between Vito Riva's visit and the new explosives expert left a sour taste in his mouth. There was one, but he couldn't connect the wormholes yet. Alex sighed and told himself, 'No point in fretting about it until I talk to Dravo.' He emptied his glass, had dinner, and retired to bed, hoping all was well with Chooli.

The next morning, he headed to the mine Ahiga owned, several hours from the capital. Once he became airborne and keyed his destination into the navigation system, he settled back and paged through reports to catch up on his administrative security duties for Ahiga. Nothing much had drawn his attention before the flyer landed on the parking bay at the site.

The ugliness of the bare ground screamed at him when he exited the vehicle. He wondered if the wealth the mine generated compensated for the raping of the planet's ecosystem. But Ahiga always rehabilitated the landscape when they exhausted the deposit. His attention returned to the reason for his visit, so he headed for the main office next to the landing pad and entered it.

A young female receptionist glanced up from her work when the door opened. She beamed with a full-lipped mouth, a round face, and black bob-styled hair. Alex preferred longer hair, but it didn't matter anymore, anyway. He approached her desk and smiled back at her.

"Is Mr. Dravo Chinko in?"

She stared at him. "Do you have an appointment, sir?" Her tone implied an appointment was necessary.

Alex's smile widened as he used all his charm. "No. But I thought Mr. Chinko would see me. I'm Alex Warner, Ahiga Powers' Risk and Security Director."

It worked. Her cheeks blushed. "Yes, he is. Just one moment, Mr. Warner, while I tell him you're here."

Alex nodded and inspected the reception decor while he waited. These offices were the opposite of those on Sirius — clean, functional, and organized. The woman talked on the office comm in a hushed voice. Moments later, a door behind her opened, and a massive man walked through it.

"Alex, my good friend," he said in a rich Slavic accent.

Alex couldn't fathom why he was a good friend. He had never seen him before today. But he smiled and extended his hand. "Dravo?"

"Yes, yes. Come this way." He gestured for Alex to enter his office. "Bring coffee," he told the receptionist.

Alex obliged and passed through to Dravo's office. It was huge. Two monstrous sofas hugged the far wall from the desk, so he headed to the furthest one and sat on it, waiting for Dravo to sit on the other. Dravo muttered some more commands at the receptionist before turning his attention back to Alex. He came over and sat, leaving the door open.

In no hurry, Alex waited for Dravo to open the conversation. He was interested in the approach the man would take. The coffee came moments later, the fresh aroma filling the office as soon as it passed the threshold. Now that he saw all of her, Alex realized the receptionist was attractive. He glanced at Dravo. A quick judgment flashed through his mind before he controlled his thoughts again.

"Thank you," Dravo said to her once she poured coffee for each of them.

"You're welcome, Papa," the receptionist said, smiling before she left.

Alex sighed inside, relieved he had cleared up the relationship between the two before he embarrassed himself. He picked up his coffee and sipped, still waiting.

Dravo did likewise before turning to Alex. "What can I do for you, Alex?"

"You heard about the unfortunate accident on Sirius?"

Dravo frowned. "No. What happened?"

"An explosion occurred at the new exploration site."

Halfway toward sipping his beverage again, Dravo's arm froze, and he stared at Alex instead. "Oh."

"The explosives expert is missing," Alex continued. "Either he's buried under the rubble or has taken off in fright. We don't know at this point whether it was an accident or intentional."

The coffee cup sat in Dravo's hand, suspended in midair, as creases developed on his forehead. "Oh," he said again.

"I'm told you recommended him."

Released from the stasis by a direct question he could answer, Dravo said, "Yes. Kansas reached out to me. Asked if I could recommend someone. At first, I was at a loss, but then I recalled a close acquaintance suggesting I contact this guy if I ever needed an explosives expert. I sent Kansas the name and the person's details. Shall I call my friend? I can arrange for you to talk to him face to face. His name is Milan Asterov. He's a reputable Procyon businessman, I assure you. I'm sure the explosion had to be a tragic mistake."

"I would appreciate it."

Dravo stood and headed to his desk. He dialed a number and waited. After half a minute, he hung up and tried again with the same result. His frown deepened as he turned back to Alex. "He's not answering. The automatic system says he's turned off his comm. But he never turns his comm off. It's his lifeblood." Dravo scribbled a note on a plasti-paper sheet. He returned to Alex and handed it to him. "That's his office if you want to chase him later."

Alex took the sheet and read it. "Thanks. I might do that. How well do you know this guy?"

"I've known Milan for a few years. We sometimes have drinks on Fridays and golf together on weekends."

"And he recommended this technician?"

Dravo shrugged. "He said he was having a rough patch and needed the money. I said I'd help the guy out. It pleased me when I heard Kansas had taken him on."

"And now they are both missing."

"Yeah." Dravo rubbed his chin. "Hope no one got hurt."

Alex shook his head. "I'll leave you to it," he said and drained the last of his beverage. "Thanks for the coffee and the chat."

"No problem."

Alex rose, said goodbye, and left to chase up Dravo's drinking companion.

He returned to the hotel to freshen up before heading out to the exotic business district, the towering skyscrapers overshadowing the urban sprawl. This guy had offices on the top floor of an edifice that resembled a crescent moon. Why the architect designed the building in such a shape, Alex couldn't fathom. He ascended to the offices, where he arrived without an appointment, hoping Asterov would overlook the interruption. The elevator stopped, and the doors opened. He walked out, entering an expansive reception space.

The floor resembled polished brass, but its surface felt safe to traverse without slipping. Alex surmised it possessed a static charge to prevent falls. The contrast of the vivid white walls with the brass floor made an impressive sight. He headed for the desk at the far end, where a woman in a formal gray pin-striped business suit sat. She glanced up from her duties as Alex came toward her.

"May I help you?" she asked.

"My name is Alex Warner, and I wish to speak to Mr. Asterov."

She stared at him as if she didn't know how to reply. "I see." She looked toward a doorway to her right and back at him. "He's unavailable at present."

"When will he be free to talk to me? It will only take a few minutes."

"Umm ... I'm not sure."

The conversation was turning bizarre. "What's the problem?"

"It's a habit of his. He disappears for days sometimes without telling us where he's going or when he'll be back."

"Oh. Can I contact him?"

"No." The receptionist realized her rudeness. "Sorry. I mean, we can't get hold of him ourselves. Odd. We can usually contact him when he leaves like this if anything important arises."

Alex frowned. It seemed odd to him, too — busy, successful entrepreneurs didn't routinely vanish without explanation and with no means of communication with their staff. An inkling of something more sinister started seeping into his gut. "I'm out of luck then. Maybe I'll try again later. I'll call next time and check that he's returned."

"Yes, do that. I'm sorry we can't be of more help."

Alex turned and left. If this were just a courtesy call, he would let the matter rest. But under the circumstances, he sensed something was wrong. Dravo had given him Asterov's home address, so Alex decided to visit his residence to check whether he was holed up there for some obscure reason. He found a taxi and keyed in the location.

Asterov lived in an exclusive suburb on the outskirts of the city, one that hugged the coastline with exquisite views of the sea and the white coastal cliffs in the distance.

Alex arrived at his house. Its ambiance reflected the suburb's prosperity. The grounds were enormous and manicured to perfection. The residence scaled three stories and sat on the edge of the cliff overlooking the ocean. The taxi stopped at the front gate, where Alex disembarked after instructing it to wait for him. Despite the gate being motorized and enhanced with state-of-the-art security, it hung open as if waiting for him. The fact it was in that position worried him.

Self-conscious just standing there, Alex headed for the house unannounced. The pathway wove in between two hedges through to the front door. He glanced around, trying to find any evidence someone was home, but the grounds were quiet. Since nothing else came to mind, he pressed the notification button beside the doorway and waited. After almost a minute, with no response, he tried it again. Again, no answer. He scratched his head in thought. He was uncomfortable snooping but needed answers to the origin of the explosives expert before leaving.

He decided to test the front door. To his surprise, it opened. He took another cursory look outside before entering the premises. It brought back memories of his days in the GIA. His inquisitive nature getting the better of him, he headed through the ground floor, starting at the foyer and investigating successive lounge rooms, dining rooms, and studies until he ended up at the rear of the mansion, which revealed an outdoor entertainment area complete with an enormous swimming pool.

Alex was about to head back inside to continue his search upstairs when an object in the pool caught his eye. He approached it, knowing what it was even before he could identify it. A male body, fully clothed, floated face down in the water. He sighed. If that were Asterov, he wouldn't be getting the answers he sought, after all.

8

CATCH UP WITH CHOOLI

A lex called in the dead body to the local police authorities, which meant he had to hang around until they had questioned him before he could leave. They asked him to remain contactable in case they needed to talk to him again. He could return to his home planet but not go out of comm range.

He got back to the hotel late that evening, feeling drained from the day's excitement. He needed to report to Ahiga, but with so much happening so quickly, he decided to message him instead, telling him he would fill him in face-to-face when he got back home. That freed him to head to the bathroom for a refreshing shower before using the hyperspace communicator to contact Chooli. He settled himself in the room's sumptuous lounge chair, sipping on a whiskey while waiting for her to respond to his contact.

A minute later, the screen activated with Chooli's gorgeous face on display. His heart raced, and he beamed at the thought of returning to his normal life.

Chooli broke into a broad smile as well.

"Hi, I miss you," she greeted him.

"I miss you too. I've done as much as I can here, so I hope to come home tomorrow."

"You'd better." She gave a feigned frown.

Alex grinned. "Or ...?"

"Or I might change the locks. I don't want strange men in my home."

Her comment made Alex laugh. "What's it like being a lady of leisure?"

Chooli sighed. "Sending me crazy with boredom."

"At least you're out of trouble."

"Ha-ha. What have you found out?"

"Not much. I've reached a dead end, literally. I talked with Kansas Salter, the mine manager on Sirius, who told me the explosives expert has either done a runner or is under the rubble. He said Dravo Chinko — he's the manager of Ahiga's mine on Procyon — recommended the explosives expert. That brought me here to Procyon to see Dravo, who told me he got the technician's name from a drinking buddy. But when I visited the guy's office, the receptionist said they hadn't heard from him in days. So, I checked his residence. This guy has a luxurious house with all the bells and whistles and state-of-the-art security, yet I found it unlocked and — wait for it — found him lying face down in the swimming pool fully clothed."

"Oh my God, Alex, do you think he's been murdered?"

"Well, it seems highly coincidental. I called the police. It's up to them to determine cause of death."

Alex saw Chooli's concerned frown as he related his findings to her.

"I don't like it," she said. "I'll feel better when you're home where I can keep you safe."

Alex smiled. "I can look after myself, you know."

"Yeah, right!"

"I agree, it *is* suspicious, particularly the explosives expert getting a job elsewhere so soon after we met with Vito and the new guy disappearing after stuffing up the charge. It's as if Vito is sending us a message: do what I want, or I will destroy Ahiga's assets — although I don't quite know how this buddy of Chinko's fits into all this. Odd that he should turn up dead, don't you think?"

"He could have had a heart attack and fallen into the pool — or committed suicide?" Chooli speculated.

"Possibly," Alex said, his tone unconvinced. "But there's something off about Chinko, too."

"Why do you say that?"

"He greeted me like a long-lost friend when we'd only just met."

She laughed. "I bet he's just a super-friendly guy, you old' curmudgeon," she teased.

He laughed back. "Yeah, you're probably right."

"Just come home."

"There's nothing to keep me here. The police said I'm free to leave Procyon — they'll contact me if they need to talk to me again. And I need to discuss all of this with Ahiga face-to-face. I'll organize my return tomorrow."

After telling her he loved her, Alex broke contact, eager to see Chooli in person again.

9

NEMESIS

After his phone call to Chooli, Alex returned downstairs for a meal. Despite or perhaps because of his hectic day, he wasn't tired, so after his meal, he walked to a nearby bar known as the Orleans to unwind.

He entered and headed to a vacant table, ordering a drink using the in-table menu as he sat and waited while fiddling with a glass coaster. The order came, a whiskey on the rocks, and he reclined in the soft-cushioned lounge chair as he pondered the conundrum of the missing explosives expert and what it might mean for Ahiga's business.

The bar had a reasonable number of patrons without being crowded, which was why Alex enjoyed visiting it when he was on Procyon. It included a section for recreational activities, the ancient game of darts, and a pool table. Various holographic screens scattered above head level displayed different visual sports and entertainment shows. That night, he wanted solitude to enjoy his refreshments while unwinding from the day's stresses. He consumed several drinks before heading for the restrooms out the back.

A woman bumped into him as he exited the restroom. She

seemed strangely familiar, a familiarity one gets from a long-term association with someone in the past, but its significance failed him. She stooped as if from fatigue or an overabundance of sorrow. He stared at her back before she scurried away like a frightened rat. With no reason to chase after her, he returned to his table and ordered another drink. Several women sat and flirted with him until they sensed his lack of interest. They then left him alone. It brought a smile to his face. Before meeting Chooli, he would have reveled in the attention, but now the fulfillment she gave him provided all he needed.

He finished the last of his drink and rose to leave, intending to return to the hotel. As he stepped over the threshold into the outside air, he paused to check his surroundings. Straight away, he noticed the woman who had bumped into him near the restrooms slumped in a seated position against the bar wall, staring at the ground. Something familiar about her struck him again, so he strolled up to her.

"Do I know you?" he asked.

The woman tensed before her head swiveled toward him, their eyes meeting. A spasm of vertigo slammed into him with the intensity of a shuttle crash. He staggered backward two steps and glared at her, exuding an animosity he hadn't experienced in years. "You!"

Ramira Lopez, the vilest person Alex had ever known, stared back at him. She had ruined his career and sent him on a descent into despair that only Chooli's qualities had healed — and now his nemesis had found him again.

"Please help me," she said with hope bridging the space between them.

Alex gave a derisive laugh. "Why would I help you? You've been nothing but trouble for me."

"I've changed, Alex. I'm not the person I was. And I have nowhere else to go," Ramira whispered as she sobbed, her gaze returning to the ground in front of her. "I know we didn't part well."

That's an understatement, Alex thought.

Ramira looked pleadingly at him as if to acknowledge the inadequacy of how she had described their parting. "Then you headed for the restrooms, and I plucked up the courage to approach you. But I chickened out with you so near me."

"How did you even know I would be here?" he asked, his suspicions fully aroused.

"I didn't. I often come to this bar when I need to drown my sorrows. And tonight was one of those nights. I saw you, and my first thought was that you would help me despite everything. Then you headed for the restrooms, and I plucked up the courage to approach you. But I chickened out with you so near me."

Alex's resolve to be done with her melted as doubt seeped into him. "Why would you need my help?"

"He has my child."

Her comment confused him. The Ramira he knew was childless, although enough time had elapsed between his leaving her and now for her to have acquired one. Still, she didn't seem the type. "Who? Who has your child?"

"My previous employer. I left him when I knew I was pregnant because I wanted a better life for my child. But he wants me to return to the awful life I used to live and stole my son to force me."

"Go to the police."

Ramira shook her head. "I can't go to the police, not on this planet. He threatened to kill my boy if I contacted the police. But you can find him."

"I'm not with the GIA anymore," Alex explained. "I left. I work for a private company now. So, I can't help you. What about the child's father? Can't he help?"

"You are my child's father," she whispered.

Another spasm of vertigo hit Alex as he stared at her in shock and disbelief.

"I can't go back, Alex. But I can't get our child back if I don't. He will kill him, and that will kill me."

A fitting end for her, Alex thought bitterly, but totally unfair for her child. He didn't believe it was his child for a nanosecond — but what if it was? Could he take the risk? Despite his doubts, her plight compelled him to help her find and recover her child in whatever way he could. He only hoped he wouldn't live to regret it.

"Why does he want you back?"

"He says once you're in, you don't get out, ever."

Knowing Ramira's past, he could believe that.

"I left so I could raise our child in peace," she wailed. "But if I return, he will only experience life in the underworld. Please, please help me."

Alex scratched his head. "I don't understand how I can help you. I'm returning to Caerus tomorrow."

Ramira's shoulders slumped, and she sighed. "I'll just have to return, then."

He could say it was all her own fault for getting involved, but that would be insensitive and wouldn't solve her problem. "Do you have any idea where they're holding your child?"

She shook her head.

"How did the kidnappers contact you?"

"They left a note in my apartment while I was working. It said to call the number on it, and they included a hologram of my child in the arms of a strange man."

"Do you have the note?"

She shook her head again. "It's back at my place."

Alex knew he should leave her and not get sucked into her predicament, but the detective in him smelled a mystery that intrigued him — and part of him wondered if it could indeed be his child. "Let's go to your apartment and check that note."

Ramira's face jerked up at him and a hopeful smile gleamed. "Thank you."

She wobbled into a standing position and staggered toward Alex, almost falling as she neared him. He stretched out to grab her arm and steady her, which brought her closer to him. The reek of alcohol confirmed her overindulgence, but he chose to overlook it.

"Let's go," he said.

10

CAPTURED BY A DEAD MAN

Alex and Ramira entered her apartment a half hour later. They had walked since it was nearby. Besides, Ramira said she needed the fresh air.

Once inside, Alex noted the unkempt nature of the premises and signs that a child had once lived there: toys, children's picture books, and children's clothing lay strewn around the living room floor and on chairs. An unmade bed was visible through the bedroom doorway, and unwashed dishes and utensils were stacked next to the sink in the kitchen. Empty boxes and cartons lay untidily next to the trash chute. It was beyond him why it took so much effort to place them through the slot to dispose of them. Either Ramira was not into housework, or the kidnappers had made a mess when they stole the child. He suspected both.

Ramira headed for the bedroom and returned with a plasti-paper note. She stared at it, tears welling as her mouth quivered. As if unable to speak, she shot the message out toward Alex. He took the few steps between them and gently removed it from her fingers. Its contents backed up her story — a phone number and a hologram of a small child held by a man. The child looked terrified, but the man beamed at the holographic camera, pleased with himself and seemingly happy to have the child under his control.

Judging by the boy's tear-streaked face, the man was a stranger to him, and a sinister aura radiated from the hologram. An open window behind them gave a view of other buildings.

Alex recognized one of the buildings. He had been there that day talking to Dravo Chinko.

"That's the Powers Enterprises building," he told her. "It's near here. He could be laid up in a hotel behind it."

Ramira dried her eyes and sidled next to Alex. Her voice rose in excitement as she realized he had identified the building and the location of the room where they had produced the hologram. She grabbed Alex's arm. "We have to go there."

Alex frowned. It seemed too coincidental that they had captured an image of the building housing Ahiga's company on Procyon. He glanced at Ramira but saw only hope staring back at him. He returned his concentration to the hologram. A nasty knot tightened in his stomach, and a warning filtered through from his subconscious. But he knew they had to investigate further. He sighed. "Lead the way."

They left Ramira's apartment, still walking, as she said it was not far. After twenty minutes, they rounded a corner, and a sign illuminated on the Powers Enterprises building lit its surroundings, almost overpowering the pedestrian lighting along the pathways.

"There! There!" Ramira called, excited as she pointed to a nearby hotel. It looked rundown and out of place in the otherwise high-profile business district.

Alex studied the hotel and the office building. Hoping Ramira was following him, he started walking toward the hotel but veered sideways so he could view the side of the hotel facing the office to judge the likelihood of them recording the hologram from a room within the hotel. Once in position, he studied the angles and rubbed his chin. "It's certainly a possibility."

Ramira grabbed his arm. "Let's go check. Maybe they're still there. We can rescue our son, and I won't have to work for them."

Alex wanted to tell her to stop calling the child their son, but he refrained. Instead, he turned his head to her, his expression doubtful. "I wouldn't get my hopes up yet."

"But we can go look."

"You're getting ahead of yourself. How will the hotel manager react when we rock up asking for a room? And you think he'll show us all the rooms facing that direction, no questions asked?"

Despite it being nighttime, he could see her blush. Her expression turned to pleading.

"OK," he said, "we'll only ask for the rooms occupied when they took the hologram. But I'm not the police, so they don't have to tell us."

With that said, Alex headed toward the lobby with Ramira at his side. The whole place yelled cheap. It was obviously frequented by those down on their luck or needing privacy for an hour. He wasn't sure what category they would be placed in, but he presumed the latter. Bracing himself, he stepped into the hotel foyer and headed for the checkout desk.

The manager emerged from the minuscule office behind the counter. He looked grumpy, as if upset at being disturbed at whatever he had been doing.

"Yes?"

"We want a room," Alex said.

"No kidding."

"No, you don't understand."

"How long?"

"You don't understand. We're looking for a western-facing one that was occupied—" Alex glanced at Ramira. "When did your child go missing?"

"Yesterday afternoon," she said.

Alex turned back to the manager. "Yesterday afternoon."

The man gave Alex a suspicious look. "You a cop?"

"No."

"Piss off then." He made to return to his office.

"A man and a small child," Alex blurted out, attempting to keep the manager's attention.

The man froze. His head turned. "What if there was?"

Alex picked the expression a mile away. The guy needed his palms greased. He knew exactly what Alex was asking, but he wanted recompense to make it worth his while. Alex reached into his pocket and pulled out his credit card, dialing in a number before showing it to the manager.

The guy returned to the checkout desk and retrieved his card, touching Alex's and completing the transaction. "A guy with a kid was here yesterday."

Ramira rushed to the counter, full of hope. "Are they still here?"

He shook his head. "They left not long afterward. Seemed strange to me. They usually stay longer."

Alex looked at him in disgust.

The man noticed. "Hey, everyone has to make a living."

"Can we check the room?" Alex asked.

"Sure." The man checked the register and scanned the key rack. He pulled out a blank key, coded it, and handed it to Alex. "Room 512. You'll have to use the stairs. The elevator's out of order."

Alex and Ramira headed for the stairs and started the ascent one step at a time to the next landing and the next until they reached the fifth floor. Alex was a little out of breath, but Ramira was puffing hard. Giving her time to recover, he gazed along the corridor in both directions from the stairs that provided access to the middle of the hotel building. They were alone, and everything was quiet except for the odd scrape and bang of someone downstairs. He checked down the stairwell but concluded it was coming from the manager in the foyer.

"Ready?" he asked Ramira.

She nodded and straightened, giving Alex a weak smile before taking her own survey of the corridors. "Which way?"

He pointed to the left. "Room 12 should be that way."

He started walking with Ramira behind him, each footstep echoing throughout the corridor, augmented by the odd creak of the floor as they progressed. They arrived at number 12 and stood in front of the doorway, Alex holding the key card and wondering what might lie behind it. He looked at Ramira. She looked nervous, expectant, exhausted, but was she telling the truth? His gut said not to trust her, but he had gone this far with her. If he could help her, his conscience said he should. Besides, his curiosity had got the better of him. He had to know. He placed the card on the pad.

A beep sounded, and a green light illuminated before the door clicked and unlocked.

Alex pushed it inward, revealing a darkened interior.

No one was there.

He exhaled the breath he was holding and entered, Ramira following him. He flicked the light switch and let the door close.

As he crept further into the room, he searched for any clue of occupation, current or past, that might show any useful evidence. He headed for the window and checked the outside view. It certainly resembled the one in the hologram.

"Where are they?" Ramira asked as she gripped his arm. "Where is my boy?"

"I don't know. But it's a good bet they were here." Alex turned and surveyed the room from his vantage point at the window. A bed was on his left, covered with a shabby grade of green comforter, ancient, neglected, and dirty. A chest of drawers stood beside it, with a bedside lamp on top. Another door was closed on his right, presumably the bathroom, hiding whatever lay behind it.

Alex headed to the light switch and turned it off. No illumination leaked between the bottom of the door and the floor. He switched the light back on and returned to Ramira, who stood staring forlornly through the window.

The bathroom door opened.

A man entered the room. He was tall, stocky, and middle-aged, his hair slicked back. He wore a trendy black business suit over a shirt that scintillated into different colors as he moved. With the nonchalance of indifference, he leaned his bulk against the doorframe.

Ramira screamed.

"Who are you?" Alex asked, aware of his exposed position with nothing to protect him.

"Milan Asterov. I believe you wanted to see me." He looked amused.

"But you're dead! I saw you floating in your swimming pool."

"You saw someone floating in my swimming pool. Did you bother to check who it was?"

"The police ... they thought it could be you."

"Ha! You're an ex-cop and you can't tell a fake cop!"

Alex kicked himself for his naivety. He was getting rusty — a result of sitting behind a desk too much. *Why was Asterov here, anyway? And why was there a dead body in his swimming pool?*

As he opened his mouth to ask more questions, Asterov pulled out a gun and shot him.

Ramira screamed again.

Alex stared with horror at the spot on his shoulder that hurt, only to find a dart embedded there. His vision blurred, and he collapsed into unconsciousness.

11

ALEX IS MISSING

C hooli parked her commuting scooter in the underground garage of their apartment building. Her anticipation of seeing Alex again filled her with excitement, and a tingle of lust warmed her. Alex's absence this time had troubled her more than she realized. He had been away many times before, but her work had always provided a distraction. With more time on her hands, the loneliness affected her more. She headed for the elevator and punched the button for their penthouse apartment. Butterflies mounted as the elevator rose, making it difficult for her to stand still for more than a second.

Once she arrived at her floor, the door to their apartment opened, but beyond it, everything was cloaked in darkness and stillness. Where's Alex? He should be home already. Something must have delayed him. He'll be home any minute now. She exited the elevator and checked her comm for a message from him, but there weren't any. Her excitement evaporated, replaced with a sense of loss; her compass felt confused as she grappled with the reality that he wasn't there.

"There's no need to panic," she mumbled to herself.

She dropped her belongings on the side table, positioned for that purpose, and headed to the kitchen for a drink. Instead of her usual juice, she picked out a local variety of white wine and poured herself a glass before heading to the balcony. She sat in an outside lounge chair, sipping her drink pensively as she watched the last Tau Ceti sun rays bleed over the horizon before beckoning in the dusk and disappearing. With nothing better to do, she prepared her supper, ate, and flopped into bed with still no word from Alex. The lack of communication sprouted a seed of foreboding as she tried to sleep. It wasn't like him to be late and not contact her.

After bouts of disturbed rest throughout the night, she woke tired, frustrated, and worried. Her heart pumped faster than usual, and dampness covered her palms. Even her aureola had developed a gray tinge. She showered, had a quick breakfast snack, and tried calling Alex again, with no success, even after several attempts.

What if he's had an accident? Her stomach knotted tighter. What if he's left me? She shook her head, castigating herself for jumping to conclusions. She put in a video call to Ahiga.

"Hello," Ahiga said, his tone breezy. "Hope Alex returned safely last night."

Ahiga hasn't heard from Alex, either.

"He hasn't come home yet, Ahiga. I was hoping you knew where he was."

"Hmm." Ahiga frowned. "No, I don't. I just assumed he returned safely and was resting today before coming to see me. So, he hasn't contacted you?"

Chooli shook her head. "Not since he called me from Procyon and said he would be home yesterday. And I can't contact him. Where could he be?"

"I don't know. Let me find out. I'll get back to you. It's not like Alex to go off without an explanation, is it?"

"No." Chooli couldn't contain herself any longer. "What if something has happened? What if he's hurt?" she blurted.

"He's fine. Don't worry. I'm sure there's a logical explanation. Let me make some calls."

Chooli's screen went blank. She continued chastising herself. She needed to be stronger and keep her emotions in check.

Unable to bear the silent apartment a moment longer, she decided to go to her office in the hope Nascha would let her stay even though she was still on suspension. She needed to be around people.

As soon as she arrived in the office, Nascha approached her. "What are you doing here, Chooli? Looks like you had a late night. Catching up on lost time with Alex?"

Chooli, in no mood for banter, was tempted to give a curt retort but remembered that she needed a favor from Nascha. Her lips quivered. "He didn't come home. He's not answering his comm, and I don't know where he is."

Nascha stared at her, shocked. "I'm such an idiot," she replied, her behavior changing instantly. "I should've known something was wrong. Have you tried talking to Alex's boss?"

"Yes, but he doesn't know either. He said he'll try to find out. In the meantime, I was wondering if you would let me stay in the office. I can't bear being in the apartment on my own waiting for news."

Nascha nodded. "Of course. Let me know what you find out from Ahiga," she said as she moved away.

Chooli was grateful to Nascha for letting her stay.

"Are you OK?" A familiar male voice asked.

She jerked her head upward and blushed as she furtively wiped a tear from her eye. Chief Inspector Shilah was staring at her.

"Nascha gave me permission to be here, sir," she said quickly, worried the Chief would blast her for appearing to break her suspension.

But he brushed that aside and looked at her sympathetically. "You're upset over something. What is it?"

"Alex didn't come home last night, sir. He was supposed to arrive yesterday afternoon. And I can't contact him."

"Do you have any leads?"

"His boss is trying to find out where he is."

"He probably just changed flights."

"But he would have told me."

"I'm sure you have nothing to worry about. Keep me informed in case there's something we can do."

"Thank you, sir," she said, relieved she wasn't in any more trouble.

Shilah walked away, and Chooli returned to staring at her tablet screen, her distress over Alex's disappearance escalating. Ahiga was taking too long to contact her. Something is wrong. She resisted an urge to call him back, knowing he might need time to find answers. Unable to sit still, she stood and paced by her desk until her colleagues started sending her curious looks. She then headed out for a coffee to distract herself.

Her comm buzzed when she returned to her desk, almost making her drop her take-out coffee. Ahiga. With trepidation, Chooli stared at it, dreading the news she might receive when she answered it.

12

SORRY, THE GIA CAN'T GET INVOLVED

Ahiga was calling her back. Her hand wouldn't move. When it did, it felt like she was pushing through molasses. Her middle finger reached for the button, and she pressed. Ahiga's face came on the screen, his expression already telling her it was not good news.

"You haven't found him, have you?" A chill ran through Chooli as if the harbinger of death stood in front of her.

"No. I haven't. He's vanished."

"No one just vanishes! Where is he?" Despite knowing how ridiculous she sounded, she felt herself devolving into hysteria.

The entire office staff stopped working to stare at her, shocked by her outburst.

Nascha rushed over. "What's happened? What's wrong?"

Bewildered, Chooli turned to her, speechless.

Seeing Ahiga on Chooli's comm, Nascha asked him, "What's happened?"

"I can't find Alex's whereabouts," Ahiga said.

Nascha frowned. "Where was he seen last?"

"I traced him from Sirius to Procyon. Kansas, our manager on

Sirius, met him and told him to go to our mine on Procyon. We know he was in Procyon because his final report to me comes from there. He says he met with the manager of my mine there, Dravo Chinko, who gave him the name of the person who recommended the explosives expert. It was in Alex's last report. Let's see, I have that guy's name here somewhere. Yes, Milan Asterov. Later, he messaged me to say he was coming home the next day. And he told Chooli the same thing. That's where the trail goes cold. There's no evidence he left Procyon."

Chooli had recovered her composure. Her inquisitive nature started overpowering her alarm. "He said he needed to talk to you face-to-face."

"He messaged that to me, too. But there's no record of him catching any commercial flights to Caerus," Ahiga said.

"If he missed his flight, he wouldn't have leased a private carrier. He would've waited for the next flight and told me of the change."

"I agree. I contacted his hotel and got them to check his room. He didn't check out. All his belongings are still there, and he hasn't slept in the bed."

"That's a worry," Nascha said as she glanced at Chooli. "What did the hotel say?"

"Nothing. They hadn't seen him for a couple of days." Ahiga's face looked frustrated. "It's not like him. I called the local law enforcement. They've received no reports on him — not that they would unless he meant to visit someone and didn't show up."

Chooli went very still for a moment and then said to Ahiga, 'The police know *nothing* about him? But he spoke to them about a dead body he found in the swimming pool."

"What body in what swimming pool?"

"The guy you just mentioned, the one who recommended the electronics expert."

"Milan Asterov? He's dead?"

"Alex said when he couldn't get him at his office, he went to his house. The front door was unlocked, so he had a look around and found a dead body floating in the swimming pool. He took it to be Asterov and that he'd been murdered. He called the police. So, why are the police now saying nothing about Alex's call?"

"I don't know. Why didn't Alex tell me about this body?" Ahiga was sounding very concerned now and slightly irritated with Alex.

"It had just happened, and that's one of the things he wanted to discuss with you in person." Chooli had been standing. She now sat and huffed in frustration. "What do we do? He doesn't answer his comm. Did you check the hospitals?"

Ahiga nodded. "The police checked. No one has been admitted under his name, and there is no John Doe answering Alex's description."

"Where is he? What if all this is connected? What if Alex is floating in a pool somewhere?" Almost hysterical, Chooli turned to Nascha. "We must find him. Do you think the GIA will let me use their resources?"

Nascha straightened. "You can ask." She rubbed her chin. "But I don't like your chances. It's not an official case for the GIA."

"But he's my husband, and he could be in peril."

"Irrelevant," Nascha said. "We have to follow the rules."

Chooli returned her attention to Ahiga. "Please keep looking. He must be somewhere."

"The first thing I'm going to do is get back to the police about that dead body," he said, his tone grim. "They've either got very slack policing practices on Procyon or something fishy is going on."

"I'm going to search, too," Chooli said. She wouldn't let a small matter of protocol prevent her from finding her life partner. She broke the connection.

After a moment, she turned to Nascha. "I'm going to the boss." She stood and walked off, leaving Nascha shaking her head, knowing Chooli had little chance of the GIA opening a formal investigation into the disappearance of the husband of one of its junior operatives.

Chooli stomped toward Shilah's office with a pinpoint-focused determination to get what she wanted.

She halted at his office and knocked on the open door. Seeing him writing earnestly at his desk, she waited for him to give her his attention, drilling her eyes into him as if she had telepathic power to stop him from working and focus on her instead. She hoped Shilah would agree to her request because nothing would prevent her from looking for Alex.

Shilah raised his head. 'Ah, Chooli — have you heard from Alex?"

"No, sir. May I have a minute of your time, please?"

"Sure. What can I do to help?"

"Alex's boss has found no sign of him. I want the GIA to search for him."

Shilah straightened in his seat and stared at her as he placed his stylus carefully on the desk. After a few moments' silence, he said gently, "We can't do that, Chooli. It's against agency policy. I understand your desire to locate your husband, but we can't start an investigation without an invitation from the planetary authority concerned. Where is he?"

Chooli gritted her teeth. "That's what I'm trying to find out."

"I mean, where was he seen last?"

"On Procyon."

"Well, unless the Procyon authorities request our involvement, we can't do anything. Even if they did, it's the Procyon office's responsibility."

Chooli almost stamped her foot in frustration. "There must be something we can do."

Shilah shook his head. "You should return home. He may be there."

Shilah was fobbing her off. She could see he would never concede.

"Why can't I contact him?" she persisted.

He shrugged. "He probably turned his comm off to get some uninterrupted sleep."

"His belongings are still in the hotel."

With a shake of his head, Shilah said, "So? He left to run an errand and forgot to turn his comm back on. I'm sure he has a reasonable explanation for not contacting you. So, go home, Chooli. I *am* sorry, but we're overrun with cases here without adding a private job to the list."

Chooli stared at him, fuming, wondering what she could say to change his mind, but she knew any further attempt was pointless and might be counterproductive. He might forbid her from getting involved. She sighed in defeat and turned, trudging back to her desk to consider her options and devise plans to find Alex. An idea came to her.

She decided to take Shilah's advice and go home.

Nascha saw her as she was about to leave. "What did the boss say?"

Chooli glanced around to make sure Shilah wasn't anywhere within earshot. "We can't divert GIA resources to investigations where the local authorities haven't requested our involvement," she replied, her tone sarcastic.

"I told you so."

"I'm not giving up."

"What will you do ...? Or shouldn't I ask?"

"What you don't know won't hurt you."

"Be careful. You're already in Shilah's black books."

"Alex is my husband. He's in trouble. And I'm finding out what happened to him. Can't anybody understand that?" Chooli's frustration spilled over.

Nascha held her hands up in a surrender gesture. "You don't have to convince me. I agree this isn't like Alex. My gut says he's in trouble too, but there's little I can do about it without the GIA's approval."

"Good. At least we agree on something." She left the office knowing she had behaved poorly toward a friend.

13

I'LL GO IT ALONE

Chooli rushed out of the office, eager to return home to carry out her plan. She wouldn't let the Chief prevent her from using GIA resources to find Alex. She had associates in high places and was not afraid to use them for a problem nothing else could fix.

When she got home, she half expected Alex to be there to greet her as she opened the door, but that was foolish thinking. He would've contacted her if that were the case. She slapped together a bite to eat and, taking a deep breath, connected the hyperlink comm unit she and Alex kept and dialed Commissioner Harris. Her heart rose in her chest, constricting her throat. Reverting to such drastic action almost overwhelmed her.

After several seconds, Commissioner Harris' face showed on the screen. "Chooli! To what do I owe the pleasure?"

"Commissioner Harris. Thank you for answering. I have a pressing problem I hope you can solve. Alex is missing. I don't know where he is, and I can't contact him."

He frowned, lowering his gaze momentarily as though considering the import of this news, and then raising it again to Chooli's worried face. "That doesn't sound like him. Where was he seen last?"

"On Procyon, where he was chasing up a lead about a mysterious explosion on a mine in Sirius — one of Ahiga Powers' mines."

The Commissioner rubbed his chin as he gave Chooli a sideways glance. "And you want the GIA to help you find him?"

She nodded. She hoped she had put her most pleading face forward to convince the Commissioner. "Alex's boss contacted the local police, but they can't find Alex anywhere. Surely that means we can search for him?"

He shook his head. "I'm afraid not. They need to ask for our help, particularly in the Procyon constituency. They become prickly if we meddle in their affairs before being asked for assistance. Besides, how long has he been missing?"

"He didn't arrive home yesterday. And it's totally out of character for Alex not to contact me when his plans change."

"The local police will insist it's not long enough for them to call for help," the Commissioner pointed out.

Chooli sensed her hopes were fading. Anger and stubbornness rose within her.

She gritted her teeth and raised her voice. "When is long enough? When they find him dead?"

He raised his hands. "I'm on your side. But we must follow the designated protocols or the entire system collapses, and that's detrimental for everyone."

"I can't wait for the police or you to decide on when the procedure says the GIA can help. If the Commissioner can't pull strings, who can?"

"Even I'm constrained, Chooli."

She looked away in disgust and chewed the inside of her cheek as she contemplated her next move. It was drastic and against her wishes, but if it meant starting her search for Alex, she would do it.

She glared at the commissioner. "You leave me no choice but to resign."

He raised his eyebrows in surprise. "I suggest you think seriously before you go ahead with that course of action."

Chooli looked at him with pleading eyes. "I can't just sit here and do nothing when Alex is in trouble. I know he is. If that's my only alternative, I will do it."

He sighed. "I can't say that I blame you. Look, I understand you're on suspension for a minor misdemeanor."

It was Chooli's turn to be surprised. She didn't realize Chief Inspector Shilah had discussed her behavior with Commissioner Harris.

"Why don't you take advantage of that time?" Commissioner Harris continued. "If you need more, I'll grant you a temporary leave of absence. That way, you can return to your duties afterward. And Chooli, while I can't help you officially, I'll give you any help and support that I can, in the circumstances, short of making it official. I want Alex back safe with you, too."

The Commissioner's words were music to her ears.

"Thanks. That means so much to me. I'd better start making plans."

"I'll talk to Shilah about your situation and square it with him. You've gone over his head, so he's likely to be peeved with you."

Chooli chuckled. "Thanks. I'm sure he'll get over it. It's not the first time I've annoyed him."

"I know."

After sharing parting words, she broke contact and sat staring out of the panoramic window of their residence, wondering what she was getting herself into.

14

CAPTURED AGAIN

Alex regained consciousness, groggy and disoriented. His blurred vision remained unfocused for several minutes until the soporific effects of the drug wore off. Once he could see, he realized he was lying on the floor just outside the bathroom door of the hotel room he and Ramira had entered. It was daytime and, by the sun's position, after midday. He searched for her and found her on the floor next to the bed. She still looked unconscious. When he felt able, he rose to a sitting position. He was unrestrained, and that confused him. What was the point of shooting him? Asterov could have just left. The purpose of luring him to the hotel also baffled him. If Ramira's child had been there, he wasn't there anymore.

Ramira stirred. Moments later, her eyes fluttered open. Alex wondered if his eyes looked as unfocused as hers when he woke. He waited for her to recover enough to speak. Several minutes elapsed before she struggled to a sitting position.

"It was a trap, wasn't it?" she said.

He shrugged. "Presumably. But what was the point? We're still free to roam unrestrained, and there's no sign of the purpose of us coming here."

Ramira sat sullenly on the floor. "They have my child." Her eyes opened wide with fear as they locked onto Alex's. "Where is my baby? Where is he, Alex?"

"I don't know. But there was no child here when we arrived. Do you know Milan Asterov?"

She shook her head. "Not personally. He's a well-known businessman on Procyon, but he also must be in the pay of my ex-employer if he has kidnapped my child."

Alex scratched his head. He ventured to stand and staggered a few paces before regaining his balance and entering the bathroom. He slurped a few mouthfuls of water from the basin and rubbed his lips dry on his sleeve before reentering the main hotel room. Ramira now sat on the bed with her head clenched between her palms as she sobbed. He wished he could console her or give her encouragement, but he had no solution to her predicament.

He headed for the door and tried the latch. It was unlocked. He opened it with ease. They were free to leave; at least they could exit the room. He wondered if they could escape the hotel itself or if Asterov and any accomplices stood guard to prevent their departure. "You want to grab a drink before we go?"

Ramira looked up, tears still clinging to her cheeks. She stared at him, confused. "We can go?"

Alex shrugged. "Apparently. We may as well use the opportunity before someone stops us."

She dashed into the bathroom. He heard slurping before she came out again and headed toward him. "Let's go." She stopped and turned to him. "Don't you think that's odd?"

Her question stumped him. "What?"

"Why let us walk away after the significant effort to lure us here, including drugging us?"

What's wrong with me? His intellectual faculties seemed to have slowed to a crawl; his usual mental quickness had deserted him. Was it the effects of the drug, or did a different psychological problem affect him? He shook his head — this was no time for psychoanalysis.

His stomach churned as he patted his clothes and cussed under his breath. "They took my comm."

With a touch of panic, Ramira searched her bag for hers but found it still in there together with her other belongings.

"At least one of us can communicate," Alex said. "We'd better go."

They left the room and headed for the rear stairwell, using that instead of the one they'd scaled earlier to draw as little attention to their movements as possible. When they arrived at the first-floor landing, they stopped.

"Should we walk out the front entrance?" Ramira asked.

"Is there a different way? Is there a back door?"

"I'm sure one exists, but I don't know where it is."

"Let's return to the lobby and search for another exit."

"Shouldn't there be a fire escape?"

"Good thinking," Alex said, annoyed he hadn't thought of it himself. He searched the perimeter for the emergency exit signs and found one near them. "Over there." He pointed to their left.

She nodded and they crept toward it, making the smallest noise that movement permitted.

The door hinges screamed as Alex opened the door, his face cringing as he glanced back to check no one had been alerted. He passed through the doorway with Ramira following him. After a search of the ground below them, he led her down the remaining steps and onto the pavement in an alleyway behind the building.

"What now?" he asked. "We shouldn't go back to my hotel. They'll have lookouts watching it."

"There's an empty apartment near here we could shelter in. I know the owners. They're away, but I know how to get in. Let's find a public transport kiosk and grab a lift."

Despite his persistent misgivings about Ramira, Alex accepted her lead. He had no better ideas to offer.

They dashed from the alley, checking the street before they headed away from the hotel to find transportation. It didn't take long for them to arrive at a kiosk. They found a vacant scooter, and Ramira voiced directions into the navigation console.

The scooter left, and they arrived at their destination within half an hour. Ramira led him through several streets before they entered an apartment block. They ascended to the 12th floor and went into an apartment, flopping into the closest armchairs, relieved as they recuperated from the intensity of the previous hours.

"I should call Chooli," Alex said, opening his eyes and glancing at Ramira.

"Who's Chooli?" she asked, remembering in time that she was not supposed to know about Chooli.

"My wife," he said, the term causing her to wince.

"You lost your comm, remember?"

"You still have yours. May I borrow it?"

She shook her head. "They'll be monitoring it. They will find out where we are."

Ramira was right. But Chooli would worry about him not returning on schedule and not contacting her to explain his delay. He knew her. She would not rest until she found a means of communicating with him or locating him. She was persistent, creative, and ruthless once she set her mind on a goal. He concluded his only option was to bide his time and send a message to her at the first opportunity.

"What now?" he asked.

"We still need to find my baby." Ramira broke down weeping again and shook her head in despair. "I'll never see him again."

"Don't give up hope. We have a lead. We know Asterov is involved somehow. He's a crook, for sure, but he's also a well-known businessman with a legit business to front. I know where he lives and works. We can track him down at either place."

"And then what? You think he's just going to tell you where our child is?"

Alex winced at the pronoun but chose to overlook it. "I'll find a way to force him to tell us what he knows."

Ramira's sobbing subsided. "He won't have my boy. They'll have him hidden somewhere else, guarded by goons in the pay of my ex-boss. He's the one pulling the strings, not Astcrov. All Astcrov needs to do is get a message to them, and they'll move him again."

"Then we'd better make sure he can't contact them." Alex had no further words of support to give her hope. Finding her child alive would become more difficult with each passing day. Yet he had to help her despite not understanding why.

The door to the apartment burst open.

15

CHOOLI'S SEARCH BEGINS

The morning after her talk with Commissioner Harris, Chooli woke early. Her slumber had again been fragmentary as her mind descended into dreams of Alex in danger and her retarded attempts to rescue him as if her feet were wading through thick mud. She sat and yawned as she rubbed the sleep from her eyes, tired and grumpy as well as nervous as the implications of her decisions took hold.

Nothing would happen if she stayed in bed, so she jumped out, showered, and ate breakfast before calling Ahiga.

"Ahiga here."

"Can I visit you this morning?" Chooli asked as she sipped on her coffee. "I need more background on Alex's movements over the past few days — up onto he went missing."

Ahiga's eyebrows rose in surprise. "Is the GIA involved now?"

"I wish. They say they can't step in unless Procyon requests their help."

"So ...?"

"The Commissioner is fine with me going it alone. I know something's happened to him. He's in trouble. And the longer we wait, the worse his trouble will get."

Ahiga fidgeted as he looked at something beyond the screen. He faced her again. "How does ten suit you?"

"Ten's good. I'll be in your office then."

"No, come to our house. Mai is dying to see you — and it's out of earshot of any inquisitive ears in my office."

"OK." She ended the call.

It was just after eight, and the trip to Ahiga's residence only took half an hour, so she used the interim to pack. She intended to travel off-world, but the length of her absence and destinations were unknown, so she needed to cater for all conceivable circumstances. That meant a large bag. She sniggered, almost hearing Alex grumbling that they were only going to be away for a few days. Reality then returned, and her mood sobered. She'd give anything to hear him grumble again.

When her departure time arrived, she headed downstairs and off to Ahiga's place on her scooter.

Mai opened the door as she prepared to press the buzzer next to it. "Have you heard anything?" she asked, her eyes wide with anxiety.

Chooli shook her head.

"Come in, come in."

After Chooli crossed the threshold, Mai closed the door and hugged her. "You must be so worried."

Chooli pulled away and held Mai's shoulders in her hands. "I am. Thanks for your concern. I need to talk with Ahiga."

Flustered, Mai said, "Of course. I shouldn't delay you. Follow me." She led Chooli through the reception foyer and into a side room, Ahiga's study, where he worked when he needed to put in hours at home. He sat facing away from them, crouched over his tablet, deep in thought.

"Honey, Chooli is here."

"Show her in," Ahiga said, eyes focused on his screen.

"She's standing right behind you," Mai said, rolling her eyes.

"Oh." Ahiga's head shot up. He turned in his chair, splayed his arms, stretched, and yawned loudly as his back cracked.

Chooli and Mai giggled.

He gave them an inquiring stare. "Have you never seen someone stretch?"

"Not like that," Chooli said.

He grunted and turned to Mai. "Chooli and I need to talk. So, you can leave now."

"I'm staying," Mai said firmly. "Chooli's my friend, and I want to help."

"Suit yourself." Ahiga shrugged and gestured to the chairs at the side of his desk. "Please sit."

Once Chooli and Mai settled, he began. "I know nothing more than I told you yesterday, Chooli. I wish I did and could tell you Alex is on his way home."

"That's what I expected." She leaned forward in her seat, her hands folded in her lap, trying to hide the tension she felt by adopting a professional pose. "But can you tell me again Alex's movements from when he left Caerus?"

Ahiga nodded. "Alex left on my request and headed for Sirius. He—"

"Why did you send him to Sirius?" Chooli interrupted even though she knew the answer. She needed to get all the facts on the table.

"An explosion had occurred at my Sirius mine. I thought you knew that. I sent Alex to investigate the cause. We were concerned that it might not be an accident. We were also concerned there could be a leak at the mine—"

"A leak?" Chooli interrupted again. This was the first she'd heard about a leak.

"We had reason to believe that someone from the mine might be leaking information to Vito Riva. It was just after we became aware of that possibility that the explosion occurred."

"Vito Riva?"

"He's a businessman of somewhat shady reputation. He's interested in buying my mine on Sirius and didn't like it when I said it was not for sale."

Chooli nodded, storing the name in her memory bank. "Go on."

"Anyway, Alex traveled there and talked to the mine manager, Kansas Salter, who told him they had just employed a new explosives technician after the last one left abruptly for a more lucrative position. The new technician disappeared after the accident. Kansas mentioned he hired the new guy on Dravo Chinko's recommendation. He's my business manager on Procyon. Alex also reported that he thought Kansas could be our leak — not intentionally, mind you, but because he's the sort of guy who might get indiscreet while on leave. He likes the social hot spots."

"So, Alex went to Procyon?" Chooli prompted.

Ahiga nodded. "He checked into the Continental Hotel. He then saw Dravo Chinko, who told him he was given the technician's name by a buddy of his. Milan Asterov. Alex never reported to me again except to say he was coming home. He messaged me that he had things to tell me but would prefer to discuss them in person. After what you've told me, I assume he was referring to the dead body he discovered in what must have been Asterov's swimming pool.

"Later, when I asked the police to inquire at Alex's hotel, they discovered that his belongings were still in his room. When they viewed the video footage, they saw Alex enter the hotel in the late afternoon and leave again just after 9 pm. That's the last we know of his movements. There's no record of him returning to the hotel."

"And what about this Milan Asterov? Have you tried to contact him?"

"Yes, I have. No one seems to know where he is either. Nor do the police know anything about a dead body in Asterov's swimming pool."

There was silence in the room for a moment as they absorbed this.

"I don't like it," Ahiga finally said.

The lack of a useful lead sent a wave of panic through Chooli. Alex could be anywhere. She thought furiously to find something else to ask Ahiga. "Did you talk to Dravo again?"

Ahiga shook his head. "I can't get him, which concerns me as well."

"Don't you think it's odd that people keep disappearing, and Alex saw a dead body that no one else saw?

In laying out the facts, Ahiga was now as troubled as Chooli was.

Chooli realized she only had one choice. "I must go to Procyon. That's where the trail ends. So that's where I'll start my search."

"That's logical." He rubbed his chin. "Do you have transport?"

"No, I haven't looked at the commercial flight schedule yet."

"She can use your yacht, Ahiga," Mai interjected. "She'll get there faster with no hassles."

"I was just about to suggest that," he said, turning to Chooli. "Use it for as long as you need it. It's the least I can do until you find him." He glanced at Mai and gave a wry grin. "And it will keep our relationship amicable at home."

Mai arched her back, returning his smile with satisfaction.

16

ARRIVAL IN PROCYON

Chooli disembarked from Ahiga's private space yacht at the Procyon spaceport, grateful he had offered her his craft to help her find Alex. She felt miserable and lethargic, weighed down with worry. Her mood deteriorated further when she stepped into the incessant rainfall once she left the terminal in search of transportation to take her into the city. She located a taxi shuttle and headed with single-minded intent to the same hotel Alex had checked into.

At the hotel, she fronted the reception desk. "I have a room reservation for Chooli Richards."

The receptionist, a man much taller than her with short blond hair and dressed in a pristine hotel uniform, radiated professional bonhomie. Yet she experienced a hint of prejudicial discomfort behind it. She decided to ignore it this time.

"Let me check." He typed in commands on the screen attached to the counter. "Yes. Three nights?"

"Yes."

"One moment." The man continued working with the screen to check her in and complete the hotel's other welcoming procedures.

He gave her the key card for the room. "Room 2617. One of our finest rooms."

She nodded as she accepted the key. "I also wish access to the room Alex Warner occupies or occupied. I'm his wife."

The receptionist frowned and responded primly, "I'm afraid it's against hotel policy to allow admission to another guest's room without their permission, wife or not."

Chooli gritted her teeth, jumping to the conclusion that her Cetusian heritage was the reason for his refusal. Before she escalated the altercation to an extent where the issue spiraled out of hand, she calmed herself and rationalized that it was a valid and common hotel policy.

"I see. I'm also a GIA agent and need access to the room."

"Do you have a warrant?" The man smiled, a hint of contempt filtering through his expression.

Her temper flared. "Listen! He's my husband, and he's missing. I must search his belongings for any clues about where he may have gone." Her raised voice drew embarrassing attention from nearby hotel guests and other receptionists, but she was beyond caring until she received a satisfactory response.

The receptionist glared at her. "We have no information about your identity or your personal life. It wouldn't surprise me if he left you for someone more to his taste."

Chooli's intended tirade stopped abruptly, her mouth open in shock and her aureola glowing a murderous black.

A vivid redness covered the man's face as he realized his inappropriate remark, his contemptuous expression changing to one of alarm. "Please ... I ..."

"How ... dare ... you!" Chooli's voice echoed through the foyer, bringing everyone within the space to a standstill, their heads turning her way. The hotel manager rushed from his office behind the reception desk.

The manager, a balding middle-aged man, glanced at Chooli, the receptionist, and back to her. "May I help resolve this issue?"

Chooli glared at the receptionist for several more seconds before diverting her attention to the manager. "This receptionist insulted me in the worst possible manner."

"Maybe you misunder—"

"I misunderstood nothing. I know an anti-Cetusian slur when I hear one. And I've heard plenty in my time. I grant it wasn't the worst one, but it's in that category."

"Hmm." The manager stared at the receptionist, far from impressed. "Go into my office. We will discuss this when I finish here."

The receptionist, perspiration pouring from his forehead, obeyed his superior. His body language screamed total dejection as he left.

The manager turned back to Chooli. "Now, what seems to be the problem?"

She took her time to respond. Calming herself, she realized she might have overreacted to the receptionist, but he had it coming. She didn't regret it. She changed her demeanor back into that of a hotel guest making a reasonable request.

"I wish to inspect my husband's room. Alex Warner. He has disappeared, and his room may hold clues to his whereabouts. Besides, there's no point in maintaining a booking for someone who isn't there. If he returns, he can stay with me." She placed her hands on the reception counter, her fingers interwoven as she presented the manager with her most innocent, straightforward, and rational expression.

"As no doubt our receptionist explained, we usually respect the privacy of our hotel guests." He raised his hand, palm outward in a placating gesture as Chooli prepared to butt in. "However, I understand your predicament and the distress you must be feeling. This time, I will overrule hotel policy and allow you to inspect Alex Warner's room in my presence. Is that acceptable to you?"

She was relieved that his proposal avoided creating another scene to get her way. She nodded her head. "I can agree to your terms."

The manager smiled. "Good. Now, please settle into your room.

When you are ready, return to the foyer and ask for me, Mr. Anderson. We can then head to Mr. Warner's room."

"Thank you." She turned and left with the porter, who had been waiting for her with her luggage.

Chooli stood just inside the doorway of Alex's room an hour later with the hotel manager beside her. Everything looked in order. Alex was always a tidy person, and the placement of his belongings in his room provided ample proof of that. She stepped forward and explored the room at a leisurely pace, taking in each object with the practiced gaze of a police investigator. His clothes hung in the wardrobe or lay tucked away in a drawer as the size and purpose of the item dictated. In the bathroom, she noted his toiletries stood on the vanity bench in his typically neat way. She turned her head and frowned. None of the belongings a person usually carried with them — card, communication unit, identity documents — were present, suggesting he had left of his own accord, intending to return.

She caught the manager's attention. "Can you open the safe?"

He began to refuse her request but then thought better of it. "Certainly."

He headed to the strongbox and punched in the overriding manager's code. The lock clicked. The manager swung the door open, but the safe was empty. She nodded. It was as she expected. Alex always carried everything with him when he left a hotel room. He had warned her, "You never know who might snoop while you're out."

She sighed. "What do you think? Should I pack his belongings and take them to my room? We can settle the account then."

Mr. Anderson rubbed his chin as he glanced at her. "There's no point in maintaining a room a person won't return to."

"Good. Place whatever is due on my bill. Inform me if you prefer an interim payment."

She spent the next half hour collecting Alex's belongings and carrying them to her room. Once she had completed her task, she stared out the hotel window, gazing at the skyline in the late afternoon sunlight and wondering what to do next.

———

The next day, Chooli tried contacting Dravo, but had the same success as Ahiga had, so she headed for Milan Asterov's office. She had no appointment with him, but his PA should know his whereabouts if he was absent. After alighting from the taxi, she breathed in the air as she studied the building Asterov's office occupied. It looked staggering. Business must be booming. She stepped inside and took the elevator to the floor of his office.

The doors opened, and she headed for the reception desk. A young female sat there. She raised her head and gave Chooli a welcoming smile, a genuine smile, Chooli noted, instead of one held there as part of her job.

"Good morning, madam. Welcome to Asterov Enterprises. How may I help you?"

"I am Chooli Richards. I wish to meet with Mr. Asterov. Is he here?"

"You don't have an appointment with him?"

"No, I don't, but it's imperative I talk with him. It's about Alex Warner."

The receptionist raised her eyebrows. "Oh? Mr. Warner was in here the other day. Has something happened to him?"

Chooli raised an eyebrow and frowned. "Why would you say that?"

Flustered, she said, "I was ill, and my replacement told me about him. It's just that he was here asking for Mr. Asterov, who was not here. Mr. Warner said he would catch him at his house, but we never heard whether he caught up with him or not. Mr. Asterov hasn't mentioned talking with him. He usually reports on any business matters that occur at his residence."

"Well, is he in? Can I ask him?"

"I'm sorry, he hasn't arrived yet today. Shall I call him?"

Chooli paused as she considered whether she should warn him of her presence. "No. I'll attempt to catch him at his house. Do you have his address?"

"I'm sorry, but we don't divulge our manager's home address. My colleague really should not have handed it out to Mr. Warner."

Chooli crossed her arms in an obvious demonstration of disapproval as she glared at her. "It's imperative I see him. Alex is missing, and I need to find out what Mr. Asterov knows. So, will you give me his address, or shall I call the police?"

The receptionist gulped, displaying signs of distress as her face reddened. "No, no." She grabbed and activated a data card and saved Asterov's details onto it. "Here, take this. It will guide you to his house."

With a fake smile of gratitude, Chooli said, "Thank you," as she took the card. "Have a nice day." She turned and headed for the elevator. As she let out a sigh of relief, she wondered why extracting information was like pulling teeth.

When Chooli exited the taxi, she stood in disbelief at Asterov's enormous mansion. Business must be very profitable, she thought. Massive Corinthian-style columns held the cantilevered portico entrance to the building, which towered three stories high. The imposing edifice discouraged visitors instead of welcoming them. She hoped it wasn't a portend of the barriers she might experience in locating Alex.

The solid oak door loomed before her as she stepped up to it and pressed the button to announce her presence. No sound filtered through the wood-and-stone barrier as she waited, and she wondered if the bell was out of order. As she considered pressing the button again, she heard footsteps approaching from behind the closed door, so she dropped her hand to her side and waited.

The door opened.

A tall, overweight, bald man stood in the doorway, jowls covering his cheeks and multiple layers of fat hung from the chin of the white-skinned human. Chooli's eyes were level with his chin. He wore a business suit, white shirt, and red tie — unusual for humans of the era. "Can I help you?" He frowned as his gaze settled on the aureola bridging her head.

His stare made her nervous. "My name is Chooli Richards. I'm looking for Milan Asterov."

The man's eyes widened as though he recognized her name. "I am he."

"I wonder whether I may ask you a few questions about Mr. Alex Warner?" She glanced past him, hoping he got the hint to invite her into his premises.

He noticed. "Please. We can talk in more comfortable surroundings." He gave a smile that, to Chooli, appeared more predatory than welcoming.

She smiled back just as insincerely. "Yes. Better than standing out here."

He stepped aside to let her pass. She entered the foyer. The door slammed behind her, making her jump and turn her head. She stared at him.

He continued smiling. "The wind caught it."

There was no wind.

"This way." The man escorted her through the mansion to the patio at the rear, where a pool extended further into the yard. Chooli assumed this was the pool where Alex had seen the dead body.

"You have a nice place here."

"The perks of a successful enterprise." He pointed to a deck chair. "Please. Take a seat. Can I get you a drink? Coffee? Something stronger?"

She checked her surroundings. A three-meter-high wall enclosed the property. Manicured lawns and a garden extended to the sides and past the pool with two outer buildings — a conservatory and studio, maybe. "Thanks. Just water will do."

"Very well." He disappeared into the house.

Chooli wondered why he didn't have servants given his obvious wealth and extravagance. She sat in a deck chair and waited, her position such that she maintained a view of the residence and the pool. Asterov returned and handed her the water.

He held a tawny-colored drink in his other hand. Whiskey, she assumed. With a glance at her as if still assessing her mood, he lowered his bulk into a deck chair opposite her and swirled his drink. "What can I tell you about this Alex Warner?"

"Do you know where he is? He should have come home several days ago, but he's vanished."

"No. I don't. Why should I?"

Chooli realized he was baiting her but let the matter slip for now. "He came to see you after visiting Dravo Chinko, an acquaintance of yours. Did you see him?"

"No. It's true he arranged to see me, but he never showed up." He took a sip of his whiskey as he studied her.

Chooli frowned. "When was that?"

He raised his head and gazed at nothing as if recalling events. "Several days ago, so just before he told you he was coming home. I would have to ask my secretary the exact date."

"That makes little sense. Why would he say he's coming home if he hadn't completed his business here?"

The man shrugged. "He may have gotten whatever he was looking for by other means."

"He told me he hit a dead end."

"There you go, then."

The inconsistency in the argument disturbed Chooli. An uneasy feeling crept over her, a slight shiver as if a cool breeze had wafted past her. The frustration tensed her muscles as she stared at him. Should she push him? Should she mention the dead body? She was undecided but her instincts told her that any mention of the dead body could be unwise.

"Holo-vision footage showed Alex leaving the Procyon Imperial Hotel mid-evening. Did he frequent any places in the nighttime?"

Asterov stood and slowly paced toward the pool, turned, and returned to her. "How should I know? I never met the man. There's a bar near the hotel called the Orleans Bar. He may have gone there."

Chooli nodded. It would fit with Alex's character to relax in a bar. "What style of bar is it?"

"Just a casual place. Nothing sleazy, if that's what you're thinking. Ex-pats congregate there. It shows sporting events throughout the Confederation, so they go there to check how their favorite home teams are doing."

It was a lead, and Chooli realized she wasn't going to get any further information from him. She rose from the deck chair and placed the empty glass on a nearby table. "Thanks for your time. I won't disturb you any longer."

Asterov smiled pleasantly. "Let me know how you get on."

17

A FURIOUS VITO

V ito rushed toward his office. Fury radiated from him, the heat even reaching his tailing subordinates as they tried to keep pace with their boss and stole sideways glances at him.

When will Ahiga capitulate? Must I show my resolve to gain control of the crystal boramide on Sirius? He had hoped Alex's disappearance would bring Ahiga back to the negotiating table, but Vito now realized Ahiga was tougher — or dumber — than he appeared. It seemed he needed to make it clearer to Ahiga just who was behind Alex's disappearance.

"Sir," Anastasia, his personal assistant, spoke up.

"What?" he snarled.

"A communication request awaits you from Milan Asterov, sir." She gulped as if expecting punishment for informing him.

"What does he want?"

"I don't know, sir."

He paused and glared at her. Intimidating her gave him a delicious sense of power, but it was pointless and childish, so he continued through the reception and into his office. "Close the door," he yelled at Anastasia behind him without glancing her way.

Moments later, he heard the door click as it mated with the doorframe. Rounding his desk, he peered at it before sitting and stabbing the comm button with his right pointer finger. "Vito."

Milan Asterov was not Vito's favorite person right now. He had stuffed up what should have been a simple job. The explosion at the Sirius mine was designed to spook Ahiga and bring Alex to Procyon. That part had worked well, but the explosives expert had got greedy and turned up at Milan's house looking to blackmail him. Milan had dealt with the matter promptly by overpowering him and drowning him in his swimming pool. But before he could dispose of the body, that infernal, meddling Alex Warner had discovered it and called the police. Admittedly, Milan had fended off disaster quite adroitly, but it shouldn't have happened in the first place. The explosives expert—chosen because he was *not* much of an expert—should have blown himself up in the explosion. Vito hated loose ends.

"It's Milan."

"Get to the point."

"Umm ... sure. A complication has arrived on Procyon."

"What complication?" Vito said, drumming his fingers on the desk.

It seemed everything Milan Asterov touched got unduly complicated. Riva thought he would have to deal with Asterov eventually, but not yet. He could still be of use.

"Chooli Richards."

"Who?"

"She's Alex Warner's wife, and she's asking questions about his whereabouts."

"So?"

"She's a GIA agent."

The news hit Vito like an asteroid had smashed into him. Why didn't he already have that vital bit of information? He did now. "When did she get there?"

"Yesterday, maybe. She came to question me."

"I take it you misdirected her?"

"Not really. I could tell she was sharp. I told her about the bar where Ramira pulled off her con. There's no harm in letting her sniff around there. They know nothing."

Vito rolled the information over in his mind. "The bar will have holo-vision footage."

"We chose blind spots as much as we could."

"A-ha." Vito rubbed his chin. "Still. We should move him. Make sure she doesn't find him before I'm finished with him."

"Where?"

"Bring him back here. We have plenty of warehouses where we can lose him and the infrastructure to deter any inquisitive agents here."

"OK."

"How many doses of chimera stardust have you given him?"

"Two."

"That's enough for now. We want the third as a threat if it comes to that. We might give it to him anyway for all the trouble he's caused us. But dose him with sedatives when you move him."

"I'll get things moving. We should arrive at Xi Boötis within the week. But Vito—"

"What is it now?" Vito was getting fed up with Milan.

"What's the point of Ramira? I grant she did a good job abducting Alex, but she keeps letting him escape, forcing us to bring him back. Why does she do that? She's becoming more of a hinderance than help."

Vito sighed. Milan could be so obtuse. "She has to do that to maintain her cover until I'm ready to bring this matter to an end," he explained patiently. "Have your thugs play along with her." Vito almost added 'you moron' but stopped himself. No point in unnecessarily upsetting Milan while he was still useful to his overall plan.

Vito disconnected the link. His ill temper abated after a while, and he started feeling pleased with himself again.

He called Anastasia back and instructed her to find out everything she could about Chooli Richards, including getting a holograph image.

With any luck, his abductee's partner would follow her mate, and Vito might get to cook two troublemakers in one still.

J ust as Vito's mind had diverted to other matters, his comm buzzed again. He frowned, annoyed at the disturbance, and impatiently pressed the connect button. "Yes?"

"When can I end this charade?" a disgruntled female voice blurted from the speaker.

Ramira. "When I say so."

"But you promised it wouldn't take long. When will you finish it?"

He sighed. "When I'm good and ready. Anyway, I thought you wanted to have some fun with him. You used to like him."

"That was a long time ago. We've both moved on since then."

"You're coming to Xi Boötis."

"What!"

"I need Alex closer at hand — somewhere I can keep a watch on him."

"And me?"

"You need to keep up your performance. There's even more incentive now." Vito grinned with sinister satisfaction.

He saw Ramira frown. "What do you mean?"

"His mate is chasing after him. With any luck, you'll meet her, too. Imagine the excitement you'll get from that."

Ramira's expression transformed from annoyance to calculation.

"It could be interesting," she mused, adding with determination, "But promise you'll let me go then."

"Don't worry. I'll arrange something when you arrive."

Vito disconnected. He steepled his fingers. *You'll get to leave when I'm satisfied, my girl, and only if you do your job right. Otherwise, I'll put you on chimera stardust too.* He smiled at the thought.

18

ORLEANS BAR

After asking a hotel porter for directions, Chooli had no difficulty finding the Orleans Bar that evening. She had considered traveling there on her return from Asterov's place but felt it best to patronize it at the same time Alex would have. True to Asterov's description, it was a typical ex-pat bar with many families using the establishment, eating their meals as they watched the holo-vision screens. It was still early when she arrived. She surmised the clientele might change as families left.

She found a quiet table by the corner and gestured to the waitress, who diverted from her intended route and headed her way.

"Yes?"

"A beer and a menu, please."

"Coming up." The waitress keyed in her order and glanced back at her before walking away, a momentary sneer crossing her face at the sight of Chooli's aureola.

Chooli stared at her back, wondering when the Terran human population would forget the distinctive features of the Cetuseans. She sighed, believing it would probably never happen.

The waitress returned with the beer and menu and left.

As Chooli sipped her beer, she scrolled through the cuisine options and selected her meal. The food came as she emptied her glass, so she ordered another one. When she finished eating, she relaxed and studied the movement in the bar as the night wore on. The families chatted, oblivious to the entertainment and the other patrons. Others sat, eyes glued to the holo-vision screens as they viewed the sport of their obsession playing out in real time, sipping on their drinks as they commentated to their friends or voiced their displeasure or glee at the proceedings.

The families had all gone by 8:30 pm, and a more upbeat younger population had begun to drift in, complete with several women on the lookout for men to exploit. Tonight, they might become her prey as she interrogated patrons and staff.

A band began playing around 9 pm. They played modern music, which Chooli liked. Some things remained universal in the Confederation.

Older men started drifting in soon afterward, men tired from a long day's work away from home, searching for company and entertainment to help unwind before retiring. What better way to unwind than with female companionship for the evening? Chooli scrutinized the ones sitting at the bar. Typically, they ordered a drink and then rotated in their seats to view the band and ogle the audience for likely candidates. Several locked eyes with her before moving on to less intimidating prey — not that she was purposely presenting a hostile presence. She hoped to blend in, but her distrustful persona must be leaking through her façade.

Nobody watched the screens anymore, the patrons socializing with each other, dancing, or searching for wait staff to replenish their drinks. The sound was deafening. Chooli smiled as she recalled a time when she had relished such high volume. These days, she preferred the loudness toned to a lower level. She marveled at the change in her taste but didn't regret it.

About to give up on anyone approaching her, she finished her drink and prepared to leave.

"May I buy you another drink?" a man asked.

Chooli guessed he was in his 40s. He approximated Alex's height and build, but his hairline had receded, and his eyes squinted as if to protect them from smoke irritation, even though the bar was devoid of it. She wondered why he had waited so long to approach her.

"Sure," she said as she returned to her seat.

He ordered a drink from a passing waiter. "I'm Maddock," he said, sitting next to her.

"Chooli."

"Haven't seen you here before tonight."

"Haven't been here before tonight."

"So, you're not from around here?"

"No. I'm from Caerus. I'm here looking for someone. What about you?"

Maddock smiled. "Oh, I'm native to Procyon."

Chooli's drink came, the waiter placing it in front of her as Maddock directed. Chooli spotted he gave the waiter a discreet rise of his eyebrows, to which the waiter returned just as discreet a nod. She thanked him as she considered the significance of the exchange. It was something she had seen many times before in the bars of Caerus: a tag team of men preying on unsuspecting young women with spiked drinks.

"Excuse me." Chooli made to stand. "I just need to use the restroom."

Maddock nodded. "I'll sit here and mind your drink." He gave her what he probably thought was an alluring smile, but Chooli detected too much eagerness in its shape and shivered inside as she moved away.

She considered leaving, but that would negate any chance of finding a lead on Alex's whereabouts. Besides, she had the means to counteract any sedative or mind-altering drug and intended to use it to her advantage. While in the restroom, she searched her purse until she found a miniature tablet container and opened it. A red tablet half the size of her pinky fingernail nestled inside. She swallowed the tablet before tidying her hair and returning to Maddock, an inviting smile fixed on her face as she met his eyes.

Seated again, she turned to him and said in a husky voice, "You didn't get sick of waiting then?" She picked up her drink and sipped it. The tainted flavor was obvious to her trained senses, but she did not show that she had detected it.

"I couldn't leave such an attractive woman without learning more about her." He gave her a smile that was more of a leer.

Chooli shivered inside again. "You are wicked." She returned his suggestive smile, hoping it confirmed her interest in him. She took a bigger gulp of the drink. "You haven't come across a man called Alex Warner, by any chance, have you?"

Maddock's guard slipped for just a moment as if he had heard the name, but he quickly refastened his interest in her. "Why talk of other people when we can talk about ourselves?" *What a cheesy line,* she thought, but she smiled back to keep up the pretense.

After talking more and consuming most of her drink, she waved her hand across her face. "It's warm in here. Isn't it warm?"

"Maybe you need fresh air," Maddock suggested, adopting a fake note of concern.

"You could be right. I should be on my way, anyway." Chooli made to rise but swayed and grabbed the table.

Maddock's hand reached out to steady her. "You alright?" he asked.

She touched her forehead. "I'll be fine once I breathe some fresh air. Must have drunk more than I realized."

"Let me help you." He steadied her, gripping her arm firmly before stepping her away from the booth and helping her outdoors.

"I don't understand." She leaned against him as if struggling to stay upright.

As they exited the building, he directed her toward a darkened alleyway.

"My hotel is that way," she said, slurring as her legs buckled before she found more strength to use them.

"We'll just walk over here."

They rounded the corner into the alley.

As soon as they were out of view, Chooli swiveled around, grabbed Maddock by his arm with one hand, and shoved him against the wall, jamming her other forearm into his throat. "You lowlife scum! I should break your neck, so you don't destroy any other unsuspecting lives."

With eyes wide and fearful, he struggled to free himself, but the more he resisted, the harder Chooli forced her arm into his throat.

"What do you know about Alex Warner?"

He gasped and coughed for breath as Chooli's arm constricted his airways. "Don't know anyone by that name," he managed to get out.

"You do. I saw it in your eyes when I mentioned the name in the bar." She gave her arm another shove.

He tried getting her away from him by pushing with his free arm, but despite his superior strength, she kept him helpless with her positioning.

"I'm waiting."

She watched thoughts race behind his eyes before his muscles relaxed in resignation. She eased her hold, and he said, "A woman was in the bar a week ago asking for him."

Chooli shoved her arm into his throat again, producing another spluttering outburst from him. She frowned. "What woman? What's her name? Where do I find her?"

"Don't know," he gasped out. "Never seen her before."

Possibly he was telling the truth, so she eased her throttle hold again. But she was confused at why a woman would seek Alex by name in this bar. "What did you tell her?"

"That I didn't know any Alex Warner. Then she looked past me as though surprised by something and raced toward the gents. I didn't see her again."

"So, you think she saw him?"

"It seemed like it."

He peeked over Chooli's shoulder, and she saw a flicker of hope radiate from his eyes. At the same time, the corner of her eye detected movement. She rotated Maddock around just in time for his accomplice-waiter to ram into him, sending them both sprawling to the ground.

She stepped out of arm's reach. "Big mistake."

Before they could collect their wits, stand, and prepare an attack, she landed a quick boot to the groin into each of them. "If I hear of you two playing that trick again, I'll come hunting for you. And you'd better pray I don't find you."

She turned toward the alley entrance and left, groans emanating behind her. She at least had a lead. But what mysterious woman had searched for Alex? And why?

19

RETURN TO ORLEANS

C hooli lay awake in her bed after returning to the hotel that night. The image of Alex with a strange woman stayed fixed in her mind. Her jealousy had been legendary in her youth, but she had never doubted Alex's trustworthiness. Maybe he wasn't. His infatuation with her might have worn off, and his so-called business trips might be excuses to slip away to secret trysts with other women.

No. She couldn't believe that, or she didn't want to believe it. It would break her heart. But the idea was driving her insane. Unable to sleep, she struggled from her bed and headed for the small kitchen in search of water.

Instead of fretting about Alex's fidelity, to which an answer was impossible at present, Chooli decided her best choice was to focus on questions she could answer. Maddock said he met the woman a week ago, which accorded with Alex's last night, so she should return to the bar to check for any closed-circuit holo-vision footage of Alex to confirm his visit and discover if he met anyone. She returned to bed, hoping to snatch a few winks before morning.

Chooli stirred late, having nodded off at some stage during the night. Her body must've demanded more sleep than she intended to take. Still, she rose with a refreshed outlook despite her concerns about Alex still being at the forefront of her mind.

She ate breakfast in the hotel restaurant and asked one of the waiters about the opening hours of the Orleans Bar. He went away and returned five minutes later to inform her it opened at 3 pm. Chooli had several hours to kill before then and wondered what she might do. She considered various strategies, but they all depended on her finding evidence of Alex visiting the bar, so she decided she might as well spend the time browsing the shops in the main retail district.

Carrying her shopping, Chooli returned to the hotel at 2 pm. The retail therapy had eased her nerves, but she needed to dispense with her purchases and prepare for her visit. After unloading the bags in her room, she ate a quick snack in a cafe next to the hotel before heading to her destination, entering the Orleans just after opening time. She headed to the counter and the person standing behind it.

The woman, in her late 20s, slim, tall, and sporting shoulder-length black hair, glanced around from restocking the refrigerator with beverages when she heard Chooli's footsteps. "Can I help you?"

"I hope so. I need to speak with your manager."

"Oh?"

"I'm interested in your security footage feeds from a week ago."

The woman frowned. "We don't show them to patrons."

"You will show them to me. I'm a GIA agent." Chooli waved her identification card.

The woman's eyebrows shot up in surprise. "I'll go get him." She placed the box she held onto the counter and left, returning presently with the manager in tow.

A middle-aged man, bald and overweight, approached Chooli. Jowls decorated his cheeks, sagging to a triple chin of fat. First Asterov, now this man — she didn't understand why people didn't do more to sculpt their physical attributes in this technological age.

"You want to view our security vids?"

His abruptness jolted her, but she chose to overlook it. "Yes. I'm interested in viewing a night about a week ago."

"What are you searching for?"

"A man."

The manager chuckled and glanced at the bartender. "Aren't we all?"

Annoyed but keeping her temper, Chooli pressed the issue. "He's missing, and I'm trying to find him."

The manager's expression turned sour. "She said you're GIA." He pointed to the bartender. "You have a warrant?"

Chooli knew she stood on shaky ground but needed to view the recordings. She decided to appeal to his better nature if he had one. She gave him her most pathetic smile. "This is unofficial. He is my husband. As you can appreciate, I'm worried about him. I'm hoping you'll feel sorry for me and let me view it, anyway."

The man continued to look unimpressed. Unable to restrain her aureola from tinging green, she added, "And the last person who made a smart joke on that topic walked bow-legged for a while."

"Sorry, miss. Partner or no partner, without a warrant, you don't look. I need to protect my clientele's reputation."

With gritted teeth, Chooli glared at him. The bartender cringed at her boss' callous response. Chooli had no alternative but to strike for his jugular. "The police might be interested in the type of business you allow on your premises in the later hours. Especially predators spiking the odd drink of unsuspecting women."

He froze, and silence filled the bar. "Follow me then." He turned and stormed back to his office.

Chooli walked behind him, entering an office once they left the bar proper. A security storage setup sat on a table in the corner together with several screens displaying views from cameras placed throughout the premises and outside — front and rear.

The manager turned to her. "What precise night are you interested in?" His voice was gruff. He certainly didn't want Chooli there.

"Footage for the night of July 17th after 9 pm."

He sat at the console and keyed in the information. The holo-vision for the night appeared on the screens, progressing in real-time. Alex was nowhere in sight.

"Can you speed it up five times, please?"

He turned and stared at her. "Won't you miss him?"

"No, I'll see him if he comes in. I have a good eye for detail."

The manager shrugged and obeyed her instruction. Everything progressed in fast motion.

"Stop!" Chooli's heart raced as she recognized Alex enter the bar.

He complied. Chooli noted the time as 9:37 pm.

"Real time."

The footage started playing again, and she viewed Alex order a drink and sit in a booth at the back, near where she had sat the previous night. He kept to himself as he watched the live band playing that night. She studied him intensely, noting every detail of his actions, and gritting her teeth as several women sat next to him and started to flirt. Alex politely shook his head, and the women all left moments afterward. She breathed a sigh of relief. She got the manager to fast forward several times when nothing much was happening.

Just before midnight, Alex stood and headed for the restroom. A woman followed him, turning from the restroom door to lean a shoulder against the opposite wall, her face averted. Chooli frowned. *Is she waiting for him? Or am I reading too much into it? Maybe the woman is waiting for someone else.*

As Alex emerged from the restroom, Chooli's pulse quickened. She watched him stop and glance at the woman's back for a second. Then he turned and walked to the bar, frowning as if he was trying to solve a puzzle. He returned to his seat, drank another beer, and headed for the entrance to leave. She felt disappointed but relieved. Her trust in him remained intact.

The footage had given her no clues about his disappearance or what had happened to him, but she still had the exterior holo-vision to view before he would disappear from the range of the bar's cameras.

Alex appeared outside, where he studied his surroundings before stopping his head's rotation to stare at something to the right at ground level. His body and head blocked Chooli's view of what he saw. He frowned as if confused. When he moved toward his goal, Chooli caught a glimpse of the same woman from the restroom earlier. The woman lifted her head when Alex spoke to her, and Chooli could see her face was covered in tears. They talked for some time before the woman rose, stumbling as though half-drunk, and Alex walked off with her.

Chooli sat frozen and speechless. Who was the woman? Did Alex know her? It seemed like he did. They appeared to engage in a serious discussion, not a flirtatious exchange. But why did he go with her? She didn't know whether to be pleased at this breakthrough or heartbroken.

"Looks like he's dumped you," the manager said with a smirk as he turned to her.

Her heart raced in her chest, her mind confused, but his sarcastic remark broke through the fog in her head, resulting in a fury she didn't know she possessed, her aureola black with rage. Her limbs lashed out and before either of them knew what had happened, the manager lay prone on the floor in a throat hold, Chooli ready to break his neck. His terror snapped her from her trance, and she released him, shocked at what she had done.

"I'm sorry," she muttered and raced in a panic from the office and out of the bar, not stopping until she reached her hotel room. What was wrong with her? She had almost killed a man for making a cheeky remark. What would she do to Alex if she found out he had left her willingly?

As her heartbeat steadied, she pondered her next step. Alex had left with a strange woman to an unknown destination. How would she trace his steps now?

20

WHAT THE HELL IS HAPPENING?

Alex returned to consciousness. His head thumped, and he felt nauseous with an unknown craving. What had they drugged him with? He groaned as he dared to crack open his eyelids.

He lay on a hard surface in a large room with high ceilings resembling a warehouse. Floodlights blazed from the ceiling, increasing his pain. The room was empty except for four chairs and a solid steel table bolted to the floor. A single door penetrated one wall, the other walls being a dirty shade of white with no distinguishing features that he could discern from his position. Apart from the lighting, air vents in the ceiling allowed cool air to circulate. Ramira lay on the floor several meters away, motionless.

His wrists and ankles burned from being restrained. With his arms tied behind his back, he could still move enough and see his feet. The restraints were ordinary cable ties. Still, they were too strong for him to break. He closed his eyes again and sighed. *What the hell is happening? Why am I here? How is Ramira involved?* Her story of a kidnapped child was sounding more and more hollow. He tried to assemble the facts. The alleged kidnapper was Milan Asterov, the man who recommended the electronics expert—who was now missing. And there was an unidentified body in Asterov's pool. Were these things connected?

His head started to throb as he tried to piece the puzzle together. He attempted to move himself into a more comfortable position, but wherever he settled sent shafts of pain from his wrists until he rolled into a prone position on his stomach. That made it difficult for him to view his surroundings, but at least it eased the pain.

After a while, Ramira stirred and shrieked. Their captors had tied her ankles and wrists, too. She was facing away from Alex, so she couldn't immediately see him.

"Are you alright?" he asked.

She groaned as she maneuvered herself to roll over to face him. "I've been better. You?"

"A splitting headache and a strong craving for something. What did they give us, do you know?"

Ramira shook her head. "I assume it was a sedative. They must've given you more. I don't have a headache."

Alex thought she showed a hint of guilt, although she covered it well with confusion. Perhaps he was imagining things. Since she was in the same predicament as him, it seemed she was no nearer to rescuing her child than ever — if there was a child to rescue. He gritted his teeth when he thought of Milan Asterov and how he had fooled him. He reckoned Asterov must work for Vito, which meant that Vito might be the mysterious employer Ramira talked about. Or was that a lie, too? The throbbing in his head worsened as his thoughts went around in circles.

"I wish they'd cut these ties off," Ramira complained. "They're killing me."

"There's nothing in here sharp enough for us to do it ourselves."

She remained silent after that, and Alex lay on the floor with nothing more to say.

After what seemed like an eternity, the door opened, and two gigantic men entered, followed by a third, pencil-thin in comparison.

The musclemen looked in their mid-30s, wore white tee shirts and blue jeans, and had crew-cuts. The third man was much older, had shoulder-length black hair with gray streaks, and wore a charcoal gray suit with an open-collar white shirt and black polished shoes. Why they needed three people to mind him and Ramira when they were both tied up, Alex couldn't fathom, but they were there, and he hoped they would give him answers.

"Cut off these cable ties. They're killing us, and what's the point of them? We can't escape from here, anyway," Alex said gruffly and with a glare at Gray-suited Man.

Gray-suited Man merely grinned, his eyes cold. "They stay on for the time being. They might encourage you to give us the information we want and obey our commands."

Ramira remained silent, presumably from the after-effects of the sedative and the pain she was enduring. Alex persisted. "What if we need the restroom?"

"You'll have to be inventive."

Alex glared at him, but he knew the man wouldn't budge. He lay back, offering no further comment.

"Bring her with us," Gray-suited Man ordered his minions.

Alex jerked his head around, watching Ramira cringe and wriggle backward in a fruitless effort to avoid manhandling. A muscleman picked her up under both shoulders and dragged her through the doorway, ignoring her screams of pain.

"Where are you taking her?" Alex demanded.

Gray-suited Man threw him a mocking look. "None of your business." He turned and left.

The door stayed open, and another thug entered, approached Alex, and cut his restraints before departing without saying a word.

Rubbing his sore wrists and ankles, Alex stared at the door as it locked, leaving him to speculate on what would happen next.

21

CHOOLI VISITS THE PROCYON POLICE

C hooli lay in bed the next morning, confused and desperate after wrestling through another sleepless night. She struggled to rationalize her behavior of the previous afternoon. Her crazy, jealous mind failed to comprehend Alex's actions on the security recording. Worse still, she couldn't understand her reaction to seeing it. Was she so insecure about their relationship?

With a sigh, she sat and rotated to the bedside, tired and grumpy. She wiped the sleep from her eyes, yawned, and stretched. A decision on her next move had defied her all night, but a thought crystalized as she reviewed the intelligence.

Ahiga had contacted the local police here. Someone may have communicated with them with further information or queries about Alex. It was improbable, but it was the only idea she had in her current mental state.

Once she had dressed and eaten breakfast, she took a taxi to the nearest police station. After she jumped out, she surveyed the station façade. It didn't look like a law enforcement establishment in a prestigious part of Procyon City. The walls were filthy, damaged, and needed maintenance. It gave her the impression that Procyon undervalued professionalism in their police force. She hoped it didn't extend to the personnel hired to protect their citizens. Without delay, she entered the station to conduct her intended business.

An officer sitting behind the reception counter glanced up at her from his tablet screen as she walked through the door. He looked bored and returned his attention to the screen. Several other people sat in the foyer. They were in diverse states of agitation in chairs lined up along the furthest wall from the counter, some looking anxious and others showing various stages of guilt or uncertainty. The police showed no urgency in attending to them as several officers in the space behind the counter stood gossiping, having no perceptible interest in helping the waiting clients. The impression made Chooli nervous. If this was a normal day for them, she had doubts about their willingness to help her with her issue. She stepped up to the bored officer at the counter, who continued to stare at his screen.

Without looking up at her, he said, "Take a seat and wait your turn."

The remark surprised and upset Chooli. He could at least inquire what her issue was to prioritize her case. She stayed where she was and stared at the top of the officer's head.

Feeling her eyes on him, the officer lifted his head to glare at her. "I said, take a seat."

She placed her fists on her hips. "No, not until you do your job."

The officer's eyes boggled and then diverted their attention to the people seated behind her. "What you looking at?"

When Chooli turned her head, she saw a row of smirks as heads busily pointed elsewhere. She directed her attention back to the desk officer. By then, several other officers had noticed a change in the atmosphere and interrupted their socializing to investigate.

The desk officer's face burned red. She couldn't tell whether it was from rage or embarrassment. "Sit down right now, or I'll lead you to more uncomfortable accommodation until you learn to obey orders."

The man's associates gathered around him.

Chooli's eyes widened. "You'd arrest a GIA agent with no probable cause?"

As soon as the words left her mouth, she knew it was a mistake to run the GIA agent angle, but there was no way of grabbing the words back and swallowing them.

Spluttering himself to speechlessness, the desk officer stared at her and then turned for support from his compatriots, who quickly found other more pressing matters needing their attention.

The crowd behind Chooli started murmuring to each other about the unusual turn of events.

She remained where she stood, waiting patiently for a response, determined not to lose control.

As if knowing he had no alternative, the desk officer gritted his teeth and spat out, "To what do we owe the pleasure of a visit from a GIA agent? You know you have no jurisdiction here."

"I know. But I got your attention, didn't I? I'm looking for a missing person and hoping someone has reported him missing or you have some information about his whereabouts."

"We have hundreds of missing persons." As if intending a sarcastic comment but thinking better of it, he sighed. "What's this person's name? We can run it through the system."

"Alex Warner."

"Why would this person be missing?"

"He should have returned to Caerus but didn't arrive. He was last seen here."

The man shrugged. "He changed his mind and got on a different spaceship and went somewhere else."

"He would've told me." Chooli sensed herself becoming frustrated. "Can you run his name through the system and check for any reports on him?"

"He would've told you?" The officer produced a knowing, sardonic grin. "What is this, a lovers' tiff?"

She gritted her teeth. "Will you help me or not?"

"What's going on?" an officer of superior rank asked as he approached the reception counter.

The desk officer turned and spoke in a sarcastic tone. "This GIA agent wants us to use our resources to find her lover."

Chooli turned red as her aureola radiated green with embarrassment.

"Is that correct?" the senior officer asked as he turned to her.

"My relationship with him is irrelevant. He is missing, and I'm trying to find him."

"And it's GIA business?"

"No. It's personal. And he said he called you about a murder."

The senior officer stared at her for a moment and returned his attention to the desk officer. "If he called us it will be on record. Run a quick search. If nothing turns up, that's it." He turned back to Chooli. "We can't divert our resources any more than that unless you report the person missing. Is he missing?"

"Nobody can find him."

"He may not want to be found."

"Or something's happened to him, and he needs help."

The senior officer glared at her as if resenting her obstinance. "We'll run a check, and that's it." He turned and marched off, leaving her staring after him and the desk officer grumbling, resentful at having to work for a change.

With reluctance, he keyed the name into the police records system before looking over Chooli's shoulder. "Next?"

After an exorbitant time, the man directed his attention back to her.

"Nothing's coming up. No missing person." The officer said in a sarcastic tone. "And no murder report."

Chooli feared that outcome but had hoped for something more.

She nodded her head. "OK." As an afterthought, she added, "Thank you," before turning to leave, resigned to hitting another dead end.

She was running out of options, and it was breaking her heart.

22

EVERYTHING POINTS TO SIRIUS

C hooli went to a cafe near the police station and found a table. While sipping a coffee, she considered the events at the station and where they left her, which was precisely nowhere.

Nascha had warned her about the Procyon police not cooperating with anyone from the GIA. She might have done better in a private capacity. She sighed. Their final agreement to search their records was at least something. *But why do they have no record of Alex reporting a dead body to them? Do Vito's tentacles reach as far as Procyon? Or are Procyon police as inept as their ramshackle buildings and bored staff suggest?*

The aroma wafting to her nose calmed her as she sipped the bitter fluid. It helped her think, but even the caffeine fix gave her no enlightenment on her next step. The dead body had to be related to Alex's disappearance. It was too coincidental. And she was no nearer to discovering the identity of the woman Alex had left the bar with. She couldn't trace where Alex went with her. The only thing she knew for sure was that there was no point in looking to the police for help.

One other avenue occurred to her as she ruminated. She would return to Milan Asterov's office and interview the receptionist again. She had gotten the impression that the stand-in girl was infatuated with Alex, so she might recall something he had let slip while talking to her and passed on to the normal receptionist if Chooli pushed harder for information. With her next step decided, she gulped the rest of her coffee and found the nearest taxi stand. A vacant one stood idle, so she hopped in and directed it to the location.

When she stepped into the office, the same receptionist's smiling face greeted her.

"You're back?"

Chooli stopped herself from replying, 'No, I'm a hallucination.' Instead, she said politely, "Yes. I have a couple more questions if you don't mind."

"I'm afraid you're out of luck again. Mr. Asterov is away for a few days."

"Oh." Chooli thought it strange she hadn't mentioned before that he was going away. "Where has he gone?"

"He didn't say." The receptionist frowned. "He never says. It's frustrating when we're trying to find him."

"I'm actually here to ask you some questions."

The receptionist's brow rose. "Oh? How can I help you?"

"Did the other receptionist talk to you about Alex Warner when he was here?"

Her eyes glazed as if remembering a secret tryst. "Yes. She gave a graphic description of him. She said he wasn't here long. Just wanted to know where Mr. Asterov was."

"Are you sure she mentioned nothing else?" Chooli considered decking her for her fantasies but resisted.

The receptionist frowned in concentration as she lowered her gaze to the desktop. "Oh! She said he'd come from a mine at Sirius where there'd been an accident and needed to ask Mr. Asterov some questions about the explosives expert Mr. Asterov recommended."

Everything goes back to that explosion at the mine on Sirius.
That's where I ought to be.

She raised her head, smiled, and made eye contact. "Thanks. You've been most helpful. They might know more about Alex's movements."

"Hope so, for your sake. He seems such a wonderful man," she gushed.

Chooli was uncertain whether she meant the comment for her or was wishfully thinking of a future tryst, but she let matters rest and headed back to the hotel.

At the hotel, Chooli called Ahiga's yacht to prepare it for a flight to Sirius. The pilot advised her the earliest he could leave was the following morning.

Leaving Procyon raised the matter of storing Alex's possessions in the interim. She wasn't even sure she would return to Procyon. In the end, she extended her room booking and kept whatever belongings she wasn't taking with her in the room until she returned or had organized an alternative arrangement.

Since the spaceship to Sirius didn't leave till the morning, she had to endure another night of worry over Alex. To distract herself, she booked a tourist tour of the planet until late that evening, after which she flopped into bed, keen to slump into the peace of sleep until she needed to wake for her flight's early morning departure. As she lay under the covers, attempting to find the realm where sleep's furtive tendrils would caress her into unconsciousness, Chooli wondered if her efforts were all in vain, and she would never see Alex again. The prospect was intolerable.

23

ONLY ONE WAY TO FIND OUT

Ramira lay crumpled on the floor after her return to the room she shared with Alex.

He stared at the authentic-looking bruises their captors had inflicted on her and felt guilty for doubting her. He wondered what intelligence they had demanded of her. His jaw clenched at the brutality. It was intolerable. What information did they want from him? He would stay clueless until she regained consciousness and could debrief him about her interrogation.

Several hours passed before she stirred.

"How are you?" he asked, hoping she could speak after her beating.

Her movements ceased as if she believed she was elsewhere. When she moved again, she repositioned her body to face Alex. A blackened eye, half shut, stared at him, contrasting with the one still good. "Could be better," she croaked in response.

"What did they want?"

"Don't know. Think they're just letting off steam. Water?"

He had conserved the water their captors had left them. "Sure." He stood and grabbed the bottle as he headed her way. Kneeling, he removed the cap and gently lifted her head before pouring a dribble into her mouth.

Ramira coughed and gagged on the first mouthful but then controlled her reflexes and gulped until she motioned for him to stop. "Enough."

He pulled the bottle away and recapped it, frowning with frustration. Gray-suited Man wouldn't allow a pointless bashing to satisfy his sadistic fetish. His eyes told Alex his demeanor was more calculating, more purposeful than that. "What did they ask you?"

"They wanted to know anything we discussed."

"About what?"

Ramira shook her head and winced in pain. "Anything at all. I told them to go jump. Hence my appearance."

He stood and paced the room. It made no sense. If they wanted to know something, why didn't they interrogate him? Why subject her to torture? If they knew anything about their relationship, they would know he would be unlikely to tell her anything, even if she begged.

And how did her child fit in with all of this?

Alex stopped pacing, turned his head, and stared at her, doubts rising again. *Was the beating fake?* That black eye didn't look fake, and he noted the bruises on her face and streaks of blood. Her torn blouse revealed more bruising on her arms and torso. It all looked real.

"Let's get you cleaned up." He grabbed the water again, but with no cloth to wipe her clean, he stepped to her, kneeled, and tore a scrap of fabric from her blouse.

She stared at him with questioning eyes.

He shrugged as he finished removing the shred. "It's not much good for anything else." Moistening it, he gently wiped the blood from her face. Despite his efforts, Ramira winced several times as the cloth passed over bruised spots.

"We have to get away from here," he said.

"How? We can't get past those thugs."

"No. But there must be a way. This place can't be impregnable."

He wasn't sure whether he believed those words. It took minimal intelligence to find a room with limited access that required little attention to prevent their escape. "Besides, another couple of sessions like this, and you won't be coming back alive. Let's get you off the floor."

Alex placed the water bottle aside and helped her to her feet. She shuffled with Alex's arm around her waist to a chair before collapsing onto it. He left her there while he continued his pacing, trying to find the chink in their captor's security that would allow them both to escape.

"Did they mention your child?"

She shook her head. "They wouldn't answer any of my pleas for information."

It made their predicament difficult since any harm to her child would place him in a compromising position, one intolerable to her. In other words, she would blame him for her child's death. Still, their only hope was to escape. He gazed upward as if beseeching the gods for enlightenment. As he did so, he noticed a large air vent high on the back wall, just out of his reach while standing on the ground — but reachable if he stood on a chair.

He grabbed another chair in the room and placed it under the outlet. Ramira looked at him curiously.

The door lock clunked, making Alex rush the chair back to its original position. He remained standing, ready for any opportunity to escape.

The door creaked open, and a thug entered, holding two trays of food and drink. Alex looked past him, but his readiness deflated as he noticed the other thug standing in the doorway, his stature preventing anyone from getting past him.

The tray-holding thug placed the meals on the table near Alex. He straightened and glared at Alex suspiciously as though he could read his mind. Alex stared back with the innocence of one attempting to cover the intentions the other suspected him of having. Without saying a word, the thug left, closing the door behind him.

"At least they're feeding us," Alex said as he inspected the contents of the trays.

"They didn't lock it," Ramira whispered.

"What?" He interrupted his cataloging of the tray's selection to give her his full attention.

"They didn't lock the door."

He jerked his head toward it. "You sure?"

"I didn't hear the bolt slide across."

All thought of the vent forgotten, he took a few steps toward the door, stopped, and glanced back at her. "They're probably standing behind it waiting for us."

"Only one way to find out." Ramira's blackened face broke into a garish smile.

Alex diverted his concentration back to the door. *Why would they forget to lock it? They didn't look like complete idiots. If they left it unlocked, they did it on purpose.* But then he realized Ramira was right. He had to try opening it and discover what lay behind it. He started toward it again, each step reverberating through the room until he reached it. The door opened inwards. If someone opened it now, it would bowl him over. He reached for the knob and turned it, tensing as fear washed over him. A bead of sweat rolled into his eyebrow. He was doing something stupid.

Jerking it open, he prepared for the inevitable assault. Instead, one thug stood on the other side with a menacing grin plastered on his face. Alex slammed the door shut again, his heart pounding, expecting the door to open, his beating for his stupidity assured. But the bolt slid across instead, preventing any further hope of escaping via that route. Laughter emanated from the other side. He frowned. It was as he expected – too easy.

"Told you they weren't idiots."

"We had to try." Ramira strained to stand. "If they were stupid enough to leave the door unlocked and unguarded, we could have grabbed our good fortune and made the most of it."

Alex shrugged, his shoulders slumping in disappointment. They needed to take any opportunity they got. His eyes moved back to the air vent. After listening for any activity beyond the closed door, he headed to the vent again, the chair in his hand.

He placed the chair in position and stood on it, his hands just reaching the bottom openings in the vent. Grabbing inside the vent grill with both hands he lifted himself until he could see out thought it. Fresh air was on the other side, a roadway traversing the rear of the building. *An escape route if I can remove the grill.*

After lowering himself to the chair again, Alex turned and said to Ramira, "We can get out this way."

Ramira stared at him with an expression that indicated anything but excitement. "Give it a try."

Alex locked his fingers around the grill bars and pulled, expecting significant resistance. Instead, the grill immediately popped out, almost over balancing him off the chair. He placed the cover on the floor, careful not to make a noise.

He stepped onto the chair again preparing to remove the outer grill. He anticipated greater difficulty in removing that grill. He also needed to lift himself and rest one forearm on the bottom of the opening while he worked on removing the outer grill.

His left upper arm muscles ached with strain as Alex punched at the grill with his right, palm forward. At first, he sensed no movement and his hopes dropped, expecting to have to concede defeat. But, with the third thump on the steel panel, it popped out, falling to the ground outside. He lowered himself to the chair again, gasping for air as he recovered from the exertion.

Alex looked at Ramira. "Ready?" He glanced at the food. "Pity we can't eat before we go, but we can't chance them returning and discovering us half way through the vent. Can you move alright, or do you need my help?"

Ramira started hobbling toward him. "Whatever we do, I'll be a liability."

"I'm not going without you." He went to her and placed his arm around her waist. She rested her hand on his shoulder, and they moved together toward the chair. "I'll hoist you to the vent. Can you pull your way through and drop to the ground?"

"I'll try," Ramira said, a quiver of trepidation in her voice. "I might break my neck, though."

"Just make sure you roll when you hit the ground. Ready?"

Ramira nodded, so Alex hoist her as high as he could. Moments later he felt her weight leave him and he gazed upwards. Her body lay halfway through the cavity on her stomach, slowly moving forward.

Alex stood on the chair and steadied her as she continued her escape. Her body disappeared soon afterwards with a thump and a groan as she hit the ground. Good. She made it and is still alive. He lifted himself again, pulling himself through with relative easy, and allowing himself to drop and land on his side on the grassy ground.

"All good?" he asked.

Ramira nodded with a sullen face. "I'll live."

Squinting as Alex surveyed their locality, he asked, "Where are we?" to no one in particular.

24

CHOOLI ON SIRIUS

The day after her arrival on Sirius, Chooli left the hotel on a hired scooter and traveled to the mine, hopeful for a clue to Alex's whereabouts. On arrival, she hopped out and started walking to the office. The air along the way was dusty, with wind-gusted particles of grit blowing past her. She shielded her eyes from the dust and sighed with relief when she entered the office, the dirt still sticking to her face and hair as she passed her hand through it.

A receptionist sitting at a nearby desk raised her head as Chooli strode inside. "Nasty day." She looked middle-aged with peppered hair and plump, wrinkled features to match the rolls of fat cascading down the torso visible above the desktop. She neither smiled nor snarled but presented a cool exterior to Chooli.

"Yes, you could say that," Chooli replied. "I'm here to meet Mr. Salter."

"I see." The receptionist made no move to contact her superior. "Is he expecting you?"

"No." The woman's stare gave Chooli the shivers. "I need to talk to him about Alex Warner. He visited here recently, and I want to ask Mr. Salter some questions."

"Are you the police?"

"I'm Alex's wife."

The woman sighed as if Chooli was making an unconscionable imposition. "And your name?"

"Chooli Richards."

"I'll check if he is busy."

The receptionist's manner raised Chooli's temperature, but she made sure she didn't show it with her aureola color. "Thanks." She gave a fake smile and ambled to the nearby window to gaze out into the developing mine.

Snippets of the woman's voice wafted toward Chooli as she whispered into the office comm, presumably talking to Kansas Salter. After over a minute's conversation, the woman told Chooli. "The manager will be with you soon."

Chooli swiveled and smiled again. "Thanks."

Alex had told her the open-cut pit was important, but it didn't look important to her. Piles of dirt rose heaped to one side of a huge deep hole in the ground where layers of solid rock lay strewn. As she watched, a flash of light emanated from the pit's far surface, followed by a crack and roar. A shudder then shook the office. Boulders projected high into the sky together with dust. She tensed in confusion, her hand reflexively reaching for the pistol she usually carried in a holster under her coat. Then she relaxed, realizing the detonation was merely a blast to fracture a wall face for excavation.

"Good morning, Ms. Richards."

Chooli jumped and swiveled to identify the person approaching her unnoticed, the sound covered by the explosion's roar. "Good morning, Mr. ...?"

The man stretched out his hand. "Salter. Kansas Salter," he said as he projected a smile. His bulky frame towered above her, toned by extensive workouts in the gym. He was square-faced and bald. His voice was a deep baritone. He was nothing like she had imagined. She had never met Kansas Salter, but she had gained the impression from Alex that he was a much slighter, more unprepossessing man.

She smiled back. "I appreciate your sparing the time to see me, Mr. Salter." She shook his hand.

"Not at all. Any associate of Alex's is always welcome, especially one as attractive as you. He has great taste."

Chooli blushed and her aureola tinged green. She wasn't sure whether to show pleasure or annoyance at the gratuitous compliment. For the sake of harmony, she decided on the former. "Thank you."

"Shall we go to my office where we can talk in private?" He held out his arm, indicating the direction.

"Sure." Chooli stepped to the open doorway behind the reception desk, which had Kansas Salter's name on it.

The man pivoted as he passed the threshold, as if to speak to the receptionist, but then changed his mind. He closed the door and pointed toward a chair. "Have a seat. Refreshment?"

"I'm fine, thanks," Chooli said as she sat.

He rounded his desk and seated himself, his chair creaking from his muscular weight. "To what do I owe the pleasure?"

"I'm here about Alex."

"Oh. How's he doing?"

"That's just it. He's missing. I came searching for information about what happened when he visited you recently."

The man frowned. "Recently? I'm sorry, m'dear, but I haven't seen Alex for months."

Chooli's heart sank, her hands clenching convulsively on her lap. A dizziness passed over her as she absorbed the shocking news. But after a few moments, she said, "What do you mean? He came here. Alex told me he came here. He said there had been an accident, and he needed to investigate it."

The man shrugged. "I don't know what he told you, but he didn't visit us. Are you sure he said that? I assure you I haven't seen him."

Confusion overwhelmed her thoughts. "So, you didn't have an accident?"

"We had an accident — if you can call it an accident. It was more a tragedy really. The so-called explosives expert blasted himself to pieces and a couple of others along with himself."

She sat staring at her clenched hands in turmoil as she considered the man's words. *Maybe Alex didn't come here. Maybe he only went to Procyon. Why would Alex lie?* She blanched as she remembered the recording at the bar, the holo of him leaving with the woman. But then her mind cleared. She gave Kansas her full attention again in time to notice a sneer, which he quickly converted into a sympathetic smile when he realized she was looking at him. "Ahiga said Alex came here and saw Kansas Salter. Ahiga wouldn't lie. Why are you deceiving me?"

"Are you questioning me?" the man asked as he rose from his chair. Sympathy and oily charm had changed to intimidation.

Chooli copied his movement, concerned for her undefendable position. "Someone is telling me lies and your information is inconsistent with what I've been told."

"It's unfortunate you're so good at your job." The man lunged at Chooli with his immense bulk, his speed belying his mass.

As soon as she saw him move, Chooli's training kicked in and she stepped to the side, hoping his momentum would prevent him from grabbing her. *Where's my pistol when I need it?*

Her presumption proved correct. His massive hands narrowly missed seizing her arm as he over-balanced and smashed into the office wall, causing the entire room to shake.

Even though she avoided his grip, Chooli realized she had moved the wrong way. The man now stood between her and the door, her only means of eluding him as he staggered upright again. He now displayed open hostility, his towering girth blocking any avenue of escape.

"Why are you doing this? Who are you?" she demanded.

"You shouldn't have come here. We can't allow you to leave now. You could pass your information on to the wrong people."

The man took a step forward.

Chooli had no choice but to use offensive tactics. She diverted her energy into her left leg to smash her foot into his groin. Unfortunately, he detected the movement and caught her ankle before she could complete the motion. He used her momentum to lift her lower body in the air, causing her to crash to the floor on her back, smashing her head. She saw stars for a fraction of a second before scrambling backward to keep out of his clutches, her heart thumping in her chest.

The man laughed.

Using her hands and feet, she continued moving backward, rounding the desk, before judging she could safely jump to her feet. As she glanced at the door, she realized it swung outwards. She needed to lure him far enough from the doorway for her to escape. It was her only hope. She needed a distraction.

"You're Dravo Chinko, aren't you?" she threw at him as she crept around the desk.

The man didn't move. It seemed he felt confident he had Chooli trapped. "Very observant."

"What have you done with Kansas?"

His grin broadened. "Let's just say he's spread throughout the mine."

"You bastard!"

It was now or never. Chooli had a direct line to the door, and she hoped the discussion had distracted him enough for her to escape. She put on a burst of speed, racing to it, bringing her shoulder to bear, anticipating the impending collision. Chinko followed her movement, but her fractional earlier start gave her sufficient momentum to reach it first, the door splintering as her body smashed into it. His hands grabbed thin air as she tumbled through the doorway, her stance changing into a roll to the floor.

A bolt of laser fire flashed past her, surprising her. But it surprised her opponent even more, as he stared in astonishment at the cauterized hole in his chest.

Chooli's eyes moved from Chinko to the source of the laser shot. The receptionist sat stunned, with the laser pistol still pointed at the doorway as her boss tumbled to the floor, dead.

Realizing she had little time, Chooli jumped onto the now recovering woman, pushing aside the pistol before it fired again. Despite the woman's bulk, her sitting position and the clumsiness of her obesity disadvantaged her. Chooli smashed her fist into the woman's face, breaking her nose on the first punch. She continued pummeling her until the pistol dropped to the floor, her head flopping sideways, unconscious.

Chooli heaved for breath as she untangled herself and stood erect again. Blood covered her hands, spots of splatter staining her blouse. She glanced at the body of Dravo Chinko, motionless on the floor, his eyes still staring with astonishment, his bulk blocking the office doorway. Chooli felt no guilt in leaving the bodies, one dead, one unconscious, without reporting the incident. She needed distance from the mine and Sirius before anyone discovered them — or before the woman regained consciousness and raised the alarm.

She used the woman's voluminous jacket to wipe the blood from her hands, grabbed the pistol, and headed for the shuttle and the hotel, intent on her spaceship flying away from Sirius back to Procyon as soon as the pilot could prepare it for departure.

25

ON THE RUN

"Any idea where we are?" Alex asked Ramira as he scanned their surroundings for a familiar landmark.

Seated on the ground and leaning against the warehouse wall, she said with a grimace, "No, I don't."

He turned to her. "We don't have any comms."

She glared at him. "I know."

Not knowing whether she was annoyed at him or the situation, he stopped talking. He glanced at her. She needed painkillers, too.

We can't stay here, he thought. Eventually, their captors would return and imprison them again. Perhaps their strange laxness was due to the whole place being a prison. Perhaps escape was impossible.

"We'd better get moving." Alex looked left and right, wondering where the fastest route to safety lay.

"We're on Xi Boötis."

He jerked his attention down at her. "Where?"

"The moons. I recognize them. The size of that one." She pointed to the large moon in the daytime sky. "It's the same as the one orbiting Earth. But there are two, so it's not Earth. The pockmarks are unique."

He scratched his head. "How did we end up on Xi Boötis?"

"They must have moved us while we were unconscious."

He stared at Ramira while he considered their options. "We still don't know where we can hide." He rubbed his chin, which by now was sprouting a beard. "Although there's a detective here from my time in the GIA who might help us—"

A hint of fear flashed across Ramira's eyes as she hastily interrupted, "We can't do that! They'll arrest me, and I'll never see my baby again." She peered past him to his left. "Let's go that way. We can follow the road. I might recognize a landmark."

"You know this place?"

"I've been around. With unsavory people sometimes. If we can get to a comm, I'll contact someone I trust to collect us."

"Let's go then." He held out a hand to help her rise from her position. His instinct still screamed at him not to trust her, but he had no choice until he found someone more trustworthy. She seemed to be aware of her surroundings better than he. He hoped he wouldn't regret letting her take the lead.

With Ramira supported as before, they hobbled together along the access road to the warehouse and then along the more defined roadway. The sun beat down on them, and the air contained a humid stickiness.

After half an hour, both perspiring and puffing from the effort, she pointed out a shop. "Go in there. I recognize it. The owner might help if he's still there. He used to look after me when I was desperate."

With no better suggestion, he followed her instructions, and they shuffled into the premises several minutes later. Relief flowed over him as they entered the building, the overbearing intensity of the sun giving way to an air-conditioned interior that chilled his overheated skin, evaporating the glistening moisture coating it. The changing light level made it hard to see until his eyes adjusted to the dimmer illumination.

The shop looked deserted.

"Just a tick," a squeaky voice called. It seemed to be coming from beyond an open doorway behind the counter.

Alex headed over that way, letting go of Ramira, who leaned on the bench top, relieving him of his burden. He sighed. "That's better."

"I'm not that heavy."

"You are to someone lugging you as far as I have."

She shrugged, admitting he had a point.

A spindly, gray-haired Asian man with a drawn face stepped through the door. He wore blue denim overalls over a white vest and came to a halt when he saw them, wariness masking his features.

"Hi, Leong," she said.

"Ramira." He glanced nervously at Alex before returning his attention to her. "What can I do for you?"

Alex thought he didn't seem surprised to see her.

"Have you heard news of the club's activities?"

Club? What club? Alex wondered. *Was the innocuous-looking Leong part of the underworld Ramira used to inhabit?*

"Nothing in particular. Why?"

"I'm looking for my child. He's been kidnapped."

Leong turned away in a typically evasive movement.

"Please," Ramira begged. "Tell me what you know."

"I know nothing."

Leong was obviously lying. Alex's temperature rose as he struggled to restrain himself from roughing the man up to make him talk. "She doesn't believe you, and neither do I."

"Stay out of it," Ramira warned Alex.

Alex turned to her. "He knows something. He needs to tell us."

Leong stepped back, his brow puckering with anxiety.

Alex took three strides, rounding the counter and grabbing Leong by the bib straps. Leong tensed, covering his face as he appealed to Ramira for help. "Tell us!" Alex shook him. "Tell us!"

"I ... I can't. The Grotto ..."

"Stop! Alex!"

Alex tossed Leong aside in disgust. But Leong stumbled. To Alex's horror, his head hit the store counter, his neck smashing into the edge hard, producing a loud cracking sound. The shop owner dropped to the floor like a rag doll and didn't move.

Alex and Ramira stared at each other in shock. They couldn't believe what had happened.

"What have you done?" she said.

"I didn't think he'd stumble over his own feet." He glared at the contorted body, angry with it for making a bad situation worse.

Now what? Alex thought.

"We can't stay here," Ramira said. "Customers will come along eventually and discover the body. It was an accident, but it won't look like that. We need a place to hide."

Still in shock, Alex thought there was no point contacting his police associate now. He would probably arrest him. But then he thought, 'Why should I feel guilty?' It was an accident, and they were fleeing a kidnapping. The worst his associate could charge him with was involuntary manslaughter. He would probably let him go.

Pulling himself together, he said to Ramira. "We need to call the police."

But the possibility of getting the police involved seemed to alarm her more than Leong's deceased body. "No, we can't do that! I'll never see my child again." She rushed to him and hung on his arm, pleading. "Please. We can't, they'll sell him or worse. I know you don't believe me, but he is your son too. You can't let them kill him. We must get away before anyone notices the body."

Her emotional blackmail trapped him. He didn't believe the child was his, but he couldn't take the risk.

"Where? Where do you suggest we go? We have no money, no comm, and no transport."

She released him and paced. "Leong will have transportation at the back. We'll take his cash chips and comm. He mentioned The Grotto — I know that place. We can hide there." She eyed the shelves of products in the store. "Take enough food with us for several days."

As if on cue, Alex's stomach grumbled. He felt dirty leaving the scene. It was against everything he had believed in from his days in the GIA. He cursed his bad luck for crossing paths with Ramira again. The police would eventually get involved, and how would he explain his actions to them — to Chooli?

But they had to do something. They couldn't just stay there. If nothing else, their captors would find them, and they'd be back where they started. Reluctantly, he said, "OK. Let's go."

"Good." She grabbed several grocery bags and started stuffing them with snacks and drinks.

Alex sighed. He took the chips from the register and patted Leong's body for his comm. He then realized they wouldn't be able to operate his vehicle without his ID. Searching for Ramira, he found her busy in an aisle. "How do you propose to start his scooter or whatever he drives?"

"I can hot wire it if necessary."

She has an answer for everything.

Ramira appeared with two large grocery bags in each hand, her aches and pains from her bashing apparently forgotten. "Let's go."

They rounded the counter and headed through the back. A scooter sat idle just outside the door. She tossed the groceries into the luggage receptacle and went to the driver's seat. After eyeing the layout of the machine, she ripped open a compartment. With a speed that stunned Alex, she had the scooter running.

"Where's The Grotto?" he asked.

"It's in the Indo Precinct. I've been there. It's safe."

He was confused. "But if he knows about it, why wouldn't everyone else?"

"Only he and I know of it. I told you we go way back. We worked together and cared for each other. He saw I needed help and was suggesting we hide there — before you spoiled everything."

Alex shook his head in dismay. Nothing about any of this made sense. He concluded he must be the stupidest or most gullible person in the Confederation. "OK. Let's go look, then."

Ramira powered up the scooter and ascended into the sky, heading for the nearest flyway and The Grotto.

He sat in silence. Apart from his hunger pains, his stomach told him trouble lay ahead. He glanced at her, thinking of an earlier time and wondering for the umpteenth time whether he could trust her.

26

FROM DESPAIR TO HOPE

Chooli's life was one long blur of fog after her unexpected brush with death at the Sirius mine. She remembered little of the trip back to the hotel as her thoughts oscillated between the mine and her confusion over Alex's whereabouts. Something far bigger than Alex being missing was happening. Something she was unaware of but had much higher stakes.

From the spacecraft on the way back to Procyon, she called Ahiga.

"I've found Dravo Chinko," she greeted him.

"That's great! Where?" said Ahiga. "Is he OK? Does he know anything about Alex?"

"On Sirius—"

"Sirius? What is he doing there?"

"Please, Ahiga, let me talk. Chinko is not doing so well. He's dead. But don't feel too sorry for him. He killed Kansas and took over the mine. He pretended to be Kansas to me and then tried to kill me. He would have succeeded, but his receptionist accidentally shot him. I had to knock her out to get away. He told me nothing useful about Alex."

Ahiga was speechless.

"Are you there, Ahiga? You can talk now."

All Ahiga could say was, "Come home, Chooli. Now. This is too dangerous. It smacks of Vito Riva's involvement."

"I'm not going home without Alex."

For the rest of the journey, Chooli mused over all that had happened and what she might have lost.

Is this what it's like to lose your life partner, never to experience the warmth of his touch again or his friendship? Will I never again feel the sensual tingle of his strokes along my spine, his soul-joining gaze, his crooning words, and his sweet lips?

She sighed and then pulled herself together. It was pointless descending into a well of self-pity. She had no evidence Alex was dead or even likely so. She felt sure he was alive somewhere out there, and she would find him. But where to start? She had already exhausted every avenue of inquiry she had discovered — until another one came to light.

Back at the Procyon hotel, still in a state of semi-depression and unfocused brainstorming, she headed downstairs to the lobby restaurant for an evening meal. She hadn't eaten since her return late that morning and wondered if a full stomach might encourage her gray matter to offer some insight into where to search for Alex next. Having secured a secluded table in the back of the establishment, she ordered a Ceti cocktail, one of her favorites, while she pondered the menu. The Procyon Kraken dish's description sounded delicious, so she ordered that with a side dish of green salad and a bottle of Procyon Chardonnay to complement the food and soothe her emotions for the evening — or dull her sorrows.

The meal was excellent. While sipping her wine, she mulled over Alex's likely fate, her GIA training guiding her eyes through the room for any signs of danger. Maybe he wasn't on Procyon anymore. She hadn't thought of that. But why would he have left? With the image of him and the woman outside the bar burned into her memory, her chest compressed in distress. She shook herself; dwelling on that image wouldn't help her in her quest. A visit to the Port Authority Office in the morning to search their records for any hint of his departure was her next step. The thought of having a plan of action lifted her spirits.

C hooli rose early, full of resolution. She wolfed her breakfast before departing for the spaceport, eager to discover any sign of Alex's movements. She arrived at the Port Authority Office just after nine local time and headed for the reception desk.

A youth — Chooli wondered whether he had hit puberty yet — looked up from a screen behind the counter when he heard the door swish open. A smile appeared on his face as he watched her approach. Despite the smile, his eyes did not look friendly. She tensed as she neared him.

"May I help you?" the black-haired youth asked.

"You may," she said with her most engaging expression. "I'm searching for someone who may have been on a ship leaving Procyon about two weeks ago. Is there someone who could help me with the passenger lists?"

The youth's smile disappeared. "Is this a police inquiry?"

"No, it's not. It's personal. A friend of mine was last seen here and has since vanished. I'm looking for him."

"I'm sorry. We don't divulge passenger details to civilians."

Chooli's heart sank. She had hoped her charm, combined with his inexperience, might gain her an opening. Sighing, she switched into woman-in-distress mode. "But it's imperative I find him. His family and I are so worried something bad has happened to him." Her voice trembled as she spoke. But the youth remained unmoved.

"Sorry. That's the law. I can't break the law."

Chooli knew that was rubbish, but it was pointless arguing with him. "I'd like to speak with your superior, please."

The youth gritted his teeth as if circumventing him was a personal insult to his honor. But she didn't care. She needed answers. She glared at him, all attempts at charm evaporating, and he glared back. The standoff ended a few seconds later when he averted his eyes in defeat. He made a call on his desk comm, muffling his conversation. When he finished, he returned to whatever had been occupying him before she had interrupted him, ignoring her. She waited impatiently for his superior to arrive.

A middle-aged man of medium build but carrying a huge abdomen that struggled to defy gravity entered the reception. He was bald except for a fringe of gray hair circling his head from ear to ear at the back. His eyes bulged, and he wore a sour expression. As he approached, she turned to greet him, and his eyes bulged further as they registered her appearance.

"What's with this inquiry for a passenger list?" he demanded as he stopped before her.

Hello to you, too.

She smiled. "Yes. I wish to find out if the person I'm chasing has left Procyon."

"It is very irregular. What authorization do you have?"

Chooli realized she was reaching the same impasse. She glanced at the youth, then at the supervisor. She knew she shouldn't do what she now intended to do, but she was desperate. "May we speak in private?"

The bald man's suspicion subsided. "Yes, of course. Follow me." He turned and led Chooli through to an office. After rounding the desk, he sat, leaving her to stand or find her own seat. He seemed eager and excited as though foreseeing what she intended to propose. As he leaned back in his chair, he folded his hands behind his head and stared at her.

She remained standing to give him a sense of power. "I need to review those lists."

"It's against spaceport policy."

"And yet we are here in your office discussing it."

"We are."

"What can I offer you?"

"You're an attractive woman."

"I was thinking more along financial lines."

His eyes hungrily roamed her body. "You're asking a lot from me."

She already felt dirty but didn't flinch. "Why? Those lists can't be that confidential."

"They've sacked people for less."

Chooli dreaded going where he was leading her. She glared at him and decided. Is this the only way? "Name your price."

"You. Tonight. All night."

Her stomach churned just imagining the scenario, but she kept her face and aureole blank. "OK. Let's get started on those lists."

"*Before* you view the lists."

"No. I need to see them now."

"I can't help you then."

He was bluffing. Chooli saw the hunger in his eyes. He was just trying to get his reward without delivering the deal. "I'm sorry." She turned to leave.

"Wait."

She stopped mid-stride and turned her head back to him, eyebrows raised.

"OK. You can view them now. But you'd better come through with your promise."

With a smile, Chooli nodded. "Where do we start then?"

The supervisor stood and approached her. He brushed his fingers against her cheek and let his hand drop to her breast while he tried to kiss her, sending a wave of revulsion through her. She raised her arm between them and pushed him back. "Tonight."

He desisted. "This way." They left his office and walked through several corridors until they entered a room with myriad screens and consoles on desks. He approached one and logged in, bringing the archive files for vessel movement details onto the display. "There."

Chooli sat and started traversing the menus until she reached the information she sought. She ran a search for Alex amongst the departing passenger ship lists — from when he should have left to the current date — and waited. A blank screen came up several minutes later. She frowned.

"You've drawn a blank," the supervisor said, standing behind her.

She turned to him. "Could he have used a private vessel?"

"It would have shown in the search result." He gave a smug grin.

Chooli deflated with disappointment. She had been so sure he had left Procyon. She sat contemplating her options as the supervisor's predatory hands crept ever closer to her.

"What about freighters?"

The hands stopped. He looked surprised. "What about them?"

"Could he have left on a freighter?"

His arms dropped as if they had lost their purpose. He frowned. "Some freighters take on passengers."

"Did the search include them?"

"No. It's a separate database."

"I need that searched, too."

He sighed as he reached in front of her to access the keyboard, his hands stalling, confused over which direction they should take until they resigned themselves to the keyboard task instead of sating themselves on Chooli. "There," he said as a fresh screen appeared.

She set up the new database search. It went quicker than the first one, and when completed, a notice flashed. 'Three unknown passengers on *Riva's Titan*.' Chooli's heart skipped a beat. She pressed the details button and read. *Riva's Titan* was a megaton freight ship that had left Procyon a week ago for Xi Boötis. Excitement welled up in her. It was the right timeframe. "Why are the passengers unidentified?" she asked as she turned to face the supervisor, noting his puzzled expression.

"I don't know. It shouldn't be possible. The ship's captain must register every person, but these three weren't."

"And no idea who they were?"

"No. Not now."

It was something she could use to continue her search. Butterflies gave a momentary flutter through her stomach. "That's it then. Thanks for your help." She stood to leave.

"Aren't you forgetting something?" the man asked as his eyes roamed over her again.

Chooli hoped he wouldn't push his payment. "Oh, that. Where do you want to meet?"

"The bar at the Fortune Hotel. Bring what you need for the night." He gave a meaningful grin.

"Sure." She was determined to stay unresponsive, even though her insides heaved. "See you at seven."

"Seven."

"Now, I have things to do."

The supervisor led her to reception, where she left him for the outside air and freedom. She would not be visiting the Fortune Hotel ... ever.

27

TO XI BOÖTIS

C hooli walked through the Xi Boötis spaceport terminal exit to a brisk breeze and overcast skies mid-afternoon two days after leaving Procyon. Rain threatened to pour at any moment, but it was exhilarating to follow a defined path again, even if it turned out to be the wrong one.

As soon as she had left the Port Authority Office on Procyon, she had returned to the hotel, packed, and headed straight back to the spaceport and Ahiga's yacht. Luck had the pilot ready to leave Xi Boötis an hour after she arrived. There was no way she would ever become the depraved supervisor's entertainment. He'd be furious over her deception, but she hoped it taught him a lesson for the future.

She found a taxi and headed to the Xi Boötis capital, the outline of its skyscrapers silhouetting the horizon in the dimmed, overcast skyline. She reviewed her plans to pass the time. Xi Boötis had a GIA office, and she intended to go there to use their resources to locate the mysterious freighter and its captain.

But first, she headed for a hotel to use as her base and prepare for action. After a search through the database, she settled on the Continental Hotel. She had brought all her belongings and Alex's with her so she would not have to return to Procyon.

It was too late to begin then. Even with an uneventful trip, she was tired and needed rest for a fresh and alert start the next day. At the hotel, she went to a rooftop restaurant in the evening for dinner. A knot rose in her throat as she reminisced about her first dinner with Alex. It seemed so long ago, and she missed him so much. She sighed and finished her solitary meal before retiring.

Light streamed through the window the following morning as she woke, the cloud cover of yesterday replaced with sunshine and blue sky. She glanced at the chronometer and grunted with surprise. She had slept in, something she seldom did. The bed felt warm and cozy, so she luxuriated for another five minutes before reluctantly easing herself from under the covers to prepare for her day.

After dressing and breakfast, Chooli headed for the GIA office a few blocks from where she stayed. She walked, taking advantage of the sunshine, the photosynthesis occurring in her aureola adding extra vigor to her step. The only thing missing was Alex at her side, but even his absence couldn't dampen her current spirits.

As soon as she arrived at the office building, she headed for the directory panel to find the floor the GIA occupied. To her surprise, it was housed in the basement. She frowned. Unusual. If that's its location, that's where it is, she thought as she headed for the elevator. Her comm buzzed before she proceeded any further. She checked the caller, confused. It was Nascha.

"Hello. Chooli here."

"Hi. Glad I caught you. It's not inconvenient to talk, is it?"

"No. What's up?"

"I received a call from a Police Detective Inspector Chiang from Xi Boötis just now."

Chooli's eyebrows rose in surprise. "Oh?"

"He's investigating a suspected homicide. Thing is — witnesses observed two people running from the scene, and one fits Alex's description."

"What? Where's this? How can I talk to this Detective Chiang?"

"Woah. Calm down, Chooli. It couldn't be Alex. He's on Procyon ... isn't he?"

"He was. But I can't find him there. And a freighter traveled with three unnamed passengers from Procyon to Xi Boötis; it's very unusual for passengers not to be named, and the timeframe matches. I'm chasing up the ship's captain right now."

"Oh." Nascha stayed silent for a few moments. "You should talk to this detective, then. He's in Xi Boötis City police headquarters. The murder occurred in one of the decrepit industrial suburbs, from what he told me."

"Detective Chiang?"

"Yes. Alex and I talked to him during the Scorpius serial murder investigation. That's how Chiang remembered him."

"OK. I'll talk to him. He might help me with the freighter, too."

"I'll leave you to it, then. I called since it seemed a coincidence. Good luck."

"Thanks. It could be the break I need, but I can't imagine Alex implicated in a homicide."

"Talk to Chiang."

"OK."

Nascha hung up, leaving Chooli staring through the glass façade of the building where she stood, wondering what Alex had gotten himself involved in. She changed her mind about the GIA. That could wait. She needed to see Detective Chiang without delay, so she found a vacant taxi and headed straight for police headquarters.

She disembarked and entered the police station, where a cacophony assaulted her ears as soon as she stepped over the threshold. Victims, felons, and police officers intermingled in the front reception space, while behind the counter, a frazzled sergeant sat rubbing his forehead as he attempted to placate his current client. As he seemed the person she needed to talk to, she lined up to wait her turn. The general hubbub drowned the details of the discussion between the officer and his client.

Chooli perused the rest of the room while she waited. Several people sat mute, their faces distorted with stress and fear. Some cried. Her urge to help them intensified her frustration, but she knew she had no jurisdiction to interfere. Two or three glared at her with naked hostility. When she looked at their wrists, she noticed restraints pinning them to magnetic clamps, preventing their escape.

"Next," she heard from the counter.

As she approached the waiting sergeant, a tall, thin Terran woman barged ahead of her. "You must help me," she said to the sergeant, her tone arrogant.

"She was first," he said, pointing to Chooli.

The Terran turned to inspect her, disgust oozing from her. She returned her attention to the sergeant. "She's just a Cetusean. She can wait."

Chooli's blood boiled as she glared at the bigot, but she decided not to make a scene.

Not tolerating the woman's presumptuousness, he said, "It doesn't matter who she is. She was first, so move aside and let me serve her."

"Well! I've never been so insulted. I wish to speak to your supervisor."

The man's jaw clenched as he considered his options. "It's OK. I can wait," Chooli said.

"You see. They're used to waiting. Now, I—"

After glancing at Chooli, the sergeant addressed the woman. "She was ahead of you. I don't care who you protest to. Go sit or do whatever you want — but wait your turn."

"Humph. You haven't heard the last of me. I've never seen such insolence." The pest located a vacant seat, glaring at the officer as if doing so would devour him with the wrath of God.

The sergeant sighed and turned his attention to Chooli. "How can I help you?" he asked in a professional tone.

"You could have served her. I didn't mind."

"She comes every second day with a complaint. We're sick of her, but you can't bar people from reporting a crime, regardless of its triviality." He smiled. "It's the highlight of my day to put her in her place."

"I wanted to speak to Detective Chiang if he's available."

"Oh?" He raised his eyebrows, surprised. "To what does it relate?"

"A homicide that occurred recently. He phoned my Caerus colleague. He was searching for information about the whereabouts of Alex Warner. I believe we might help each other if I can meet him."

"I see." His forehead creased as he considered his next move. "I'll call him. What is your name?"

"Chooli Richards."

"Just one moment." The sergeant picked up the station comm and disconnected after a brief conversation. "Detective Chiang will see you momentarily. Are you in the GIA by any chance?"

She smiled. "Yes, I am, but it's a personal matter."

"I see. Well, take a seat, Ms. Richards. Detective Chiang'll be here soon. Now for the wrath of the fiery dragon," he said as he winked.

She chuckled, turned, found a vacant spot, and settled herself down to wait.

She didn't wait long. A man opened the locked door connecting the inner office to the reception vestibule. He was middle-aged and wore red trousers and a tunic with a blue shirt, his hair black and cropped short. He surveyed the space before his eyes settled on Chooli, smiling as he approached her. "Chooli Richards?"

She stood. "Yes."

"I'm Detective Chiang." He held out his hand.

"Thanks for seeing me," she said as she stood and shook it.

"Come with me."

He headed for the doorway he had exited. She followed him as

they threaded their way along a corridor before they came to an interview room. He gestured for her to enter, which she did. The room
was bare, apart from a table, two chairs, and electronic equipment
hanging from the ceiling behind security glass. A two-way mirror
lined one wall.

"Am I being interrogated?" she asked with a smile, making small
talk.

"Not at all. It's the only room available. Would you like a drink?
Tea? Coffee? Water?"

"Water, please."

Chiang left to arrange the refreshments before returning a
minute later.

During that time, Chooli sat staring at the mirror, nervous,
knowing anyone on the other side would suspect she had something
to hide. Maybe she did. What if Alex had committed a crime —
murder? What should she do? And what should she tell Chiang? She
didn't believe Alex had intentionally killed anyone. *I mustn't jump to
conclusions myself. Let him tell me what happened and what evidence
implicates Alex.*

Chiang returned and placed the water on the table in front of
Chooli. She thanked him and took a sip. The cool liquid provided the
right burst of lubricant to a throat dried by tension.

"Now," he said as he sat opposite her, the table between them.
"The sergeant said you were enquiring about Alex Warner. May I
ask why?"

The detective's phrasing instantly intimidated Chooli. Her
muscles tensed even more, and she pushed back in her chair until the
backrest prevented further retreat. "Alex is my husband, and he's
missing."

"So, you're the mysterious life partner. His history is vague on
that score."

"Because I'm a GIA agent. They keep their agent profiles confidential for operational reasons."

"So, why isn't the GIA investigating?"

Her tension deflated, replaced by hopelessness. "It's not a GIA matter, even if I am an agent. We must be asked before we can offer our services."

"So, you're here in a personal capacity?"

Chooli nodded before staring at him, desperate for answers. "But I was contacted today by a colleague, Nascha, who's also a friend, to say you've sighted him here and think he's involved in a homicide. I can't believe Alex would kill anyone, not intentionally. Please tell me if you have any idea where he is. I'm going nuts searching for him."

Chiang glanced at her with calculating eyes as if weighing her words and how much he should disclose to her.

"Before I divulge any information — and I have no obligation, mind you — what do you know of his movements?"

Chooli saw through his tactics, but she couldn't blame him. She'd do the same. She sighed. "He went to Procyon, and I traced a security video of him leaving a bar there. That's the last anyone has seen of him. I traveled here because a freighter came to Xi Boötis with three anonymous passengers on board, and I hope to talk to the freighter's captain. I'm convinced they were Alex and his captors."

Chiang's brow rose.

"OK, I'm desperate and out of options. When Nascha mentioned you spotted him here, I decided I should approach you first."

"You saw him on Procyon?"

"I watched a hologram recording of him."

"Was he alone?"

Chooli squirmed. She was reluctant to reveal her intelligence but knew her obligations. "I saw him leaving with a woman." After a micro-second, she added. "It wasn't what you might think."

He raised an eyebrow. "What might I think?"

She blushed. "You know. He picked ... her ... That's not like Alex."

"I get the picture." He stood and paced the room, rubbing his chin, before fronting her again. "I want to show you something." He grabbed the tablet he had brought with him and tapped the screen several times before turning it toward her.

A holographic recording started rolling, showing a derelict district of Xi Boötis City from a camera on a road intersection. A shop stood to the left. After half a minute, two people entered the screen-shot — male and female. Chiang froze the footage and zoomed in on their headshot. Only the backs of their heads were visible until the female turned hers.

"Is that the woman?"

Transfixed by the image, Chooli gulped. "Yes." The male fugitive had to be Alex.

Chiang fast-forwarded the recording until a vehicle emerged behind the shop and rose. He zoomed into its forward side window, revealing a man's face. Chooli's head slumped. *It couldn't be. He wouldn't kill anyone. It's a mistake, or he acted in self-defense. Or perhaps the woman killed the man.* She raised her eyes to Chiang. He was staring at her, waiting.

"Is it him?"

"It resembles him," she prevaricated. "But I don't understand why he would be there. Or with that woman. Do you know who she is?"

"We'll know all that when we catch them."

"Where is he?"

"We don't know. They've disappeared."

"Just like on Procyon." Chooli's tone reflected bitter disappointment. "I'll never find him." Her heart ripped further with defeat.

"Can't you put the GIA's abundant resources to use?"

She jerked up her head at the condescending tone, meeting his eyes. She wanted to lash out at him but refrained. "As I said, they can't help without your explicit invitation."

"Yeah, well. Our procedures won't allow me to, yet ... unfortunately."

"What else can you tell me?"

"Nothing at present."

She sighed. "I'll go then. Thanks for your time." She stood to leave.

"Keep in touch. We'll get a lead, eventually." Chiang moved to the door and opened it. He led her to the exit.

The passage exiting the station seemed much longer than it was entering it, Chooli thought as she left and requested a taxi to return her to the hotel.

28

RAMIRA DROPS A CLUE

Alex and Ramira arrived at a dilapidated shack in the Indo District. He wondered how well it would conceal their presence and for how long. The Grotto, the man called it. Its appearance resembled a rubbish tip. They hid the scooter and went inside.

Alex paced the floor, depressed at having to stay there, while Ramira checked the rooms for suitable bedding and facilities.

She returned to him. "We have two beds and running water," she said, pointing to the next room.

"We can't live here for long." He glanced at her. "I know a guy. We can contact him. He'll offer us a hideout until we work out a plan."

Panicked, Ramira rushed over to him and grabbed his arm. "You can't, please! They might kill our child."

Alex was getting tired of her standard objection to everything, especially as he was doubting more and more whether there was a child at all, let alone *their* child.

Filled with suspicion, Alex asked, "How? They don't know our whereabouts. We escaped, remember?"

"But they'll wait until they find me. If they discover we used someone to throw them off our trail, they might get impatient and kill our child, anyway. I can't take that chance."

"Your logic makes no sense." He stared at her, his temperature rising. "What's really going on here, Ramira?"

Ramira burst into tears. "You're right. I have been tricking you about that. But not about our child. They really have kidnapped him, and they will hurt him if I don't do what they demand." She pointed to her face, where the welts from her beating had faded into a brownish yellow. "These bruises — I got them because I didn't want to trick you." She sniffed and wiped her tears from below both eyes.

Alex felt like a jerk, but he still knew she wasn't telling him everything. "What do they expect you to do?"

"Keep you isolated, trapped."

"Why?" He threw his arms out, flabbergasted.

"Some mine or something."

He gaped at her, trying to process her words. A mine? Then it hit him. He burst out laughing. "Vito thinks this will convince Ahiga to hand over his holdings on Sirius? He's crazy. Ahiga won't give in to extortion, and neither will I." He shook his head, amazed. After pacing the floor space, he returned to her and stared hard at her. "So, we're meant to stay here until we're found?"

Ramira shrugged. "I guess so. They didn't say."

Uneasiness still flowed through him. "Why did you want to escape, then? Wouldn't it have made more sense to stay where we were?"

"I had to make it look like I'd been captured along with you and had just as much interest as you in escaping. And I had to stick with you."

Alex thought it highly likely Vito's thugs would capture them again very quickly but kept that to himself. His mind teamed with questions. *Does Vito really think he can acquire the mine this way? Or is he just being vindictive because I advised Ahiga against conducting business with him? What should I do? Run? But where?* He knew someone would have discovered Leong's body by now and alerted the police. He was probably a wanted man.

Events seemed to be drawing him deeper into a quagmire not of his making. It was all Ramira's fault. His resentment of her rose with each supposition. *Why am I such an idiot whenever I encounter her?* But he had no time for psychoanalysis. He turned to Ramira. "So, what do we do now?"

29

COMMISSIONER HARRIS OFFERS HELP

Once Chooli returned to the hotel after meeting with Detective Chiang, she headed for her room and sat cross-legged on the bed, moping. She would not sit there doing nothing; it wasn't in her nature. But what her next step should be remained elusive to her. Chasing up the freighter captain was pointless now since she knew Alex was on Xi Boötis. She considered whether she should verify the third person's identity but decided her time was better spent on other inquiries. She had to find Alex before he incriminated himself beyond redemption. *But where should I start? Where?*

Chooli needed higher-caliber help. The time for asking nicely was over. She required the sort of interrogation resources and ruthlessness that the local GIA office couldn't give her. She wasn't sure the GIA as an organization had the mettle. Her only choice was to call Commissioner Harris for help.

There was no better opportunity than the present, so she grabbed her hyperlink comm and dialed the Commissioner's number. After waiting impatiently, she heard him answer.

"Harris here."

"Hi, sir. It's Chooli Richards. Can you talk?"

"For you, Chooli, always. I've been worried about you. Have you made any progress?

"I've traced Alex to Xi Boötis, and he's in a spot of trouble. But I still can't find him."

"What trouble?"

She paused, not sure if she should tell him. But she realized she had to stick her neck on the chopping block if she wanted him to do likewise. "He's implicated in a homicide. Circumstantial at present. Security footage shows him and another person fleeing the scene."

"Oh." After a moment, he continued. "That's unlike Alex ... Who's the other person?"

Chooli blushed and was pleased the Commissioner couldn't see her. "He and a woman. I don't know her. But he left the Orleans Bar on Procyon with her the night he was last seen. I saw security footage of them."

"What does she look like?"

"I didn't notice." Despite not seeing him, she sensed him raising his eyebrows in disbelief, deepening her blush. "About his age. Blonde. Slim. Similar height. Not bad looking, I guess. Why?"

"I hope it's not who I think it is. For Alex's sake."

"Why? Who do you think it is?"

"A gremlin from his past. It was almost his undoing. She was trouble then, and she's likely trouble now."

Chooli frowned as she reviewed the footage of Alex meeting the woman on Procyon in her mind. It explained why he accompanied her and why they seemed familiar with each other. But he had mentioned no incident to her like the Commissioner had suggested. "What's her name?"

"Ramira Lopez. She's bad news. She's associated with Vito Riva, amongst other things."

Vito Riva? Where have I heard that name lately?

"I must find her. I must find them. And I need help."

Silence issued from the comm.

"Are you there, sir?"

"... Yes," he said. "What precise help are you requesting from me?"

"The GIA here providing resources to track down Alex." As soon as she vocalized her appeal, she cringed inside, waiting for a disappointing answer but hoping she was wrong.

"I'm afraid that's not possible. The local police have issued no request, and the GIA can't get involved without that, or it might cause a Confederation incident."

"Please. There must be something you can do?"

More silence. "Not officially."

"And unofficially?"

"I'll help you in any way I can."

Chooli pondered her requirements as she stared at the comm. "Can you get the GIA to release some weapons to me?"

Silence. "Why?"

"I might meet unscrupulous characters during my investigations. I'd like to think I had a modicum of protection."

Silence. "Fine. I'll call the Xi Boötis office manager and tell her to issue you with your needs. But I don't want news of trails of destruction."

"You won't." *I hope.* "Thank you, sir."

"Is that it?"

"Yes."

"I'll be on my way. And Chooli ..."

"Yes, sir?"

"I hope you find Alex. Ask me if you need more support. I'll help you if I can."

"Thank you, sir. I appreciate it."

Commissioner Harris disconnected.

She sat back. The lack of official GIA backing disgruntled her but didn't surprise her. Unofficial was better than nothing. She sighed. *What do I do now?*

30

CHOOLI STARTS CONNECTING DOTS

I t was late afternoon, so Chooli couldn't visit the GIA office until the morning. The Commissioner had to make his request to them first, anyway. She undressed and showered to wash away the day's grime. Her thoughts wandered as she lathered her hair until her eyes jerked wide open.

Riva's Lion

Alex had mentioned meeting Vito Riva not long before he left for Sirius. Ahiga had told her Vito wanted to buy the Sirius mine, and he had mentioned him as the person most likely to be behind Chinko's takeover of the mine. *The name of the freighter can't be a coincidence.*

She quickly finished showering. Once dressed, she grabbed her tablet and searched for the owner of *Riva's Lion*. A microsecond after placing the query, she had her answer. The company in charge of the freighter was owned by Vito Riva. For once, the stars aligned, but she couldn't fathom how to use the information to her advantage.

With a sigh, she went to the living space of her suite and flopped on the couch, switching the holo-vision streaming service on to find a show to distract her. She ended up watching a tabloid Who's Who current affair program when a well-known celebrity,

Sabrina, appeared on the screen. Fascinated, the segment held her attention.

"Welcome to Xi Boötis," the reporter said to Sabrina.

"I'm glad to be here."

"Everyone is waiting with bated breath to see your new movie."

"Yes, yes." Sabrina flicked her hair back. "It's my best performance so far. I'm here for tonight's premiere."

"Do you have any celebratory plans after the viewing?"

"Yes. Vito Riva has kindly invited me to an after-show supper at the Crimson Lotus."

The interview continued, but Chooli didn't hear any of it. She stared at the screen, dumbfounded. Vito was on Xi Boötis and in the city. Rage flared within her. *He's getting an unexpected guest.*

After getting directions to the Crimson Lotus from the concierge, Chooli readied herself for an upmarket restaurant that enforced high dress standards on its patrons. She prepared her makeup and dress carefully for the occasion, ensuring her clothes allowed plentiful freedom of movement. When ready, she checked the timing for the movie's completion and gave her prey another hour before she ventured to the establishment.

Butterflies fluttered in her stomach as the Crimson Lotus entrance came into view. Her motion became rigid and unnatural as her muscles tensed for action. Knowing her condition was unsuitable for confrontation, whether physical or psychological, Chooli stopped and took several calming breaths before continuing.

A giant crimson lotus flower rose from the semi-circular raised porch decorated as a lily pad at the restaurant doorway. Two security guards stood expressionless on either side of the tunnel, bifurcating the central petal, their hands clasped in front of them.

Chooli made to enter the restaurant, but they stepped laterally, blocking the entrance. She stopped and looked up at them, wishing they would make eye contact with her, but they stared straight ahead. "I'm dining here tonight," she explained.

"Restaurant's closed," the left one snapped.

"No, it's not. Please let me through," she said in what she hoped was an authoritative upper-class voice. She also hoped her temper was not about to fracture.

"You're not eating here unless Vito has invited you." The brute lowered his gaze to meet her eyes. "And he didn't invite you."

"Is that right? I'm out of luck then." She made to leave but immediately dashed around the thugs and headed inside the premises. Both their arms jerked toward her to grab her, but she was too fast and unexpected for them to get a hold of her.

She slithered through the doorway into the restaurant dining room, the staff staring in surprise. One burly guard stomped in after her, his expression reflecting an intent to kill her if he caught her. She glanced behind her and dashed to the side, gambling that her size gave her an advantage over his bulk in unexpected changes of direction.

The vast hall was empty except for a table in the secluded rear of the restaurant, where she saw Sabrina, whose self-satisfied expression changed to confusion when she spotted the disturbance heading her way. Beside her, Chooli caught sight of an overweight man with a ball-shaped face and a bald scalp. He wore a black tuxedo with a dazzlingly blue bow tie. It had to be Vito Riva.

Chooli turned to the guard with a table between them. They traded tentative maneuvers in one direction and then another as they tried outsmarting each other. Amusement flashed across Chooli's mind in imagining the entertainment they must be giving the onlookers.

Knowing she couldn't keep this up all night, she made a final dash to the diners, expecting to sail past the thug in triumph. But she felt a burly hand grab her by the forearm, the vice-like grip threatening to crush it and crumble her bone to dust.

"Let me go, you over-muscled ape!" Chooli's temper was well and truly exploding. She struggled as she fought with the brute while trying to move closer to Vito's table.

Finally noticing the disturbance, Vito turned and frowned at the ruckus upsetting his private meal. But when he saw Chooli, his annoyance morphed into a delighted smile. He waved to draw the guard's attention, after which he gestured to let her pass. Confused, the guard released her and straightened the cuffs of his sleeves.

Chooli, surprised by her sudden release, glared at the brute again before straightening her outfit and preparing to traverse the rest of the distance to her goal. She came to a halt in front of Vito, who welcomed her like an honored guest. Self-conscious with everyone staring at her, she stepped forward, suddenly unsure how to proceed.

"What a delightful surprise," Vito said. "Welcome to our little dinner party, Ms. Richards."

The warmth of his greeting perplexed her. She wondered how he knew her identity as they had never met. "Where is Alex?"

He laughed. "No small talk? Straight to the point. I like that. But please, take a seat." He gestured to a vacant chair, his features still showing unalloyed pleasure.

"I prefer standing." She glanced behind her to see the thug still where she'd left him. Giving Vito her attention again, she asked, "How do you know who I am?"

With a Cheshire cat grin but shifting scheming eyes, he replied, "You're famous in the Confederation. Franconia and other such heroic acts."

"Just doing my job. Where's Alex?"

"Why do you think I have him?"

"You transported him on *Riva's Lion*."

His smile faltered but returned a moment later. "You're thorough. I'll give you that. His location is unknown to me."

"That's a lie. You have him."

"I tell the truth. But I wish I did." He frowned, a fleeting look of concern crossing his face before the smile returned. "Has Alex talked to you about his lovers?"

The question threw Chooli as if a sledgehammer had smashed into her. Why was he asking her that? *Is the woman an affair of his?* Alex had revealed his romantic and somewhat promiscuous past, but she had always suspected he hadn't told her everything. She hadn't pushed him, believing it better to let sleeping dogs lie should they haunt her at a future time. Maybe they were snapping at her heels now. She glared at Vito. "What do you mean?"

"My dear," Vito purred, "you don't flee halfway across the Confederation with a casual friend. Years ago, your oh-so-loyal and trustworthy partner was far more deeply in love with another than with you."

"You're a lying space viper."

Vito's smile disappeared as he took in her angry eyes. "Don't you not know I have the power to order you removed — permanently — by one glance at the thug behind her? I do not lie about this," he continued. "Since you know so much about Alex's current movements, you must know he is not traveling alone. He has company. Female company. I wonder what they're doing now?"

Chooli's fists tightened as each word left Vito's mouth. Her rage ascended and darkened, as did her aureola. She had lost control but didn't care. She threw down the gauntlet and tossed her own daggers at him. "They were both escaping from you."

"You keep deluding yourself with that. It may morph the truth long enough for your delusions to transform into reality. I doubt it. You see, she's the love of his life. They've reunited and rekindled the flame. They even have a child together, a dear little boy," he goaded.

Another smash of the pile-driver crashed into her before she snapped. "You bastard!" She rushed for Vito, her arms raised and hands ready to crush his throat. The distance disappeared like a hyper-jump. The pleasure of seeing fear wash across Vito's face sent her into an even greater frenzy. Two steps from achieving her goal, she felt monstrous hands grab her arms, jerking her to a halt.

She gasped for breath, both from her exertion and from her continuing fury. She struggled but couldn't break the iron grip. Her effort was pointless, but it helped vent her rage.

"Remove her," Vito commanded.

"Let me go!"

But her body started moving away from the table despite her scrambling legs intent on resisting the backward momentum. As she reached the restaurant entrance, she realized her defeat, and the anger and determination drained from her, leaving an empty shell of desolation and humiliation as her actions crowded her memory. The thug threw her onto the pavement with such force that she scraped her hands and knees and ruined her dress. The abrasions stung less than the indignity.

If Vito thinks this will stop me, he knows little about me. Since he won't tell me where Alex is, I'll find him my way.

She picked herself up from the ground, fuming. Glancing back at the restaurant entrance and the two guards standing like statues again, she could swear she could see suppressed smirks. She turned and plodded back to her hotel, wondering what she could do to discover a lead to Alex's whereabouts — and what secrets he had withheld from her about that woman.

31

A PRODUCTIVE VISIT TO THE GIA

Seated in her hotel room, Chooli stared gloomily out the window into the Xi Boötis night, her thoughts racing past her confusion to find a new course of action. Her only way forward, she concluded, was to visit the GIA to get more details on Ramira Lopez. If she knew who she was, where she came from, and her current history, Chooli might gain enough information to give her the next step toward Alex and answers.

In the morning, she headed for the GIA office to begin her quest into the world of Ramira Lopez. She arrived at the reception mid-morning and asked for the office manager before sitting down to wait. After five minutes, a tall, middle-aged woman walked through the security doors. Her hair was blonde streaked with purple, a style Chooli had seen extensively on Xi Boötis, and she wore a jade-toned hanfu. Chooli noticed intelligent brown eyes inspecting her as she stood to greet her.

"Hi, I'm Chooli Richards."

"A pleasure to meet you. We've heard interesting reports about you from time to time."

Chooli blushed.

"I'm Li Meng, the GIA office manager on Xi Boötis."

"Thanks for your time. I hope the reports have been favorable."

Meng raised an eyebrow but didn't comment. "How can I help you?"

Uncomfortable with discussing her petition in public, Chooli asked, "Can we go somewhere more private?"

Meng smiled. "Of course. Follow me." She led Chooli through the entrance to the secure office space and toward the far end, where a row of offices lined the wall with windows overlooking the grounds of the building.

A dozen people sat at desks in an open-plan workspace, busy with their tasks. Some glanced at Chooli as she passed them before returning to their work. She and Meng entered a large office at the farthest end, one of a line of separate offices, and Meng invited Chooli to sit. She closed the door behind her before rounding her desk and seating herself.

"Now, what is this cloak-and-dagger business needing such secrecy?" Meng gave Chooli an amused smile as if she was having fun at Chooli's expense.

Chooli blushed again, her cheeks burning as she searched for the right words. She didn't want to get on Meng's wrong side. "It's a delicate matter. I'm undertaking a private investigation—"

"To find Alex Warner," Meng finished the sentence for her.

Chooli offered a weak smile. "Yes. I see someone's already briefed you of my affairs."

"When you have the GIA Commissioner call you in the middle of the night requesting a favor, you source any intelligence about the matter you can grab."

"Oh. I don't mean to abuse the agency's resources." She lowered her gaze in embarrassment.

"You aren't. Not yet anyway." Meng's voice softened. "What do you need?"

After fidgeting in her seat, Chooli said, "I want more information on a woman called Ramira Lopez. I figure she might lead me to Alex's whereabouts."

Meng gazed up at the ceiling as she tapped her chin. "Ramira Lopez? Where have I heard that name?" After several seconds, she returned her attention to Chooli. "No. I can't remember. I will. In the meantime, ..." She pressed a number in her desk comm. "Can you come to my office?" Meng smiled at Chooli while they waited.

The door opened, and a young female agent entered, petite and similar in height to Chooli. She had jet-black shoulder-length hair and wore a white tee shirt and blue denim jeans, a highly casual outfit for work, in Chooli's opinion, her tacit disapproval slipping past her passive expression. The girl chewed gum and shot Chooli a defiant look.

"Chooli, meet Wu Chin. She's currently working undercover on a case. Hence her appearance. Don't let it deceive you, though. Chin, Chooli Richards."

Chin stopped chewing, her jaw dropping as she stared at Chooli. "*The* Chooli Richards?"

Chooli's embarrassment returned. "It's getting hot in here." She waved her hand across her face.

Both Chin and Meng laughed.

"Have a seat, Chin," Meng invited, gesturing to her, "and close the door behind you, Chin."

Chin obeyed and sat, remaining silent.

"Since you're here in a private capacity, I can't let you use our resources yourself," Meng explained. "But I can get Chin to delve into your matter, and you might coincidentally glance over her shoulder." She smiled at Chooli.

Chooli looked at Meng and Chin before nodding. She saw enthusiasm in Chin's eyes before she returned her gaze to Meng. "I'm happy with that."

"I need the history of a person called Ramira Lopez," Meng instructed Chin. "The name's familiar, so we should have current records of her, and it shouldn't divert your attention from your assignment for long."

"Sounds easy," Chin said while chewing her gum again. "Is that it?"

"Make sure Chooli sees what you find."

Chin nodded and looked at Chooli. "Shall we start?"

"Yes." Chooli smiled as she stood. She turned to Meng. "Thank you so much. I realize I'm stretching the rules."

"Don't thank me," Meng said. "Thank Commissioner Harris. He must hold you in high regard."

"Still, thank you."

"Come see me when you finish. We can discuss other potential support *then*."

Chooli smiled. "I will." She nodded to Chin, who opened the door and led her to her desk.

"You on terms with the Commissioner?"

Chooli flushed again. "Not really. It's through Alex more than anything." She wanted to avoid unwelcome publicity circulating through the agency but understood the power of the rumor mill.

"It shouldn't surprise me, given what you've done. You're gutsy."

"Well, it's not helping me at present."

"So, why are you checking into the Ramira chick?"

Chooli told Chin about her discoveries so far.

"Wow!" Chin had stopped chewing as Chooli's story unfolded, but it restarted at an increased tempo. "That's some story." She arrived at her desk and booted up her tablet. "Let's search our database." She opened the GIA records and typed in Ramira's name.

Several seconds later, the screen filled with information.

Chin whistled. "She's got quite a sheet," she said as she started reading. Remembering Chooli, she turned to her. "Pull in closer." She shoved her chair sideways to accommodate her.

Chooli obliged and leaned inward to get a closer view while they both read the display.

The report started off by listing Ramira's petty crimes on Earth until she joined a crime syndicate. During that time, she befriended a police officer to extract information from him. The officer's name was redacted, but Chooli felt her temperature rise. When the police noticed the leak, Ramira went to jail for a year. It didn't say what happened to the lawman. She moved to Xi Boötis and continued in organized crime, this time with an organization run by Vito Riva. While there, she allegedly engaged in drug trafficking and other illegal activities, but the authorities never had enough evidence to charge her with any crime.

Informants reported she retired eighteen months ago and had stayed clean ever since.

The file said she was single and childless.

"Quite a hard-assed bitch," Chin said afterward. "But how does it help you? She seems dormant."

The name Vito Riva shone out to Chooli in neon lights. She couldn't stop staring at it as her confrontation of the previous evening replayed in her head. *He had lied about the child. What else had he lied about?*

"What do you have on Vito Riva?" she asked.

Chin stared at her. "How much time do you have? You name it, he's probably done it. Problem is, we can never convict him. They don't call him 'Teflon Vito' for nothing. He runs significant legitimate businesses and seems to call in favors to make any *indiscretions* disappear."

"His name pops up wherever I turn. I'm sure he's involved. I just don't know how."

"Maybe, but this Ramira chick is retired. She must be acting on her own."

"She might have come out of retirement with suitable inducement from Vito."

Chin shrugged. "Not much to go on."

"No." Chooli seemed to run out of questions her agency helper could answer. "What are Vito's legitimate businesses?"

Chin typed the query into her tablet.

A list of companies and products scrolled down the screen, but one had an asterisk next to it.

"What's that one?" Chooli asked, pointing to the asterisked item.

Chin pulled up the details. The business supplied crystal boramide to the government and other private enterprises. It listed the mineral's end products and its regulated status.

"Why is crystal boramide regulated?" Chooli asked.

"It's used to make chimera stardust."

"What's that?"

"The most addictive and destructive substance in the galaxy. Three decent doses, and you'll do anything for another fix, I'm told. Problem is, it also eventually kills you. Drug syndicates will do anything for a supply of it. It's worth a fortune."

"Oh." Pieces started falling into place. The mine on Sirius had crystal boramide deposits. Vito dealt in the mineral. It produced an extremely addictive narcotic that demanded a high price. Control of supply gave you an open credit chip to print money. Alex had gone to the Sirius mine to investigate an accident. She had encountered nasty business at the same mine. All of that could be no coincidence. She had to discover how Ramira was involved with Vito and chimera stardust trafficking. "I think I'm done here."

"That's it?" Chin's eyebrows rose.

"For now. I need to do some digging myself." *But where do I start?* "Thanks for your help."

"You're welcome. It's such an honor to meet Chooli Richards! Hey, contact me if you need anything." She typed on her tablet, and Chooli's comm pinged. "Being undercover gives me a lot of leeway. Call me, even if it's just for a chat and a drink."

"Sure. Thanks." Chooli appreciated the girl's admiration teetering on hero worship but doubted there would be any time for chit-chat in the foreseeable future.

Standing up, she considered what else she needed while in the GIA office. Some protection would be nice. She wondered how far Commissioner Harris had told Meng to help her. She could only discover Harris' generosity in one way. "Can you take me back to Meng now?"

"Sure." Chin led her back to Meng's office and knocked on the glass door.

Meng looked up and waved them inside.

"Get what you wanted?" she asked Chooli.

"Yes, thanks," Chooli replied. "Chin was very helpful."

"Good. She's one of my best information moles. She can uncover just about anything." Meng smiled at Chin, who lowered her head modestly. "Sure you don't want her to do something else for you?"

"No. I have enough to start. But I have one other matter to discuss with you."

"Sure. Thanks, Chin. Sounds like you've been your usual efficient self."

"You're welcome." Chin left, closing the door behind her.

"Sit down, Chooli. What's this other favor?" Meng's eyebrows rose questioningly.

Chooli didn't bother sitting. She shuffled on her feet before answering, "I know it's irregular, but I wonder whether you can supply me with some weapons to protect myself."

Meng laughed. Chooli thought she was acknowledging her audacity in asking, but she said, "Commissioner Harris expected you to ask that."

"I'll understand if you can't." Chooli held her breath, waiting for a reply.

"Harris ordered me to provide you with what you wanted within reason."

Chooli exhaled. "Thank you so much."

"Mind you, we can't let you loose in the arsenal, but we'll arm you well enough to defend yourself. Just make sure you don't use it to start any wars. We might have some sticky questions to answer if you do." She pinged the details and authorization for accessing the armory.

"I won't. And thanks. That's all I wanted."

"My pleasure. I hope everything works out with tracking Alex. Please come see me again if you need any more help. I'll do what I can."

"Thank you, Meng."

Meng called the receptionist, who escorted Chooli from the office.

A smile crept over Chooli's face as she left the building. They were exceptional people, but she mustn't abuse their generosity.

As it was lunchtime, she found a cafe and ate a light meal before heading for the arsenal and sorting through the equipment she thought she needed for the days ahead. She still wasn't sure what her next step should be.

32

ENTER VAPDOG

Chooli's night was restless as she tossed and turned while considering her next step. Her semi-conscious brain told her that the best way to find Ramira and, through her, Alex, was to penetrate the Xi Boötis underworld. *But how?*

She could think of no agent who would help her take the first step. Using the GIA for such a nefarious undertaking was out of the question, even with the support of Commissioner Harris.

As dawn broke and her bedroom brightened, she sighed in frustration while staring at the ceiling. Her mind buzzed from lack of sleep and too much mental exertion throughout the night. Rest escaped her grasp, so she threw off the blankets and crawled from her bed, grumpy and dejected. She showered and dressed before heading to the breakfast cafe downstairs.

She knew she had thought of a lead overnight, but her drowsy and fuzzy state had sent her into a restless but momentary slumber before she woke again, making her forget the idea like it was a dream.

The cafe stood on the ground floor with a window facing the exterior pathways, and she sat where she could get an outside view. Once she had finished eating, she sipped her coffee, staring through the window vacantly when a man walked past her. He wore the most atrocious attire she had ever seen, with mismatched, torn and dirty clothing, spiked hair, and solid metal chains dangling from his shoulders and waist. She scrunched her face at the sight in disgust. The man reminded her of someone Alex had told her about. As she prepared to take another sip of her coffee, a light bulb flashed inside her head — Vapdog! With it, she remembered her idea of the night before: she needed to penetrate the underworld. For that, there would be no better helper than Vapdog.

Vapdog's home was the Xi Boötis underworld. He had helped Alex with their murder investigation on Franconia as a favor to Alex for services rendered previously. Alex and he had a history going back to Alex's policing days. Alex had advised her to contact him if she ever got into difficulties with organized crime anywhere in the Confederation. She considered her current predicament qualified.

After gulping the rest of her coffee, she rushed back upstairs to search for his comm details in Alex's belongings. After sifting through mountains of data cards, she found a contact number to try, although it had a question mark next to it. She shook with trepidation as she tapped the number into her comm, wondering if she was making a mistake and whether Vapdog would help her for Alex's sake.

After several rings, the line connected with voice only.

"Yo."

"Is that Vapdog?"

"Who wants to know?"

"Chooli Richards, Alex Warner's wife."

Silence came from the other end, seconds elapsing. "What's he gotten himself into now?"

She lost control. Her emotions welled up inside her as her hope of finding Alex escalated. Her throat tightened, tears threatened to escape her eyes, and her voice trembled. "He's in trouble. I think someone has kidnapped him, and I can't find him. Please help me."

"Damn moron ... Sorry, that wasn't meant to slip out. Typical

Alex. I bet the big softie was pulling some sort of Sir Galahad stunt."
Vapdog sighed. "Where are you?"

"In the Hotel Continental in Xi Boötis City."

"I can't help you now. But come to the Jiang Shi Bar tonight around midnight. I'll meet you there."

"What do you look like?"

"Don't worry. I'll find you. Alex has boasted about your looks to me often enough — with holographs."

"Oh." She had not known Alex had kept in touch with Vapdog. "OK. Thank you so much. I'll see you tonight."

Vapdog disconnected the link.

Chooli spotted the bar straight ahead as she stepped from the taxi. As expected, it looked trashy, with multicolored LED lights flashing images of naked women dancing above the doorway, half the lights blown, and a bouncer standing by the door, clad in a tee shirt and jeans, looking totally unlike the stylish goons at the restaurant the previous night. She had dressed casually and sighed with relief at choosing well.

The bouncer stared at her as she stepped up to the threshold but didn't prevent her from entering the bar. She felt his eyes follow her as she passed into the noisy, smoke-filled interior. The ventilation struggled to filter the haze from the air and keep the temperature to an acceptable level, considering the horde of customers inside the place.

She felt exposed and uncertain but kept her nerve as she threaded her way through the crowd, searching for a spare table. Ogling eyes followed her, accompanied by snide or snickering smiles, as the people took a break from their discourse to note the intrusion of a stranger before continuing their business. She spotted a vacant table out of the way toward the rear, butting the side wall. She sat on the padded bench seat — with her back to the wall as she always did when encountering strangers with unknown intentions.

After scanning the bar for anyone resembling Vapdog and finding no one meeting her mental image of him, she ordered a beer using the in-table ordering service. The drink arrived, and she reclined in her seat as she slowly sipped it, waiting for him to show himself. Several men glanced her way but lost interest for reasons Chooli didn't understand. She kept her eyes trained on the entrance, hoping to spot Vapdog as he arrived. Then she sensed a presence beside her on her blind side, making her jump in surprise. She jerked around to view the intruder.

A man sat next to her, face disfigured with tattoos and piercings. His stiffened black hair stood spiked across his head from front to back in a mohawk style. His head's dark guise complemented the black tee shirt and chrome spike that accompanied the fake leather jacket and pants. Brown eyes stared at her with a mixture of interest and contempt.

"Told you I'd find you," he said.

"Vapdog?" Chooli raised her eyebrows.

"Yeah. But why are you dressed like a tourist?"

Offended, she said, "I'm dressed casually. What did you expect?"

"What do you want? I could damage my reputation sitting with you."

"Why? Not interested in women, or am I not your style?"

"I admit you intrigue me — might even see you as a challenge if you weren't Alex's. But your style risks people getting the wrong idea about my tastes. That and my solitary existence is legendary. Again, what do you want?"

"I want to find a woman called Ramira Lopez. I hope she can lead me to Alex."

Vapdog glanced around, searching for eavesdroppers. "Don't say that name here. She's trouble, and you won't find her."

Chooli's hopes deflated. She'd been certain Ramira was her best chance. "I give up then." As the words of defeat left her mouth, she recalled a time when nothing would have prevented her from achieving her goals — and a spark ignited in her. Her papa had often chastised her for being too focused on her goals at the expense of others. She glanced at Vapdog as she tapped into that stubborn determination. "You will help me."

Vapdog's eyes widened in surprise. "Why?"

"Alex saved your life more than once. You owe it to him."

"I helped him on Franconia. That was repayment enough."

"I'm calling it only partial payment. And if you don't help, I'll make sure your business goes bankrupt."

Vapdog glared at her. "Be careful whom you threaten. It might get you killed."

She gritted her teeth. "At least I will have died trying."

Silence grew between them as they stared at each other in a standoff.

Vapdog's eyes wavered, and he sighed, acknowledging defeat. "What is it about Alex?" he muttered. He inspected Chooli again. "You won't find him in that attire and prancing like an exotic Eridani pony."

She gave an inward sigh of relief but then frowned. "Why? What's wrong with how I look and act?"

"Look around you. Can you spot anyone dressed like you?"

"So?"

He stared at her as if he doubted her intelligence. "Come with me. I'll have to show you." He moved to stand.

"I thought you didn't want to be seen with me?" she joked.

He glared back at her. "I'll make an exception." He stood and waited.

Chooli followed, letting him lead her from the bar and out into the street. Instead of exiting via the front door, they headed out the rear doorway, many patrons giving them both more than a passing glance. She noticed him gritting his teeth, his shoulders sagging and his head bowed as if the humiliation taxed his dignity. She stared at the crowd, wondering how he considered their behavior to be any different.

They passed through dark alleyways as he led her into parts of the city she would never venture into on her own without a weapon. She cast furtive glances into dark corners and vacant alleys, expecting assailants to spring out at them at any second. Her nerves kept her in constant readiness to defend herself. Still, she trusted him to keep her safe, for Alex's sake, if nothing else.

They arrived at an entertainment thoroughfare that had seen better days. Vapdog led her down a set of steps to a basement landing, the path blocked by a steel door with a peephole shutter. He smashed his fist on the door. The shutter opened and closed before the door yawned inward, and he led Chooli into a room packed with clientele beyond anything she had ever experienced. Music blared and thumped throughout, people dancing or swaying to the rhythmic beat. She suspected many had imbibed the odd opiate or other drug to dull the pain of reality for one night at least.

Vapdog threaded through the crowd, Chooli following him until he reached another doorway and entered. He glanced back and gestured with his head for her to follow him. She wondered where else he thought she might go. They entered a second packed room. As the door closed, the noise level diminished to one conducive to conversation without shouting one's lungs out. Many of the occupants interrupted their business to check who had disturbed them.

"Vapdog!" a man shouted across the crowd. "What brings you here tonight — and who's the trussed-up slag with ya?"

Chooli froze in shock. No one had ever insulted her appearance before. And yet, given the welcoming smile and casual tone, it seemed like a normal opening line here. It bothered no one else.

"Zapper," Vapdog replied to the greeting as he headed toward him. "Hoping you can do me a favor."

"Depends. I'm hanging low at present."

"Nothing to trouble you. Just tell her why she doesn't fit."

Zapper laughed. "That's easy. She lacks the get-out-of-my-way sneer, for starters. One good fright and I reckon she'd die on the spot."

To demonstrate, he sneered at her with inches between them and added, as if to emphasize his point, "Boo!"

She jumped and felt an instant surge of resentment at his mockery. "I'm not that timid," she said through gritted teeth.

Zapper laughed again. "It talks."

His abusive challenge aroused Chooli to lunge at him, but Vapdog held her back, grabbing her by the shoulders. "Cool it. Understand what I mean now: he's being nice to you."

"I'd like to see him insulting someone then." Her temper cooled, but she still glared at Vapdog's friend.

"Fighting bitch," Zapper commented approvingly. He inspected her up and down before reaching behind him and fetching a beer from beyond Chooli's view. He grinned. "Here. Sip on that," he said as he held the beer out for her.

Chooli grudgingly accepted the drink and nodded her thanks.

Zapper shook his head despairingly.

Her hand holding the bottle stopped halfway to her mouth. "What?" She glared at Zapper and then at Vapdog. "What did I do?"

"You shoulda told him to shove it where it fits before you accepted it," Vapdog explained.

She stared at him, dumbfounded. She had much to learn about their weird etiquette.

33

TRAPPED AGAIN

Alex and Ramira left The Grotto, Alex relieved to be away from such a depressing hut.

Alex followed Ramira through the streets of Xi Boötis City as the day's light faded. He was tired and hungry, the snack food they had stolen from the store long gone. Anxiety accompanied him. He feared capture by either the police or Vito's gang, both undesirable outcomes — although he would much prefer the police.

Ramira was searching for a landmark but wouldn't tell him what it was, saying she'd know it when she saw it.

"Found it!" she exclaimed.

"At last."

They stood in front of a dilapidated apartment block four stories high in a rundown suburb. Few people occupied the streets, and those few hung their heads low, intent on reaching their destination without encountering anyone else's business. The building was so old it was made of bricks and concrete instead of the cerami-plastic used in modern buildings. Rubbish littered the footpath in front of it. The façade included windows on each floor.

Alex gazed upward. "Which one?"

"Top floor."

He shook his head and muttered sotto voce, "That'd be right." Just what he needed after walking for most of the afternoon: four flights of stairs to scale. He was sure the building would have no elevator — or it wouldn't work.

"Let's go inside before someone sees us," Ramira said as she mounted the two steps to enter the foyer.

Alex followed her and entered a rundown space, dark and musty. The meager installed lighting came from one ancient incandescent globe that had probably been stolen from a museum. He didn't think anyone made them anymore. A line of personal lockboxes sat flush against the wall on the left. A closed door stood on the right, presumably an apartment entrance. At the far end, a set of stairs rose to the upper floors. He sighed as he headed for them to start the trudge to the top floor, hoping their destination contained comfortable beds and food. He could use a solid meal and a good night's sleep.

At the top, he bent forward and grabbed his knees as he gasped for air. He needed to improve his personal fitness. He glanced over at Ramira and noticed she, too, had stopped to catch her breath, leaning against the wall.

After a moment, she straightened and headed for the far end.

Alex followed her, wondering if he would ever get any respite from this ordeal.

Ramira knocked on the door. Seconds passed before it opened a fraction, then fully. A tall, elderly Asian woman with a frightened expression poked her head out, checking for prying eyes before gesturing for them both to hurry inside the apartment.

They entered, and the owner closed the door.

"Why you here?" The person spoke in broken English, but the sneer she gave Ramira was universal.

"I had nowhere else to go," Ramira pleaded, hands upturned.

The woman inspected Alex. "I'm Bai," she finally said, grudgingly.

"Alex. I'm grateful for your help."

She huffed and glared back at Ramira. "Entire planet after you. I give you tonight, and then you leave. Only time before someone come check on me. Better for everyone you disappear."

Ramira returned her stare. Alex could tell she was panicking as she considered her options. Finally, she nodded. "I'll take what I can get at present."

"Come, I make you meal." Bai, half-stooped, trudged into the kitchen, where she started preparing a meal.

A food preparation bench stood on the far wall. Bai went there. A table and four chairs stood near the entrance. They looked old and well-used. Dents and scratches covered the table. The chairs, worn from use, appeared fragile and ready to disintegrate.

As weariness overcame him, Alex sat uninvited. Bai stopped and glanced at him but then nodded and returned to her chores. She started cooking, and the aroma of spiced and hot food soon filled the room, making Alex's stomach grumble and his mouth salivate in anticipation.

Ramira stood in the corner with her arms crossed, staring at Bai. Her face reflected someone in two minds about what to do next. Then she sighed and sat beside Alex as Bai spooned the meal into bowls and carried them to the table. Bai placed the bowls in front of them and left to collect cutlery. The steam wafting up tempted Alex to start eating with his fingers, but he forced himself to wait until Bai returned and sat with them. She slid a spoon and fork across the table for them both but kept chopsticks for herself and started eating.

Alex took his first mouthful and reclined, savoring the taste as he chewed. "That's delicious," he said, as much to himself as to Bai.

Bai jerked her head toward him. "Thank you." She bowed before glaring at Ramira again.

Silence hung over the meal like an impending storm with lightning threatening to strike, but they got through it without an outburst. Afterward, Bai served tea before showing them both to their beds.

Alex was stone tired, wanting nothing more than rest, so he immediately jumped into bed. But when his head settled on the pillow, sleep escaped him. He lay staring at the ceiling, pining for Chooli and fearing the path ahead of him. He still distrusted Ramira but saw no choice but to continue with her for now. If he fled, her child, should she have one, might die, and he didn't want that. He needed to achieve both outcomes.

As his eyes started drooping into the realm of dreams, Alex thought he heard Ramira and Bai arguing. His consciousness had drifted too far into sleep to return to wakefulness, but some words wafted to his mind.

"Why you not let me be? Let my little girl stop her disgusting job?" Bai pleaded.

"Stop moaning. We all pay a price for our peace," Ramira said.

"Ha! Don't see you pay price. You go, you come back. Decide."

"Shh! Don't wake up Alex."

Bai sighed. "What you want then ...?"

Alex woke alarmed as he struggled to reach wakefulness and failed. The bedroom light blazed, and a gigantic monster grabbed his upper arm and tossed him across the room to the far wall. His head smashed against the thin paneling, dulling his mind before the pain registered. The monster stormed toward him. Alex cowered in a defensive position, preparing for the next blow while he desperately tried to work out what was happening.

"Don't harm him ...," a male voice commanded. Alex didn't recognize the voice. "Not yet." The man held an injector. "Hold him still."

The brute pulled Alex up and smashed him against the wall, one huge forearm across Alex's shoulders, pinning his neck and constricting his breathing. His other hand grabbed Alex's wrist and extended his arm.

The man with the injector pressed it into Alex's biceps. He felt a pinprick before returning to unconsciousness.

34

A NEW IDENTITY

Chooli slept in after her rendezvous with Vapdog and his friends. She woke mid-morning to sunshine streaming into her bedroom at the hotel. She rubbed her eyes as she yawned and rose to a sitting position. Last night was weird, but Vapdog had convinced her she needed to infiltrate the world he lived in if she had any chance of finding Ramira and, through her, Alex. It meant she had to create an undercover persona for herself that the underworld would believe. She had undertaken minor covert assignments in the GIA before, but nothing like the depth necessary for this undertaking. The immensity of the task put butterflies in her stomach. She took several deep breaths. It was essential to save Alex.

After brunch, she headed for a secondhand clothing store, which the hotel concierge directed her to, for the first phase of her makeover. She had first considered buying new clothes but realized they wouldn't be convincing unless they showed signs of wear and tear, which they never would in the timeframe. Hence the excursion to this store. The scuffed and worn outfits it contained were what she needed. The air smelled musty as she entered the premises. A hint of residual body odor complemented the air's fetidness. She scrunched her nose in protest until she spotted the store assistant looking at her. She quickly changed her expression to curiosity as she explored the bowels of the store.

Aisles of clothes filled the floor space before her, some hanging and others piled on shelves for people to flick through. She knew what she wanted in her head, so she scanned the signs above the merchandise to locate the sections she needed.

Before she could begin her browsing, a voice behind her asked, "Can I help you?"

She jumped, turned, and smiled.

The woman before her was taller than Chooli and older, about her parents' age. Wrinkles lined her face, etching the record of a hard life, her smile accentuating the contours. Her clothes hung from her emaciated body. She examined Chooli's attire. "Are you searching for something for a friend?"

"No." Chooli tried putting emotional distress into her expression but couldn't tell how convincing she was. "For myself. I'm looking for black leather clothing. That type of apparel."

The woman nodded solemnly. "I have the very thing. This way," she said as she turned and paced along an aisle. Chooli was amused to hear her mutter under her breath, "Young people and their fetishes," as she started to follow her.

After leading Chooli to the rear, the woman pointed ahead. "This section should contain your needs." She walked off.

Chooli concentrated on her task. Leather was still a common material for clothing, as much for durability as style, so an extensive selection stood on the racks before her.

She flicked through the pants until she spotted her size. They were black, with several scuff marks. There were no studs, but she decided studs would be overkill for her intended identity. Another pair was next to it, and she picked that, too. Skirts were further along. She searched through them and found a couple suitable for her, if much shorter than she usually wore. If things worked out, she might consider wearing one for Alex. Realizing the detour her mind was taking her on, she forced herself to focus on the task at hand.

After half an hour, she held a bundle of tee shirts and tank tops as well as pants and skirts. She considered a costume bra but decided that was taking her transformation too far and would reduce her ability to conceal weapons or other necessary items. As the *pièce de résistance*, she added a black leather jacket with two rows of spiked silver studs stretching from the collar to the cuffs on both sleeves. The ornamental studs buttoning up the front and the cuffs had a skull pattern on top. What most attracted her to the article was the thick lining with several internal pockets, which she could use to hide pistols or other items.

Once she confirmed that the clothes fit her, she headed to the counter to pay. The woman stood there waiting for her, palpably pleased at having made such a big sale.

She returned to the hotel afterward, the lingering presence of the store clinging to her the whole way back. Washing the clothes was an option, but it would remove their neglected character, so she tolerated the stench, telling herself she'd get used to it.

After a snack, she stood in front of the bathroom mirror, staring at her hair and wondering how to make it more suitable for the milieu of her self-imposed assignment. She recalled the wild hairdos she had seen the night before and imagined them on herself, deciding on one she considered best matched the shape of her head and her facial features.

Still, she dreaded cutting her long hair and changing her sophisticated hairstyle to something more suited to the underworld. She sighed in resignation. She had to do it.

When she sat in the hair salon chair in the hotel lobby shop arcade and told the stylist what she wanted, the woman's mouth dropped. "Are you sure? Your hair is so gorgeous."

"I'm sure." *I can always grow it back afterward*, Chooli thought.

The stylist shrugged her shoulders and started cutting and dying her client's hair without further comment. It was late in the afternoon by the time she finished. Chooli's once gorgeous hair now looked jagged and unkempt. Her original black color had streaks of red, green, and yellow through it, the selected dye providing a glittering appearance as the light caught it. After dark, the coloring would become luminescent, the current fashion in the Xi Boötis underworld.

The patrons in the hotel lobby stared at her disapprovingly as she made her way to the elevators, the attention breaking Chooli into a sweat. The elevator doors closed. She sighed. She'd have to tolerate it.

Half an hour later, dressed in her new old clothes, all Chooli needed was a new name to complete her transformation. Something short, memorable, and in keeping with her new look. 'Siren' seemed about right, she decided.

She felt confident that with her new hairdo, grunge clothes, and bold name, the world she intended to enter would accept her as one of its own.

35

BLENDING IN

Chooli had arranged to meet Vapdog in the Jiang Shi Bar where they first met.

Once satisfied that her appearance reflected her legend, she headed out, receiving stares of disbelief and disapproval as she passed through the hotel lobby, this time dressed in the clothes she had bought that afternoon and still wishing she could have washed them beforehand. They held a conspicuous odor she couldn't shake even with the dash of perfume she used to mask it — she feared using too much would expose her cover.

She arrived early and received as many stares at the bar as before — but of a different kind. Her drink ordered, she sat in the same spot waiting for Vapdog, determined not to let him sneak up on her again. He didn't keep her waiting long. This time she spotted him coming as if her change of persona had given her extra powers.

He looked her over. "Impressive."

"I don't need your approval."

"Ha! You're learning." He sat down and ordered a beer.

Once his drink came, and he had taken a sip, he turned his attention to Chooli again. "But you have much to learn. You get any response from anyone here?"

"Just ogling stares when I arrived. Why?"

"This bar's tame, but you should've had a few nibbles. Your attitude still reeks of conservatism, maybe even the law."

She shrugged. "So, what do I do?"

"Finish your drink and follow me. I'll take you to the people you need to convince to perfect your role. If you can fool them, you'll blend in anywhere in the underworld."

They gulped down their drinks and hired a taxi to a part of Xi Boötis Chooli had never seen on any planet she had visited before. Multi-colored LEDs illuminated every establishment along the pathway where they disembarked. Sundry people, dressed in similar but even more anti-society clothes than she wore, stood and sat in front of bars and eateries. She caught several drug exchanges occurring as Vapdog led her to a bar. No one took any notice of either of them.

The throb of grunge music assaulted their ears when they entered the place, lights hanging above a dance floor flashing in rhythm with the beat and overpowering the general low-level illumination in the rest of the premises. Chooli wondered how anyone could even hear themselves speak. She tagged along with Vapdog as he pushed a path to the rear.

Hands groped for her as she weaved past perverts while she crossed the floor, but she hit back as soon as she felt their menacing talons and glared at their owners, who sneered with impish mischief. Piercings of every description decorated the people's heads and other exposed flesh. Chooli wondered how many they placed in hidden spots and shivered as she considered the adornment process.

As she neared the rear of the bar, she spotted Zapper again. He grinned when he saw her and raised his beer glass to her. She glared at him, which widened his grin.

"You're learning," he said when she was within earshot.

"Go play ping-pong," she replied, hoping the response was derogatory enough.

He burst into laughter and turned to Vapdog. "She learns quickly."

Vapdog raised an eyebrow at him. "Not quick enough." He scanned the bar as if searching for snitches before returning his attention to Zapper. "We need to introduce her to the hard end of town."

Zapper coughed as he lowered his glass after just having gulped a mouthful. "She ready?"

"One way to find out."

"How about talking to me?" Chooli said, punching Vapdog's arm.

He lashed out with a speed she wasn't expecting, but before he could grab her, she had him on the ground with her foot on his spine and his fingers pushed back in the hand she grasped. Her reaction was pure instinct.

Vapdog winced in pain. "You can let go now. You've made your point."

As she released him, she noticed nearby onlookers gape, astonished, at them both. She was surprised that it was possible to astonish people in this bar.

Vapdog raised himself from the floor and rubbed his shoulder as he clenched and unclenched his sore fist. He glanced at her. "That was spectacular, but I'd keep those theatrics to yourself until you need them. They might give away your cover."

"Sorry. You caught me by surprise. Besides, I can't be the first one with a badass reputation with those skills to uphold."

"True. Let's get out of here. I want to show you something."

With no choice but to trust him, she followed him as he led her to the rear entrance. Zapper followed behind her. She felt simultaneously anxious and safe since she figured they provided an imposing barrier to any threats they might meet. When the back door closed, silence engulfed them again as she kept pace with the two, one on either side of her, en route to their intended destination. They didn't catch a taxi, so she presumed their destination was nearby, but they walked for ages, her feet becoming sore, before they turned the corner into a darkened street.

She stopped and stared at Vapdog. "What's this?"

He glanced back. "Education." He started walking again. "Come."

She glanced at Zapper. He shrugged and followed him. She sighed. Knowing she had no choice but to acquiesce, she strode next to them as she cautiously took in her surroundings.

A man and woman sat propped against a building wall, both staring with blank expressions, either dead or near death, Chooli thought, until one blinked and the other coughed, confirming their status but giving her little reason to change her opinion of them.

"What's wrong with them?"

"Chimera stardust, more likely," Zapper said. "Dangerous. Don't touch the stuff. Three decent doses and you're hooked for life. You can't live without it. Most die within weeks or days if they don't get another fix."

Chooli shivered as she stared at the two addicts with a mixture of compassion and revulsion.

Vapdog stopped at a spot where several monstrous thugs stood leaning against the walls of sleaze bars, flashing signs advertising their merchandise for potential customers to choose from — anything from strip clubs of every sexual persuasion to an establishment selling more perverse wares. He turned to Chooli. "This is your schooling. If you pass this test, you're ready."

"How?"

"Get out of here without getting bashed, abducted, or raped, and you graduate."

She stared at him and gulped before taking a closer inspection of their location.

"Don't worry," Zapper added. "We're here."

Chooli wasn't sure whether to be relieved by those words or terrified. Regardless, she took a large breath and headed to the nearest bar advertising topless waitresses — *nothing like a sexist underworld to cement my reputation,* she thought. Vapdog and Zapper followed close behind her.

She stepped over the threshold of the bar, appropriately named Satan's Furnace, to a rowdy group of drunken men and women amusing themselves, the female waiting staff receiving contact with more than the patrons' eyes. Chooli noted the serving women's frustration, her temperature rising in sympathy for them, but she knew she could do nothing to intervene. Spotting a vacant table, she headed toward it with the two men in tow, sitting with relief at receiving no harassment along the way.

"Order me a beer," she said to Vapdog, glaring at him.

Zapper rose and drifted elsewhere, leaving her right flank exposed. She wondered whether he went as a coordinated tactic worked out between them beforehand to increase the likelihood of her being attacked. This left Vapdog to study her response and offer feedback for her *education.* If so, she was determined to succeed in spectacular style if a predicament developed, which it did within minutes.

As Chooli gulped her beer, she spotted an approaching monster resembling a man, she presumed, out of the corner of her eye. Tattoos covered his face. The only natural features visible were his eyes and lips. The tattoos glowed with implanted luminescent dyes powered by phyla burrowing into the person's skin. She pretended unawareness of him as he lumbered closer.

He flopped beside her and grabbed her thigh as he stared at her, half intoxicated. "Haven't seen your flesh here before."

"And you won't see it again if you don't remove your hand, you moron." Chooli glared back at him with challenging intent.

"Feisty? I like that. Let's find a corner."

She sighed and glanced at Vapdog, who pretended to be deeply preoccupied with his comm device. "Move your hand if you want to use it again."

"Ha! This will be fun. Come on, let's jigger."

"Last chance. Or you won't jigger again either."

The brute increased his hold on her thigh and started pulling her toward him. That was the trigger for Chooli to teach him a lesson. She grabbed his hand and pressed on the pressure point to force it to surrender its grip. Within microseconds, she had the hand rotated and forced backward with her hand gripping his fingers with increasing pressure. She raised her free elbow and slammed it on his palm, fracturing his wrist. The guy yelped in pain as he jumped, propelling the table across the floor, the beers flying into the bar and smashing.

"You bitch!" he yelled as he turned to attack her.

Before he could begin any action himself, Chooli smashed her steel-reinforced boot into his groin, forcing the wind and any residual fight from him as he collapsed to the ground, bellowing in agony. Two bouncers arrived within seconds and dragged him away. She never saw him again. She had warned him. With a fierce glare, she challenged any one of the spectators who had interrupted their business to view the entertainment to take her on. No one did. They returned to their companions once the bouncers had deposited the injured brute outside.

Vapdog retrieved and righted the table and ordered more beer. "You could've saved our beers."

Chooli glanced at him, unsure whether he was joking since his expression stayed bland. "I'll remember next time." His lips rose in a slight upward twinge before they returned to their nondescript position.

"That was impressive," a male voice said from Chooli's blind side, heavy with a distinct Xi accent.

Her head jerked toward the voice, producing a glare when her eyes latched onto him. "Who are you?"

The man leered down from his towering, thin frame. The face had a certain appeal to it with his almond brown eyes, strong jawline, and enchanting smile. "Lingo. And you?"

Chooli intended to tell him to disappear but reconsidered at the last moment. No need to be obnoxious to everyone. He hadn't annoyed her yet. And besides, he might come in useful in locating Alex. "Siren," she told him, using her new name for the first time.

His eyes twinkled as if he were in on her secret but wouldn't divulge it. "Siren. Nice potent name." He raised his hand and stroked his chin as if considering his next words. His attention returned to her. "I can see you dislike sharing space with the uninvited, so I won't linger. We should talk." He kept staring at her.

She maintained eye contact, determined not to be the one to break it, out of principle, if nothing else. After several seconds, Lingo relented and stepped a few paces away before glancing back at her. "I'll see you sometime," he said, dissolving into the crowd.

Chooli turned to Vapdog. "What was that about?"

"I'm not sure." He stared after the man.

36

THE TABLES TURN

Drinking coffee in the hotel lobby, Chooli digested the events of the night before, the coffee's pleasant aroma at odds with her frame of mind.

Vapdog had given her a glowing report, as had Zapper, who had been watching from a distance. Her reaction to the over-enthusiastic pig wanting some action was slightly excessive, in Zapper's opinion, but well within the bounds of expected behavior. She grinned. He had pleaded with her to warn him if he ever overreached. She had promised she would.

Now that she had *graduated*, she wondered what to do next. Time was elapsing with no progress toward finding Alex, which worried her. She had to act with more urgency and focus. Her thoughts wandered back to Lingo, the man who had approached her after her altercation. He wanted to talk with her — but privately. She took a sip. Hmm! She must talk to him. He looked like the sort of guy who dealt it information. Chooli decided to discuss it with Vapdog later and set up a way to get Lingo alone long enough for her and Vapdog to interrogate him.

She ordered another coffee. Despite secluding herself, she was getting too much attention from the hotel guests. It wasn't good for keeping her identity secure. She sighed. She needed to find accommodation more fitting to her façade — which meant leaving the hotel and finding temporary dilapidated lodging in a slum neighbourhood nearer the action. The thought of it sent a shiver down her spine, but it was necessary.

Once she emptied her cup, she returned to her room to pack the clothes she would use. She had decided to keep her current room to avoid having to find storage space for the belongings she couldn't take with her. It also gave her an emergency fallback if she needed one. When she returned to the lobby, she paid a one-month advance on the room. She'd return to extend the booking if she hadn't completed her undercover activities by then.

With her accommodation organized, she headed to the part of Xi Boötis where Vapdog lived and checked into a run-down hotel in that neighborhood. The manager ogled her when she entered, but his mind disengaged from his leering long enough to extort a high price for her lodgings. Chooli considered haggling but didn't bother. Instead, she glared at him and uttered profanities, declaring her intention to mutilate his genitalia if the room wasn't what she expected or if he laid a finger on her. His lechery changed to anxiety as he handed her the digital key card.

The room smelled disgusting. Reeking, stale cigarette smoke permeated every surface. Several cockroaches scampered away when disturbed in their silent habitat; without doubt, they'd return later. Of all the creatures throughout the galaxy, cockroaches seemed to have infiltrated the entire habitable space. She suspected the sole chair in the room was bug-infested, though the bed seemed bug-free. Apart from all that, it was clean enough for someone called Siren.

She threw her bag on the bed, which creaked from the extra weight, an ominous sign for when she slept. Once she decreased the window's opacity setting, the outside became visible, not that the view was worth the effort. A plasti-crete wall a few meters from the hotel blocked any hint of the surrounding landscape. The room was so cheap it lacked any in-room entertainment. Or perhaps it had been wrecked or stolen.

Chooli sighed. She hoped she found Alex soon so she could return to her normal life.

To occupy herself until nightfall, she went grocery shopping and checked her surroundings for cafes and eateries to use during the daylight hours. Returning to her depressing hotel, she noticed her floor had a common room that, on inspection, she decided to avoid. No one had cleaned it recently. It was filthy, with stained lounge seats and food scraps scattered everywhere. And it reeked of body odor.

"Hi," a feminine voice said behind Chooli, making her jump before she turned.

"What do you want?" Chooli growled.

"No need to bite my head off."

Embarrassed by her outburst, even though it was in character, Chooli cooled her temperament. "Sorry. You live here?"

"Yeah. Room 13. You?"

"Temporary. 21."

"Make sure it's temporary. I've seen too many times where temporary turned into permanent until they met an untimely end."

Chooli shrugged. "Can't predict the future." She gazed at the woman. She was young, about Chooli's age, and skinny as a matchstick with unruly black hair. Piercings adorned her face, and tattoos covered the visible upper part of her torso. She wore old gray jeans and a matching black tank top. "What's your name?"

"Agate. You?"

"Siren."

"You don't look like a siren."

"Can't choose your birth name."

"S'pose not."

They fell silent, the time elapsing until both felt uncomfortable.

"I'd better go," Chooli said. "I've got things to do."

"Yeah. OK. Tell me if you need anything. I know where to purchase most things." Agate turned to leave but glanced back to Chooli. "Can we hang out sometime? I get little company here."

"I'll keep it in mind."

Agate started walking away, and Chooli followed her until she reached her door. Agate's room was further down the hallway.

Chooli entered her room, closed the door, and leaned against it. She couldn't pick what it was, but something seemed off about Agate. Too inquisitive perhaps. Or Chooli was just too jumpy. She sighed and grabbed a bottle of juice before flopping onto the cushioned chair. Despite the body odor and possible bugs, she resigned herself to it as she sipped with an upturned nose and thought.

She woke with a jump. Everything was dark. No light entered from outside. It was nighttime. She realized she had been asleep for several hours. How she had done that in such a gross chair dumbfounded her. Standing, she stretched the kinks from her back, hearing several cracks as she raised her arms. When she checked the time, she panicked, realizing she had to prepare to return to last night's bar.

She contacted Vapdog first and, on the assumption that Lingo should show if he portrayed the habits of most patrons, they agreed on a plan to interrogate him. She examined her appearance and left. She didn't see Agate, but Chooli sensed she was spying on her. Agate might consider her competition for her trade. The hotel carried the ambiance of temporary accommodation services rented at an hourly rate.

The Satan's Furnace came into view half an hour later. After scanning the premises, she headed for her usual table at the back.

Several patrons were recognizable from the night before, but she didn't greet them, and they ignored her.

With a beer in hand, she watched and waited. And watched and waited. *Why did I rush to get here?*

By the time she finished her sixth drink, not all of them alcoholic, she was starting to think that both Vapdog and Lingo were no-shows. Vapdog's absence disturbed her the most. He had assured her he would be there. Time to return to her uninspiring hotel to sleep. But when she made to rise, she spotted the elusive Lingo entering the bar and changed her mind. She ordered her seventh drink and kept her attention on him.

He headed to the bench-top counter. After collecting a beer for himself, he disappeared, to Chooli's annoyance, vaporizing into thin air. With her prey lost, her eyes drooped, and she stared at the table, brooding over her ineptitude.

"Fancy meeting you here," the familiar male voice said from two meters away. "I'd come closer, but I thought I'd check it's safe first."

She gave him a sour smile. "I won't bite."

After a tentative inspection of her temper, Lingo, deciding she was in an amiable mood, headed to the chair next to her and sat. He placed his glass on the table, turned to her, and smiled.

Chooli studied him. He seemed innocuous on the surface, but a viper could lurk underneath, threatening to attack the instant his prey let its guard slip — something she was determined not to do.

"Your reputation's spread."

"Why d'you say that?" she asked, intrigued but maintaining her sour façade.

"You don't have anyone entertaining you, and I haven't heard of any further hospitalizations."

She chuckled. "You might be my first, then."

Lingo's smile disappeared.

"You're safe for now. What d'you want?"

Reassured, he grabbed his beer, took a gulp, and leaned toward her while keeping a safe distance between them. "You're new here, although you were with familiar faces."

"So?"

He paused before answering, studying her. "Where are you from?"

"Bloody Franconia's royal palace. Where do you think I'm from?"

"Caerus?"

"I have Einstein in my midst." Chooli glanced up to the heavens.

Lingo gave her a perplexed expression as if she spoke an unfamiliar language. "What brings you here, then?"

"What is this? Twenty questions? You the secret police or something? I might rough you up after all."

With a jerk backward, he raised his hands in surrender. "Just making small talk. That's all."

Chooli eyed him, feigning suspicion, although she needed little acting talent. She was suspicious. "Where are you from then?"

"Here, but the other hemisphere. I work here."

"Can't pay much if you visit a shit hole like this."

"I enjoy mixing."

She studied him, wondering why he was there. To give herself time to think, she gulped more beer and emptied the glass. "You said we should talk. What about?"

"One more?" Lingo's eyes glanced at the empty glass.

"If you're paying, why not?"

He drained his glass and ordered two more beers.

Just then, she spied Vapdog materialize like a specter in the distance. He gave a barely perceptible nod and jerked his head sideways before blending into the crowd again. Her attention returned to Lingo. He seemed reluctant to answer, but she waited until their drinks arrived.

After taking another gulp, she said, "So?" She noticed an unusual taste but pretended she hadn't.

"What? ... Oh. What did I want to discuss? A rumor of a stranger in town asking questions. You fit her description."

She pushed her chair back. "You a cop?"

Lingo shook his head. "No. Gossip says she's searching for some-one. I thought I might be of help if it were you."

She eyed him with increased suspicion mixed with interest and shifted closer to the table again. He knew a lot about her.

Once she'd gulped another mouthful of beer, Chooli was in no doubt that the waiter had spiked her drink. Lingo was trying to kidnap her. She was thankful for her foresight in inserting an anti-spiking antidote capsule under her skin. Any trace of a sedative drug triggered the release of a neutralizing agent into her bloodstream.

"What help could you give me, supposing I was her?"

"I know people."

"Oh." Chooli touched her head as if she suddenly felt dizzy. "I need to go to the restroom." She rose and swayed before taking a few shaky steps.

"Are you alright?"

"Fine. Stay where you are."

She staggered toward the restroom but never made it. Lingo's hands grasped her arm. "I'll help." But instead of helping her to the restroom, he led her through the back entrance to the alleyway. She grinned to herself. It was easier than she thought it would be.

He directed her into the darkened alley. Just as she was wondering where Zapper was, he materialized and zapped Lingo with a neural paralyzer. She now understood the origin of his name. Lingo collapsed, threatening to topple her with him.

"About time," Chooli said to Zapper. "Where's Vapdog?"

"Here." Vapdog stepped from complete darkness into semi-light.

"I was getting worried."

"You can handle him yourself."

"But we need him in one piece and in a condition to talk."

"Let's move before someone gets suspicious."

Vapdog and Zapper loaded Lingo into a scooter parked in the darkness behind them. Once secured, they all piled in and headed to their destination and the second stage of their plan.

L ingo groaned as he emerged from his coma. His eyes fluttered open, and he lifted his head to try to make sense of his surroundings. "Where am I?"

"Somewhere safe," Chooli said.

He thrashed at the restraints she and Vapdog had placed on him. "What's this?" He glared at her.

"I could ask you the same thing. Why'd you try sedating me?"

He broke eye contact. "You looked like easy prey."

She stared at him. "Easy prey? You're lucky you still have your reproductive bits. Try again."

"So, what do you want?"

"Information." Chooli grabbed a chair and placed it in front of him, straddling the chair. "Why do you give me the impression you have more on me than you're admitting?"

"I heard someone new had appeared. I wanted to see who it was." He avoided both their eyes.

She lashed out, toppling the chair and Lingo to the floor. He yelled in pain as his head bounced on the hard surface.

"Careful," Vapdog said. "We still need him in a condition to talk."

"I don't like liars."

"I'm not lying," Lingo muttered as he groaned.

"Not telling the whole truth, then."

"Rumors circulated of you sniffing around. I was curious."

"Why?"

"Information is money."

Chooli glanced at Vapdog. He shrugged. "Help me get him up," she said.

They both manhandled the chair to the upright position.

She returned to her seat, facing Lingo. "What can you tell me about Ramira Lopez?"

Lingo's eyes widened with fear. "Nothing."

"You want another tumble?"

"Preferable to word getting to her that I snitched."

"Don't be too sure. Why? Who is she?"

"She's involved with unpleasant people. She had retired, but word's out she's working again."

"Thought you knew nothing?" Vapdog said.

Lingo glanced at him and back to Chooli, panic-induced sweat dripping from his forehead. "She'll work me over anyway when she hears I got snatched."

She stared at him with intense interest. "So, apart from your more carnal desires, you wanted material to sell to her."

"Word's out for information on someone looking like you."

She glanced at Vapdog and then stood and paced the room. "Where is she?"

"I don't know."

Vapdog pulled Lingo's head back by his hair.

"I promise, I don't! You don't find her. She finds you."

Chooli sighed. She'd understood it wouldn't be easy but had hoped to gain a morsel of useful information on the woman's whereabouts. "What do we do with him now?"

With a shrug, Vapdog made a cut-throat motion.

Lingo's eyes widened. "Please, I have nothing more on her — except ..."

"Except what?" she prompted.

"I've heard she has a contact at Madame Bengsei's, but I don't know who it is."

Chooli frowned and shot an enquiring eyebrow at Vapdog.

"A brothel."

"Oh." She turned back to Lingo in the hope of beating a name out of him, but he had passed out.

"I'll take him back to where we picked him up," Vapdog said. "You should disappear."

"You sure you don't need help?"

"I'll find it if I do. You should lie low for now to avoid suspicion."

"I'll see you tomorrow then." Chooli left, unenthusiastic about her destination or the prospect of a night shared with cockroaches and bugs.

37

WHERE ARE WE?

Alex woke in a darkness beyond the black of a moonless night as if he lay in a windowless space. It confused him. It slowly dawned on him that he was in a room but still restrained by the wrists and ankles, although his mouth was unmuzzled. *Where am I? Why am I here? Where's Ramira?* As if on cue, he heard shuffling nearby.

"Is that you, Ramira?"

"Huh! Ow! What happened?" Ramira's voice sounded groggy, strained. Silence reigned for a time, broken only by further intermittent shuffling. "They found and nabbed us," she said from almost next to him.

Alex jumped, surprised by her proximity. He considered her words. An intense frustration overcame him. "How? How did they discover we were there? Did Bai betray us?"

"No. She wouldn't. We shouldn't talk."

"Why not?"

"It's dark. Who knows who's standing ten feet away listening to every word we say."

"If they're that interested in our conversation, they'd just use holo-vision cameras. Hell, they could use nano drones if they wanted to stay real secret."

"How do you know that?"

"Professional development."

Alex's mind raced for answers. *They are always one step ahead of us. How?* He turned his head as memories of times past flashed through it. He only had Ramira's word that she was as deep in their predicament as he was because they had her child. Child? She was not the type to be bothered with children. They would cramp her lifestyle too much. That had to be it. She was the reason they kept getting caught. "You're telling them."

"What?" Ramira whispered, exasperated.

"Every time we move, you tell them where we are."

"What are you talking about? How could I?"

"There's no other explanation. You've been taking me for a fool just like last time."

"You're not thinking straight."

"Why? Let's examine the situation. They have your kid, supposedly, and they want me. You lose me, they lose me, and you lose your kid. If you even have a kid. Whether you've got a kid or not, you're working for them. Your escaping tricks are a ruse to make me think we're on the same side. Either way, you need me captive for whoever's running this. It's Vito Riva, isn't it? You went to work for him when you got out of prison, didn't you? And Milan Asterov is in his pay."

Light flooded the room, glaring into Alex's eyes. He closed them, waiting to adjust to the change before opening them again. Ramira must have found a light switch and was now staring at him. A mixture of frustration and cunning flashed across her expressive face, sending a shiver down his spine before her features returned to those of a frightened and tormented victim.

"Why say that? Don't you care about our child?" she asked, descending into self-pity.

One thing Alex had learned over his years with Ramira was never to doubt his first impressions, although he seemed to have done a great job of forgetting that axiom since she'd re-entered his life. Now he suspected her of the same duplicity that had brought about his last downfall.

The door to the room crashed open. A man with rippling muscles stood beyond the threshold, glaring at Alex before stomping toward them. He headed for Ramira, unshackled her, and dragged her toward the door. She screamed all the way to the entrance. Just as they disappeared, she turned her head to Alex, fear radiating from her face. Despite the thug's rough treatment and her desperate resistance, Alex knew it was all an act.

38

TORTURE AND THREATS

Ramira returned to their prison an hour after the thug had taken her, apparently no worse for her experience. He pushed her into the room, not bothering to re-shackle her. As soon as he had released Ramira, the thug's eyes turned to Alex with a predatory smirk spreading across his lips, sending a spasm of dread to the pit of Alex's stomach. Despite his usual assertiveness, Alex cowered as the thug paced toward him, knowing he was helpless with the restraints restricting his movements. With one muscle-bound hand, he grabbed Alex by the collar and dragged him over the floor and through the door. Alex tried to rise and walk but found it pointless and buffered the bumps along the hallway as best he could until they arrived at another door and entered.

The room Alex now occupied smelled of violence, urine, and bleach. It was featureless apart from a two-way mirror on the opposite wall and a chair bolted to the floor in the geometric center facing it. His stomach clenched as he anticipated the events to unfold here in the immediate future; he could already feel the dampness of perspiration breaking out under his armpits. The brute lifted him onto the seat and strapped him to it with a leather belt around his waist. He stepped back, with Alex between him and the mirror, and faced him, inspecting his handiwork, a grin plastered across his face. Alex noticed Milan Asterov standing to one side.

Without warning, the thug lashed out, his fists pummeling Alex's face until his eyes closed from the swelling. Bruises covered his cheeks, and blood dripped from his nose and mouth. His head lolled forward as he struggled to stay conscious. He had no choice but to suffer the abuse.

The door opened. "That's enough," another man said.

The voice sounded familiar. *Where have I heard it before?* Alex thought as his muddled brain struggled to clear. He attempted to lift and turn his head, but the pain overwhelmed him. He could barely open his eyes to see.

"I need him conscious for now."

He finally remembered the voice's owner. *Vito Riva?* He tried saying something, but the only words emerging from his mouth were gibberish, his facial muscles unable to form the right shape to construct the sounds.

"You're causing me a significant loss of income at present," Vito said from behind him. "You and your advice to Ahiga are driving his obstinate stubbornness beyond belief. He says it's not ethical. His ethics are a joke. Doesn't he understand how much wealth's just sitting there? You're here to tell him to change his mind." He stepped in front of Alex.

Alex found the energy to lift his head and stare at Riva with his slits of eyes before accumulating a quantity of saliva and blood and spitting on the floor, just missing Riva's shoes.

The thug stepped forward, but Vito motioned for him to desist.

"Why suffer when you can give Ahiga your approval and go home to your lovely wife?"

Alex jerked his head to meet Vito's eyes again. Bringing Chooli into the argument worried him. *Does he have her locked up somewhere too?* He hoped not. He would kill Vito if he did anything to her. "My assent would make no difference to Ahiga," he managed between gulps of air. "Once he understood your intentions for the crystal boramide, he decided without my help. The galaxy has enough illicit drugs destroying countless lives without you making more."

Vito laughed. "We shall see." He glanced at the thug. "Get the camera."

The brute left, returning moments later with a camera mounted on a tripod. He set it up in front of Alex, Vito giving minor directions as he did so, before gesturing for Asterov to stand beside Alex while he moved behind the camera.

"Let's see how he receives this message. I wonder how much he values you?" He motioned for the thug to start filming, which he did with a remote unit, and nodded when a red light blinked on the camera's face.

Asterov stood next to Alex, facing the camera but wearing a face mask. Alex rolled his head forward, unable to keep it raised.

"Good day, Ahiga," Asterov said. "I trust you are well and enjoying your life. Your friend isn't at present. You might take Vito seriously now." Asterov folded his arms across his chest. "His patience is running out. Vito carries through with his threats when he doesn't get what he wants. Give him that mine now, or I'll start sending you bits and pieces of Alex to prove his point. I expect—"

"Don't do it," Alex rasped, a bubble of red saliva inflating from his mouth before it burst.

The thug stepped into the frame and smashed his fist into Alex's cheek, jerking his head sideways before it rolled forward again, almost rendering him unconscious.

"I expect an answer within two days, or I will start fulfilling my promise." Milan glanced at the brute and gestured to stop filming. The red light went out.

"Good work," Vito said to Milan. Turning to the thug, he added, "Send that via normal hyperlink."

"Not encrypted?" the thug checked.

"No. I don't care if someone intercepts it. It might get a quicker response."

"Yes, boss." The thug took the camera and left.

"Let's see how much your employer values your life," Vito said to Alex.

Alex knew Ahiga would never relent, even if it meant he died because of it. He also knew Chooli was tearing her hair out trying to find him. It was his last hope of ending this alive. She would rescue him in the end. He just had to live long enough.

Several minutes later, the thug returned, unstrapped Alex from the chair, and dragged him back to the room where he was held captive with Ramira. He was more convinced than ever that she was in some way connected to the scheme to extort Ahiga out of the crystal boramide mine. Time would tell — time he realized he may not have.

39

SOMEONE IS FOLLOWING ME

The information Lingo provided disturbed Chooli. All that mattered to her was finding Alex, but she was shocked at the implication that he had visited a brothel. Then she recalled that Lingo had said *Ramira* had a contact there, not that Alex frequented it, so her fear lessened.

Later that afternoon, she headed to the local store to refresh her supplies. The westering sun was fading fast as the rays blazed between the buildings along the streets she traversed, their last vestiges leaving shadow and gloom behind them, a darkness suggestive of danger and roaming eyes searching for predators and prey.

She turned a corner and stopped. A premonition of being followed gripped her with ever-tightening dread. When she cocked her ears to listen, the city's white noise was all that hummed in the background. Despite her better judgment, she continued her journey, the distinct clopping of footfalls filtering through to her whenever she directed her attention to her hearing. Still, it wasn't getting louder or closer, so her fear subsided.

At the store, Chooli purchased the groceries she needed and left to return to her room. The sound of footsteps from behind her returned as soon as she started walking, their foreboding presence sending shivers through her with increasing annoyance. She turned a corner, stopped again, and waited.

This time, the footfalls continued and grew louder. She prepared to attack her stalker. The person appeared.

"Agate?"

Agate jumped when she saw Chooli about to pummel her. "It's me!" she yelled as she raised her arms to protect her face.

"I know that. Why are you tailing me?" Chooli relaxed her stance but remained guarded.

"What do you mean? I'm just walking home from work. I didn't even see you until you jumped at me."

Her alibi didn't convince Chooli, but she had no proof she was following her. "Someone's following me. I heard footsteps as I walked to the store. And I thought I heard them again. But it was you. You sure you didn't follow me there?"

"Why would I do that? You're jumpy. What shit are you into?"

"Nothing." Chooli averted her eyes. "I'm just sick of my ex chasing me. Hoped I'd moved somewhere even he couldn't track me."

Agate shook her head. "Nowhere's safe if someone's desperate and persistent enough." She smiled. "Anyway, we can keep each other company the rest of the way. Two against one."

Chooli still felt uneasy around her but didn't refuse her offer. It made sense. "Yeah. OK."

They continued strolling next to each other.

"Where did you come from?" Chooli asked.

Agate glanced at her before answering. "I work a few hours at a nearby cafe. It gives me the few credits I need to live."

"Oh. I thought ..."

Agate rolled her eyes. "Everybody thinks that. There are other ways of making a living, you know."

Chooli blushed. "Sorry. I shouldn't jump to conclusions." Still, the reply seemed evasive.

"What do you do?"

"This and that. I'd rather not talk about it." Chooli averted her gaze, conscious that she was being even more evasive.

They continued walking in silence until they arrived at the hotel. As they passed through the entrance, the manager appeared at his office doorway and glared at Agate.

"You got your rent?"

Agate glared back at him. "Yeah, yeah. You'll get it when I'm paid tomorrow."

"You're already a week behind. You'd better make sure you pay, or you'll be looking for somewhere else to stay."

Chooli watched on with interest but chose not to interfere.

"I said I'll pay tomorrow!"

The manager gripped the desk counter that separated him from Agate as if ready to leap over it, his fuming expression billowing across to her, but he said nothing more.

Leaving him to his obsessive debt-collecting, the two women climbed the stairs. "People might pay on time if he did something about providing decent rooms," Agate muttered under her breath.

Chooli grinned but didn't comment. When they reached their floor, they parted and headed for their respective rooms.

With nothing to do, Chooli puttered around and prepared a snack as she pondered over the riddle of her mystery pursuer. Someone had followed her. If it wasn't Agate, then who was it? She munched on a sandwich, which lacked any real taste, but she had to make do with what she could get without rousing suspicion, given her present persona. Her comm buzzed. She picked it up and checked who was trying to contact her. Raising her eyebrows in surprise, she pressed connect.

"Hi, Meng. Wasn't expecting you to call."

Meng's face stared out at her from the screen, her features displaying an air of concern. "Is that you, Chooli?"

Chooli chuckled. "Yeah, it's me. I needed a makeover to blend in with the crowd I'm currently mixing with."

"Our surveillance people have just intercepted a holographic message transferring to Ahiga via the hyperlink communications network. It's not pleasant to look at, but it will interest you." She looked to her side as someone offscreen spoke to her out of earshot. Meng nodded and turned her attention back to Chooli. "I'll send you a link to a cache for you to view it. As I said, it's unpleasant, but I know you'll want to see it."

Chooli wondered why she didn't relate the message's content, and the intrigue tensed her muscles as a sense of foreboding flowed through her. She wanted to ask her, but somehow, she knew Meng wouldn't tell her.

"OK. Thanks. I'll watch it straight away."

"Look after yourself and contact me if you need any help I can offer." Meng broke the connection, leaving Chooli staring at a blank display.

Moments later, her comm pinged with a new message. She opened it and stared at the embedded link as her thumb hovered over it, suspended in movement as she contemplated what opening it would reveal. Her heart pounded and her mouth felt dry as she willed herself to press the button.

The screen activated and an image appeared. She gasped. A wave of vertigo washed over her. She stumbled and staggered for a seat to drop into before she fell to the floor. The display projected a scene with Alex holding center stage, his bruised and bleeding face catching Chooli's entire attention as her hand went to her mouth and tears welled in her eyes. Alex's head flopped forward as he struggled to stay conscious. A man stood to the side of him looking directly into the camera. He wore a face mask, but Chooli recognized the overweight figure of Milan Asterov and his expensive suit.

"You might take Vito seriously now, Ahiga." Asterov folded his arms at his chest. "His patience is wearing thin. Vito carries through with his threats if he doesn't get what he wants. Give him that mine today, or I'll start sending you bits and pieces of Alex to prove his point. I expect—"

"Don't do it," Alex rasped, a bubble of red saliva inflating on the side of his mouth before bursting.

Somebody else stepped into the frame and smashed his fist into Alex's cheek, jerking his head sideways before it lolled forward again, apparently unconscious.

"No ..." Chooli sobbed, looking away, unable to continue viewing the physical abuse inflicted on her husband.

Asterov continued speaking. "I expect an answer within two days, or I will start fulfilling my promise."

The screen blanked, but she kept staring at it, tears flowing freely, her cheeks wet, and droplets dripping into her lap. The image of Alex's battered body remained burned on her retinas as she despaired over finding him in time. A wave of rage and fury she hadn't known she possessed swept her entire being. *They will pay for what they've done,* she promised herself as she wiped the last of her damp cheek dry and brought her mind back into focus. She now understood the urgency of her predicament. She had two days to find Alex before they started chopping him up and sending Ahiga the pieces.

It was time to catch up with Vapdog, so she tidied up the remains of her snack and left, heading for their rendezvous point. She hurried. Every second counted now, the need for speed burned into her by the holographic message.

Her concentration lapsed as she dashed through the streets, weaving along one and then another. As a result, she didn't notice the person following her until he was almost upon her. She turned her head in surprise when a shadow projected from the street lighting fell in front of her.

The assailant moved to grab her, but before he did, Chooli lashed out, booting him in the groin with a subsequent kick slamming into his chin, knocking him backward. He staggered, fighting to keep his balance, while she advanced, intent on finding out who he was and why he was following her. But before she could nab him, he rushed off and disappeared, leaving her staring after him and almost wondering if she had imagined the whole incident.

It seemed to her that the assailant had not been trying to kill her but to kidnap her. *What was going on?*

She snapped out of her trance and dashed off, eager to find Vapdog, safety, and a plan to move forward. She knew her luck might run out next time.

40

A VISIT TO MADAME BENGSEI'S

C hooli crept through the doorway of Vapdog's latest rendezvous point. He allowed no one to visit him at his residence. She fidgeted after scanning the location and finding it empty. *Where are you, Vapdog?*

The space was filthy, with the detritus of society scattered throughout. She gazed up to the open sky and twinkling stars in the cloudless expanse as twilight retreated over the western horizon. The entrance was stretching her imagination. It was positioned at the end of an alley with a sheet of thin plasti-crete standing across it. Still, it provided privacy for clandestine trysts away from most prying eyes. She wondered why he wanted to meet where satellite surveillance continued overhead.

After an agonizing time, the sheet rattled and Vapdog stepped through.

"About time," Chooli said.

"Sorry. I was delayed." He studied her. "What's got you so agitated?"

She told him about the holographic message and the attempted attack in the street.

"Oh."

"We need to chase up this lead that Lingo talked about."

"At Madame Bengsei's?"

"Yeah."

"But we don't know who he meant. Just that the person frequented the place."

"I'll find out. Someone there must know." Chooli paced the limits that confined the meager space where they stood.

Vapdog stared at her. "You're like a loose maser cannon. One twitch of the finger and you'll blast a hole through an entire city block."

She saw he was reluctant to take immediate action, but she needed to hurry, so she laid on her most pitiful charm. "Please. It's for Alex's life."

He sighed. "You can't manipulate me that easily. But you're right; we've got to speed things up." He rubbed his chin in contemplation. "OK. I'll escort you to the brothel, but then you're on your own."

"Great. Let's go." Chooli made to exit their cubby space.

"Whoa, steady there. Let's decide on a plan first. For instance, what are you going to say when you get there?"

She placed her hands on her hips. "I'll just walk in and ask for Lingo. And then I'll make Lingo tell me who the contact is."

"Mmm ... not sure how successful that will be. But remember, act your legend."

She nodded.

When they arrived at their destination. Chooli jumped from the taxi scooter, took a deep breath, and headed for the entrance. Crossing the threshold of the bordello was like entering a parallel universe. She had seen gentlemen's clubs on Franconia, but this was something else.

The reception lay before her, the walls glowing red and black in the dimply illuminated atmosphere. Two black divans lounged against one wall, curtains concealing the view behind them, and the reception desk stood along another. A middle-aged woman sat slouched in a chair, staring at her comm, searching the social media pages. Clothed in lingerie, she reflected the mood of the establishment, looking like a withered retiree — too old to service customers but valuable enough to keep employed as the receptionist. She either hadn't noticed or didn't care that Chooli had walked into the place. Until she said, "Three hundred for half an hour, five hundred for the full hour."

"I'm searching for a man," Chooli said.

The woman jumped, not expecting a female to answer her monotonic drawl. "Aren't we all," she said as she turned her attention from the screen to Chooli. She stared at Chooli before scanning her body with her eyes. "You want a job? You could earn good credits with looks like that."

"No, I don't." Chooli frowned, frustrated. "I'm looking for a regular client of yours."

The woman's stare became suspicious. "You a cop? Our license is up to date."

"No. Are you going to help me, or should I tear the place apart?"

She noticed the receptionist's hand disappear beneath the desk and wondered whether it was to grab a firearm or sound an alarm. "Don't do that," she warned. "Put your hands where I can see them."

The woman froze, her eyes wide with fear. "You got a name?"

"Lingo."

"Never heard of him."

The woman's words were emphatic, but Chooli's experience told her she knew who Chooli was talking about. "OK, have it ..."

A large, burly man entered. He glared at Chooli and glanced at the receptionist. "She giving you trouble?"

Chooli stared at the woman, furious she had somehow called for help despite her warning. Before the receptionist could reply and the brute could react, she flew into action, using every martial arts skill in her arsenal to pummel him into a stupor significant enough not to bother her anymore. Furniture lay strewn around the room, smashed and unusable. She heaved to catch her breath again as she turned her attention to the woman. "I warned you."

The woman started crying. "Please. I only work here. I have a family to support."

"You should have considered that before you lied to me. Now I'll check the rooms to find the person I'm searching for."

"He's not here. Not today."

Chooli grinned. "So, you *are* acquainted with him. I'm searching, anyway. And I want no more interruptions." She stormed through the curtained partition into a hallway lined with doors on her left and one at the end. The rear doorway had a green emergency exit sign above it. *Good. I can make a quick getaway.*

She reached the first door, standing before it, wondering what to do, how she would recognize her goal, and what her intentions were for Lingo. She had the answer to the last question — she'd wring his neck. Still, she'd told the receptionist she meant business, so she had better act the part. With one swift kick, she smashed it open, much to the occupants' consternation. It was at once plain they had nothing to hide despite their frantic and desperate search for clothing.

She repeated the exercise to the three next doors with the same result.

The last door stood ajar, restraining Chooli to caution as she wondered why it was ajar. Instead of standing in front of it as she had with the others, she positioned herself to the side, pushing it open with her hand. When she hazarded a peek inside, her mouth fell open until her brain started functioning again.

"Agate?"

Agate cowered, frightened, in the room's corner with a sheet covering her naked body. "Siren? What are you doing here?"

Chooli was unsure how to answer that except to respond with her own question. "What are you doing here? I thought you worked at a cafe."

"That's my day job. That can't keep me fed. I get extra cash here."

"But why? I thought you said there were better ways to earn a living."

"What's wrong with this? It pays well," she said defiantly.

Chooli changed the topic. There was no time for passing judgment. As she considered what she knew and her immediate distrust of Agate when she met her, the pieces of the puzzle fit into place, but she needed more information. "You know a guy called Lingo?"

Agate averted her eyes. "Maybe. I'm popular. Don't have everyone's name."

"But you know Lingo?"

"Why? What's he to you?"

She decided to take a punt. "He said you might know how to contact Ramira Lopez."

Agate gasped. She had slowly regained her confidence, but her bravado deserted her when Chooli mentioned Ramira, and Chooli couldn't understand why. Except that was the way everyone seemed to react to Ramira's name.

"Don't say that name anywhere if you value your life," Agate whispered.

Chooli frowned. "Why is everyone so scared of her?"

"She's ruthless and heartless."

Were they talking about the same woman? The one Chooli saw in the holo-vision recordings was destitute and pitiful. Was she an excellent actor or both? Still, how did Agate recognize her? Was Ramira an overlord of this business? As her mind struggled to assemble the information she had gathered, a conversation with Lingo flashed from her memory. "Your boss asked you to keep a lookout for someone looking like me?"

Agate looked confused and shook her head. "No. Why?"

"No reason. Just wondering."

"So?"

"So what?"

"What do we do now you've demolished this place?"

Chooli blushed. "Umm ..."

Loud footsteps running along the corridor came to Chooli's ear. She turned her head and yelped with surprise. New brutes were thumping toward her. She glanced back at Agate. "I have to leave."

With every ounce of momentum she had, she raced to the emergency exit, just avoiding the clutches of her assailants. Ensuring she slammed the door closed behind her, she dashed down the stairwell into an alley and sprinted to the front of the building complex, where Vapdog sat waiting with his eyes on the brothel's entrance, not toward the alleyway from where she emerged.

At the sound of her running, his head jerked in her direction. "What's happening?"

"Tell you later. Let's go." She didn't stop to explain as she ran past him and retraced the path they had come.

After gaping at her for several seconds, he must have decided Chooli had an excellent idea because she soon heard his frantic steps behind her.

41

ARE YOU ALRIGHT?

Ramira rushed to Alex once the thug deposited him back in their prison cell. She tried rolling him onto his side, as he was lying face down, but he yelled in agony as her hands touched him and attempted to move him. Perhaps she meant well, but the brutality of his torture still lingered in his body memory. Fortunately, he had no broken bones ... yet. Next time, he might not be so lucky.

"Sorry," Ramira said. "Are you alright?"

He groaned as he peered at her through the slit of one eye. "Do I look alright?"

"No. Just trying to help. Everything I do makes things worse." She slumped to the floor and sat, moping in her misery. She gave a sob before containing her emotions again.

Alex felt a twinge of guilt for his blunt reply. *Am I misjudging her?* But he lacked the energy to convey his mixed feelings to her in words. He became increasingly uncomfortable lying on his stomach, so he summoned his reserves and, bracing for the pain, used his right arm to roll over. By the time he managed it, sweat lathered his body, and he heaved a raspy breath. The world looked very different now that he gazed at the distant ceiling instead of the floor. He had more hope than that only moments ago.

He let his head flop sideways to watch what she was doing. She still held her head low as she muttered to herself.

"Don't blame yourself," he whispered. At least he now knew the reason for his imprisonment, but he still couldn't figure out why she was involved. It seemed redundant. She might be a contingency, a puppet in an alternative plan to set in motion if Vito needed to use extra motivation.

Ramira glanced at Alex, tears brimming in her eyes. "Why not? I'm the one who got you into this mess."

"You wanted help to find your child."

"Who's likely lost to me, a slave in the human trade market by now."

"Don't give up hope. We'll save him. We just need to escape and find out where we are."

She shook her head as she broke down into more convulsive sobs. Alex was impressed at her acting ability and then felt ashamed of himself for the thought.

Ramira's cries abated, and she reverted to a morose sulk.

"Can you get me water?" Alex asked.

His request woke her from her reverie. "Sure." She rose and walked to the remnants of their food and water, returning with a bottle half full of liquid. He fumbled it in his condition, so she helped him by holding it while drizzling the water into his mouth a gulp at a time.

The fluid quenched Alex's parched throat and washed the congealing blood from his mouth. When he had satisfied his thirst, Ramira used a few drops to wipe dried blood from his face, nose, and eyes, taking care when she touched his bruised spots.

"Thanks," he said afterward. Regardless of whether she was the cause of his predicament, he appreciated the help.

She gave a sad smile in acknowledgment and returned the bottle to where she had collected it.

A guard came with more food and left.

Alex had recovered enough by then to drag himself into a sitting position and eat what Ramira handed him. As he chewed, grimacing when his chewing aggravated one bruised spot after another, a mantra started up in his brain: *I need to escape from here.* He had two days to devise and enact a plan, or he would leave in bits and pieces. He knew the thugs guarding him would relish the opportunity to dismember him. He glanced at her. "Any ideas?"

She stopped chewing and stared at him, confused. "About what?"

"Getting out of here."

She shook her head in response. "Can't think of anything. There's only one door, and the ceiling vent is too high to reach."

Alex sighed, knowing she was right, but determined to find a means of escape, regardless. "She'll be distraught when Ahiga shows her the recording."

"Who?"

"Chooli."

"Who's she?"

"My wife. Didn't I tell you?"

"Maybe you did. I can't remember."

Despite Ramira's offhand manner, he sensed she was not disinterested.

Proving him right, she said after a moment, "I thought I was your one true love."

Alex almost choked. "Since when? You almost destroyed me."

She shrugged and returned to her meal.

"I wonder how intelligent our minders are?" She asked no one in particular.

"Intelligent enough to stop two prisoners from escaping a room with one exit."

"Yeah, but supposing we had an emergency?"

"They'd shoot us."

"They can't. That would lose them their bargaining power."

Alex sighed, wondering where Ramira was going with her line of thought. "What's on your mind?"

"What if you needed medical treatment? They need you alive for now."

She had a point. "But I'm fine."

"You might have internal bleeding. Start complaining of pain."

"Maybe. But I presume they've heard every word you just said. They must be listening. I would, especially after the trouble we've caused Riva so far. Besides, won't that jeopardize your seeing your child again?"

Ramira sighed. "You're probably right. It was worth considering, though."

Alex didn't respond but kept mulling over her idea, wondering if there was another angle to try without endangering Ramira's child if she indeed had one. He doubted it more and more, but his character made it impossible to discount it altogether. He did not want to have the death of a child on his hands.

He failed to find a means to save them both, but he wondered if he should escape on his own. That way, he might be able get help before they had a chance to blame or punish her. He considered discussing it with her but reconsidered it. She might object to being left behind. The only question now was whether he had the strength to move on his own.

42

A NAME

Chooli and Vapdog returned to his hideaway after running to the nearest taxi stand and traveling the rest of the way by scooter. As they flew, she told him what had occurred at the brothel in detail, including her surprise meetup with Agate. Her misery increased the more she debriefed him.

"Not much to go on," Vapdog said.

"No." She lowered her head, despondent. "But Agate might know of someone if I catch up with her at the hotel."

He sat in silence before offering his opinion. "Worth a try. But she won't return until the morning. She'll be working through the night."

Chooli gave a guilty grin. "Not sure it's fit for business — not in the condition I left it."

"Ha! They'll find a way. There's always someone desperate enough for some action not to care. Besides, there would be unpleasant ramifications for the owner if they don't continue to make money. They have bills to pay, especially bills to investors who don't tolerate excuses for a reduction in their income."

"What can we do before morning, then?"

He shook his head. "Nothing."

"I could go back."

"And get crucified? I don't think so. They'll be prepared for you this time."

They reached their destination and exited the taxi.

"Go sleep, and we'll start fresh in the morning," Vapdog advised.

She wasn't ready to go to bed. Time was too precious a commodity. But ideas failed her, and exhaustion overwhelmed her. "OK. I'll contact you tomorrow after I talk to Agate."

They parted, and Chooli caught another taxi back to her hotel. The manager ogled her as she passed through the reception, for which she blasted him with insults and putdowns. He hastily retreated into his office before she made good on any of them.

Once locked in her room, she flopped into the bug-infested lounge chair and moped before dozing. She woke with a start when a rapping on the door interrupted her slumber. Stretching and rubbing sleep from her eyes, she crept to the door cautiously.

"Who is it?"

"Agate."

Surprised, Chooli opened the door a crack and checked the hallway in both directions before allowing her to enter.

"What's the time?" Chooli asked.

"Two in the morning."

"A bit early to finish in your line of work."

Agate grinned. "After your demolition job, management decided it was pointless trying to stay open. A few customers arrived but retreated when they saw the state you left it in."

"You must have lost money tonight, then."

"It was a quiet night, anyway. I'd prefer I wasn't there, but the extra income is handy, and I have no alternative."

Chooli frowned. "There's always a choice."

With a head shake, Agate replied, "It's a condition of keeping my mother safe."

"That's not fair."

"That's life."

"Who's your mother?"

"Her name is Bai. She lives in a one room unit on the other side of the city."

They stood in silence.

"Want a drink?" Chooli asked.

"Thanks. What you got?"

"Water, tea, or something stronger. I have vodka."

Agate's eyes lit up at the mention of alcohol. "Vodka."

Good choice, Chooli thought. A bit of liquor might loosen her tongue. "Find a seat or use the floor. Take your pick."

Agate looked around and settled on pulling up a Plasteel seat near the lounge chair and coffee table. Chooli found a couple of glasses, rinsed and dried them, and poured a large shot of vodka into each of them. She strolled over and handed Agate one before sitting in the chair.

"To demolished brothels," Agate said as she raised her glass before taking a gulp of liquor and descending into a fit of giggles.

Chooli grinned, raising her drink, too. "Demolished brothels." She took a sip and studied Agate, wondering how to raise a most pressing topic. She decided just to come straight out with it.

"So, you know Lingo?"

Agate's expression turned glum. "You have to spoil it."

With a shrug, Chooli said, "I need to find someone in a hurry." She picked up the bottle of vodka and refilled their glasses.

"He's a client. Asks for me sometimes. Dunno why. He finds it hard to … you know," Agate giggled, holding up her pinky finger and wiggling it before slowly bending it into a drooping position.

Chooli understood the enactment and grinned. "Does he blame you?"

"Used to, until I brought in our best girl, and he couldn't perform with her, either. He still asks for me."

Lingo had said Ramira had a contact at the brothel, but Agate wasn't it, nor did she seem to know who it was. Maybe Chooli just wasn't asking the right question.

Chooli took a sip from her glass while she thought. "Does he ever bring someone ... you know ... for a threesome or anything?"

A burst of laughter erupted from Agate's mouth, and she shook so much she had to put her vodka on the table before she spilled any of it. "He's shy enough as it is," she got out between spasms. "I can't imagine him sharing with anyone else or wanting an audience."

Chooli smiled. She couldn't picture the Lingo she had seen being the same person as the one Agate was describing. Or maybe she could. He needed to force himself onto someone to arouse himself enough to complete his orgasm, as he had attempted with her. She refilled their glasses.

After calming and taking a sip, Agate frowned with concentration. "But he brings a friend sometimes. They don't come into my room together. The other guy goes off into the manager's private space, where the bodyguards relax."

Now we're getting somewhere. "You ever find out his name?" Chooli could see the alcohol was affecting Agate. She hoped it wouldn't cloud her cognition too much before she received the information she wanted.

"Travis." Agate stood with effort and stumbled to her shoulder bag left on the kitchen bench. She rummaged through it until she found a packet of cigarettes. Extracting one, she placed it in her mouth and dumped the packet back in her bag. She continued searching until she conceded defeat. "You got a light?"

In normal life, Chooli didn't smoke, but she had taken up the habit as part of her cover. "Sure." She patted her jacket and found a lighter. "Here," she said as she tossed it to Agate, who dropped it.

Agate wobbled before using the bench to lower herself to the floor. She grabbed the lighter, lit her cigarette, and threw it back to Chooli, except it went nowhere near Chooli, flying across the room instead. "Sorry." Agate giggled as she attempted to stand. She tried twice before crawling to her chair and sitting on it. "Where were we?"

"Travis," Chooli said, reminding her. "That's an unusual name for these parts."

Agate shrugged and said, "We can't all have diablo names."

Chooli's eyes bulged at Agate using diablo to mean interesting and popular. She thought she was the only one who used it and hadn't done so since her youth. Returning to the topic, Chooli wondered why Travis came to the brothel if he didn't seek out one of the girls. "Who does he see?"

"Dunno." Agate sucked on her cigarette and drew in a lungful of smoke before exhaling it in a long stream as she flopped her head back. "But he goes in where the minders hang out. I don't think he sees them, though. No one's allowed in there when Travis comes ... except for the manager."

"Who's the manager?"

"The one who sits out front. You would have seen her."

"I thought she was the receptionist."

"She's both."

"And this Travis guy only comes with Lingo?"

"Yeah. If he visits at other times, I haven't seen him."

At last. Useful information. Chooli became annoyed. Lingo could have saved her a lot of bother by simply telling her. But as helpful as the intelligence was, it didn't make it any easier to trace Travis. She was wondering how to do that when disturbing noises from Agate became audible.

Agate's stomach was convulsing until her head lunged forward. Before Chooli could take evasive action, a stream of vodka-filled vomit sprayed all over her. *Serves me right*, she thought, repulsed. She had made sure Agate received the lion's share of the alcohol. Agate had overindulged, and the foul puke stench proved that point. She tried wiping the bits of solid and mucus-congealing liquid from her clothing with little success. When she glanced back at Agate, she had flopped into the chair, comatose, and was snoring.

Chooli stood, looked at the revolting mess, and sighed. She'd have to clean it up before catching some sleep herself, or everything would reek of the regurgitation when she woke, something she refused to endure.

Agate ejected an enormous burp before settling again. Chooli wondered what she should do with her. She couldn't drag her back to her room. With another sigh, she resigned herself to leaving her there.

43

CONSEQUENCES

When a thug delivered their next meal, Alex made sure he had a prime view of the doorway and what lay beyond it. Unfortunately, the other thug standing on the threshold, along with the dim background light, gave him little information to help him with his escape plan. His physical condition also hampered him. His beating meant his movements remained constrained. Still, with a choice between escaping his captivity or losing body parts, he saw no option but to attempt the escape. It couldn't be any worse than the alternative.

He suspected the lack of light outside the door meant it was nighttime, although he had no concept of time within the confines of the windowless room. When he glanced at Ramira, he saw she was already dozing on the uncomfortable floor surface. He should sleep, too, but the pointlessness of trying in his heightened state of alertness frustrated him.

Once he pushed himself to a standing position, he staggered over to the door and tried opening it, knowing it was a waste of time. To his surprise, the door opened. *Why?* Despite Alex describing the thugs as lacking intelligence, he didn't think them that stupid. They would already be dead instead of having jobs as high-level minders for someone like Vito. He hazarded a look through the doorway and didn't spot anyone. With his confidence rising, he leaned out for a more thorough study of the space beyond it. It looked deserted. *Where were they?* Dim fugitive luminescence lit the warehouse, but he saw no light filtering from under the doorway of the thugs' ready room.

He re-entered his prison cell and rested against the wall. His gut said this was a trap, and they'd recapture him within two steps of freedom, but it might be his only chance. Ramira was asleep, too, making it easier to leave her behind. To justify his actions, he convinced himself he had better odds without her, and she had a better chance of recovering her child without him.

Deciding, he went to open the door again but paused when Ramira stirred. Forced to retreat, he distanced himself from the doorway and watched her while he waited for her to wake or return to sleep. His luck held as she muttered and rolled over away from him. He let out his breath in silence.

After lingering long enough to ensure she was soundly asleep again, he returned to the door. Opening it, he slipped out, closing it behind him. This was too easy. It had to be a trap. Regardless, he had to try. The alternative of doing nothing was akin to waiting on death row. As his eyes adjusted to the dim light, he stood motionless, watched, and listened. No movement or sound disturbed his escape. *Where is everyone?* While he waited, he studied the layout of the space, something he should have done before.

A door penetrated the far wall. Next to their cell was another door, a padlock preventing entry. *Was this the torture room?* Not likely. Even with solid plasti-crete walls, too much sound would have filtered through to their prison. He squatted and looked under the door. No light escaped through the slit. He saw no other doorways from where he stood. *Where did they torture me?* It presented a mystery he lacked the time or interest to solve. His escape route led to the opposite end, through a field of crates and to the outside air and liberty.

Instead of heading straight across the warehouse, Alex considered it prudent to circumnavigate the perimeter and stay undercover despite the extra time it took. He crept to the side wall, keeping alert for any movement or sound that might indicate danger. After reaching the corner, he took several deep breaths, relieving his stress, and continued along the wall to the next corner. He made it with just fifty meters to the doorway and freedom.

Glancing around him, he edged toward the door. The tension ate at him, but he'd be through the door within seconds. When he arrived, he took more deep breaths and extended his hand to the door handle, hoping it was not locked. He wrapped his fingers around the handle, rotated it a fraction, and smiled. It was unlocked. His luck had held. Once he completed rotating the handle until it stopped, he cracked the door ajar.

His face dropped, the anticlimax dampening his drive to continue. Another warehouse space extended in front of him — a space full of crates stacked two and three high. Other equipment lay scattered between them. He sighed, pushed the door open, and walked across the threshold. At least he was still free, with no sign of anyone occupying the warehouse. Once he closed the door again, he searched the visible part of the building before him without moving from his current position.

The space was the same width, but its length extended much further. He frowned. Entry to the space he left was via the just-used restricted access. *Why? Did I miss another opening elsewhere?* With no time to solve the puzzle, he crept sideways to gaze along an aisle. The end, 200 meters distant, contained a large, closed door to move freight in and out of the premises. He discerned no office or other partitioned-off space from where he stood.

Having got this far, Alex decided he might as well continue with his plan, so he started slinking along the corridor lined with crates, stopping whenever he reached a side passage to check for others in the building. He became more confused as he moved closer to the large door. *Where was everyone? Where were the two thugs?* After several minutes, he arrived at the last line of crates but still had at least twenty meters of vacant space to reach the freight door. He scanned the frame for the mechanism that opened it but found none.

An office with windows overlooking the warehouse stood alongside the doorway. Movement inside the office caught his eye, forcing him to withdraw under cover of the crate stack, hoping no one had seen him. That explained where they were. It didn't explain their laxness. Before his withdrawal, he spotted the door to the office. It must be the only other exit. How would he get past the thugs?

"This is a delightful surprise," a familiar voice said behind him, making him jump.

Alex spun around, perspiration dripping from him as his adrenaline spiked. "Riva!" He made to attack Vito, but before he could lunge, someone grabbed him from behind and pinned him with massive hands. He struggled to free himself with no success.

"Out for a stroll? Or trying to escape?"

"Stretching my legs."

Vito gave a wry smile. "We'll have to teach you a lesson." He peered at Alex's captor. "Take him back."

The thug dragged Alex through the warehouse to the prison, where Ramira still slept. She woke with a start when the door burst open. The thug threw Alex on the floor and booted him in the ribs, winding him. Vito followed them both into the room. He glanced at her before returning his attention to Alex.

"Did you really think you could escape?" Vito asked.

"You shouldn't leave doors unlocked and unguarded."

"I wondered if you would succumb to the temptation." He turned to Ramira. "You should have warned him against such folly, for your kid's sake. Don't overvalue your worth." He returned his eyes to Alex. "We inflict consequences for such actions." He nodded at the guard.

The thug removed all restraint from his attack as he kicked Alex in the ribs and head. Alex rolled himself into a fetal position until he could take the punishment no longer and lapsed into unconsciousness.

44

CORNERED

Chooli couldn't sleep. She rose and checked the time: 4 am. She considered returning to Satan's Furnace to see if Lingo still frequented it. He might be persuaded to divulge more information about Travis and his whereabouts. Knowing the bar stayed open all night, she changed and headed out.

The streets were dark and quiet, as she expected. She hurried to the taxi stand and hopped into the one she ordered. It dropped her off a few blocks from the bar since she wanted to check out the place before approaching it. After a quick scan of her surroundings, she started strolling toward it. At the intersection, she veered off into a side alley that ran parallel to the major thoroughfare to improve her chances of not being detected.

After she crossed the next junction, she thought she heard footfalls behind her like last time. She halted and listened, but the noise stopped. She stole a glance behind her to check for anyone, but the street was empty, so she continued. The footsteps started again. With her nerves tingling, Chooli veered into the next side alley, found a dark place to hide, and waited. Her wait was short-lived.

A female figure came into view and paused. She looked lean and fit, but the darkness and the cap she wore shrouded her face and obscured any other features. The person hesitated, undecided, as she looked searchingly ahead and into the alley. Finally, she entered. Chooli tensed, waiting for the confrontation.

The person crept further into the alleyway until Chooli could almost touch her. Amazed the woman hadn't detected her yet, she stayed hidden. Then, with her patience exhausted, she sprang like an enraged lioness and wrestled the woman to the ground. The women fought frantically as they both strived to gain the advantage. With a deft maneuver, Chooli rolled her face down and pinned her arms behind her back, and both women heaved for breath.

"Who are you?" Chooli hissed.

The woman struggled to escape and then gave up. "No one."

"Why are you following me?"

"I'm not."

Chooli pushed her elbows higher up her back until the woman yelled in pain. "None of your business."

"Wrong answer. Give me the right one before I dislocate your shoulders." Chooli shoved her arms harder.

"I was told to."

"By whom?"

"I don't know."

Chooli increased the pressure on the woman's shoulders.

The woman screamed. "Stop. I really don't know. I got paid."

Reluctantly, Chooli decreased the force, guessing the woman was telling the truth. While deciding on her next course of action, she patted the woman's clothing, checking for weapons. She found a knife of very lethal length strapped to her leg and extracted it. She was tempted to keep it, but as she had her own, she tossed it away. Continuing her search, she tipped out the woman's carry bag. A small kinetic pistol, easy to conceal and illegal, fell out. She picked it up and placed it in her pocket. There were no other weapons on her.

"You picked the wrong person to follow."

"So, it seems. What d'they want with you, anyway?"

"What does who want with me?"

"The dark web has notices plastered everywhere to keep a lookout for you. A hefty reward's waiting for anyone providing info about you. A snort of chimera stardust as well if they capture you."

The bounty on her worried Chooli. Who was after her, and why? It wasn't the brothel owners. She was being followed before she visited it. She considered her options as she continued sitting on the woman. It had to be Vito. It was the only rational explanation. With his taking Alex as blackmail bait and after her harassing him at the dinner, capturing her would exact revenge on her and up the ante in his extortion of Ahiga. But she didn't have time to ponder it further.

A shot rang out from the alley entrance, missing Chooli by a fair margin, which meant they were either bad shots or out to capture her, not kill her. She rolled off the woman and used her as a shield between her and her attackers, whoever they were. The woman struggled with frantic convulsions as she realized her danger.

Chooli pulled the pistol from her pocket as she endeavored to control her captive. She checked the ammunition. The firearm contained a full clip of fifty projectiles, judging by her limited vision in the poor lighting. It should be enough if she had unobstructed lines of sight of her assailants.

More shots rang out, the woman convulsing backward and then slumping in death, caught in the crossfire. The shooters were either unaware of her presence or uninterested in her life. Fortunately, Chooli saw the flashes from two guns and fired shots in those directions. One person yelped and fell, but the other blasted splinters from the plasti-crete building.

Still using the now-deceased woman as a shield, Chooli tried searching for her enemies to assess their number, but the darkness prevented her. She glanced behind her to check the alley layout to her rear, but when she looked, she discovered she was in a dead-end. Her sole exit was past the people who wanted to capture her. She returned her attention to that direction and waited, her pistol at the ready and her thoughts thanking the woman for having it on her.

Several projectiles whistled past her as covering fire for the two people sprinting forward. Chooli aimed and shot one of them, who fell to the ground. She started worrying. The distance between the alley entrance and her position was short, and too many people could overwhelm her before she either killed them or convinced them to retreat.

At least three guns had fired, so that made four assailants, counting the still-living person that had run forward. Wiping perspiration from her brow, Chooli scrutinized her surroundings, waiting for any movement she could target.

A round of covering fire echoed throughout the alley, and two more attackers dashed forward. This time, they stayed in the open longer, giving Chooli time to aim and fire at them, both with success as she watched them fall. The pistol impressed her. It was lightweight, but the ammunition was lethal. *Two more dead, two to go, hopefully.*

Now accustomed to the darkness, she concentrated her surveillance along the alley, her pistol ready for another shot. She roughly knew one assailant's location but remained unsure of the other. She presumed the latter was still hiding at the entry. If she got the chance to, Chooli decided she would aim for the person at the entrance when he provided the other person with covering fire to move forward or retreat. That strategy gave higher odds of killing them both and, if fortune prevailed, her leaving the alley a free woman.

She waited.

After what seemed an interminable time, shots reverberated from both the entrance and further forward, but both shooters aimed wide with no plain target in sight. Chooli had her chance. She targeted and fired at the entrance. A man yelled in pain as the bullet smashed into his hand and wrist. The foremost person lost patience waiting for backup to cover him and dashed for the exit, giving Chooli an easy shot. She fired, and he fell. The other person, for no fathomable reason other than his injury driving him insane, ran across the entrance, so she took a potshot at him. Her aim being true, the hit dropped him dead as well.

She still lay on the ground behind the deceased woman, waiting, as she listened for predatorial movement in front of her. After five minutes, she deemed it safe to crawl into the darkness before standing. She edged along the wall, passing dead bodies as she did so. They must want her badly, but did they want her dead? She was worthless if she was dead.

Once she reached the alley entrance, she poked her head into the major thoroughfare, confirming her danger had disappeared. The experience reaffirmed the need for constant vigilance.

45

A CLUE AT LAST

Chooli's path to Satan's Furnace was uneventful after her skirmish with what she presumed were bounty hunters. Everyone ignored her when she entered, so she sat in the far corner and ordered a drink while she checked out who else patronized the bar at this hour. Her sour expression, one that complemented her mood, drove away anyone adventurous enough to contemplate approaching her.

Her beer arrived, and she sipped it while spying on those entering the establishment via the front or back entrances. Halfway through her second drink, she stopped sipping and smiled as her eyes spied the person she had come there to see. She watched him head to the serving counter, pass a joking remark to a patron while he bought a drink, and then turn nonchalantly to find a spot to sit.

Their eyes met. Beforehand, his posture radiated arrogance and confidence, but that changed when he recognized Chooli. His eyes widened with surprise and fear before darting around for an escape route with the best chance of avoiding her.

She rose with lightning speed and had closed the distance

between them before he regained his reflexive reactions from his fright. "Fancy meeting you here."

Lingo produced an anxious chuckle. "Yeah, I could say the same."

"Let's go back to my table for a chat, shall we?"

"I was just going to catch-up with a friend ..."

"It will have to wait ... unless you don't want to leave here alive."

He gulped. "I can spare a few minutes."

Chooli smiled as she pointed to her spot and prompted Lingo to take the lead. He checked behind him a few times as they threaded through the crowd as if to confirm her continued presence. She just flashed another smile. When they arrived at her table, she gestured to where she wished him to sit and slid in next to him.

"This is cozy," she said, "and reconsider any thoughts you might have to take me by surprise. I have a pistol trained on you. So, behave and you'll live beyond our chat ... maybe."

Lingo's eyes widened as he glanced under the tabletop, where she flashed the weapon from her pocket before hiding it from view again.

"How did you sneak that in here?"

"Persuasion and a winning smile." She studied him as she took a sip of her drink. "Are you aware of there being contracts out to bounty hunters to capture me?"

Lingo's hand shook as he raised his glass for a mouthful. "Nothing to do with me." He kept his eyes on her.

"Good, because they're dead."

His face darkened with terror.

"I don't want to eliminate you, too." She gave a fake smile. "I'm taking a liking to you."

He sculled what remained of his drink and ordered another while taking deep breaths to calm his nerves.

"Are you anxious?"

"I wasn't expecting such pleasant company."

This time, she laughed with sincerity. "Still the charmer. What's say we do our business, and we can both leave peacefully? It is getting late."

He nodded.

Lingo's drink came.

"Who's Travis?"

"Never heard of him."

His body language betrayed his lie. She didn't need the information she already possessed. She sighed. "Your charm has diminished. You want to try answering again? Or maybe step outside for a quick romp?"

His jitters returned. "His name might be familiar."

She sat and stared at him in silence, each second infuriating her further and pushing Lingo into final submission.

"We meet now and then and visit Madama Bengsei's."

"Why?"

He gave her a knowing grin. "Why else does one visit a brothel?"

"I don't know. Enlighten me."

His sneer morphed into embarrassment. "To ... you know ... with a woman ... you know."

"What, both of you? At the same time?"

Lingo's face turned red. "No. He goes off while I get my pleasure."

"Where? Where does he go?"

"Out the back. He talks with the owner and the security guards."

"What about?"

"No idea. Tried to find out once. But they told me to mind my own business if I wanted to enjoy visiting with my manhood still intact."

That tallied with Agate's information, and Chooli was sure he told the truth about Travis' dealings. "So, is this Travis guy Ramira's contact?"

"What?"

"You told me before that Ramira had a contact at Madame Bengsei's. If it's not you, and it's not Agate, is it Travis?

"Did I say that? I don't remember."

She frowned. He was playing with her. "What's your association with Travis?"

"I can't tell you that."

Chooli sighed.

"True. I value my life too much. We just met one day, and I had no choice."

"So, how do you contact him? Where does he come from?"

"He contacts me. I don't ask who he works for. It's too dangerous."

She sat back and studied him. As pleasurable as throttling him would be, she detected no uncooperative responses or withholding of information. He had no knowledge, probably by design, so no trace of his association with anyone was possible.

"Well, the good news is, I believe you. The bad news is I want to meet this Travis today."

Lingo's eyes bulged. "That's impossible. I told you — he contacts me."

"You must be able to contact him."

"I could—"

A shot rang out in the bar and people screamed and yelled. Chooli ducked under the table. She wondered why Lingo didn't do the same. When no further gunfire occurred, she ventured to raise her head above the table to search for the shooter.

The other patrons stared toward the bar's rear exit, but she detected no suspicious movement.

She started turning to Lingo. "What was that ...?" She completed the motion. "Oh."

He sat back in his seat, eyes blank, with a bullet hole in his forehead. If nothing else, the assassin was an impressive shot. But Chooli had lost any chance of flushing out Travis through Lingo.

46

A VISIT FROM THE COPS

After her deadly encounter with Lingo at Satan's Furnace, Chooli returned to her room and rested. Agate was still out to it when she arrived but woke sometime later. With a groan and apology, she stumbled from Chooli's room to return to her own. Chooli continued napping until ten. She had breakfast, showered, and called Vapdog to update him on her adventures.

He chastised her for not getting him involved when she told him about her ambush and the shootout, but he then relaxed and ordered her to meet him at a diner near his apartment for lunch at noon.

Just as she prepared to leave, a knock rapped on her door, stopping her in her tracks. No one knew she was there — supposedly. The door rattled with another louder rap. If she didn't answer it, they would demolish it. She checked her recently gained gun and tucked it behind her in the top of her pants before bracing herself and opening the door. She stepped two paces back. Three men stood glaring at her. The one in front wore a suit. The other two stood behind him, dressed in the uniform of the Xi Boötis police. Chooli spotted at once they weren't real. She was familiar with that uniform, and what they wore was close but quite right. The men were fit, solid, and towered over her. Suit Guy had a scar across his left cheek. She would never defeat so many in close combat.

"Who are you?" she asked.

"Siren?" Suit Guy asked.

"Who wants to know?"

"I'm Detective Wong with the Xi Boötis Police Department. Mind if we come in?"

"Show me your ID first."

Suit Guy smiled. He reached behind his jacket front, watched like a hawk by Chooli, and pulled out a police ID wallet. He flashed it open and closed it again, too fast for her to get a decent look at his credentials, but she was sure it was counterfeit.

She knew it. He knew it. They stood staring at each other, him grimly challenging her to resist him further, she grimly challenging him to persist.

Without her permission, he stepped into the room, his two cronies following behind him. Chooli took two paces backward and leaned against the kitchen bench, offering a casual pose but positioning her hand to grab the pistol in an instant. She could also dive for cover from where she stood.

"What do you want?"

"We're investigating a disturbance at a bar called Satan's Furnace last night." Wong made to look inside his electronic notepad. "This morning."

"So?"

"We understand you were there."

"Earlier. I left before midnight."

Wrong gave a knowing smile. "There was a murder. You know anything about that?"

Chooli shook her head.

"Strange. The CCHV shows you talking to the victim when the killer shot him."

"So? That proves I didn't kill him."

"Please accompany us to the station."

"Am I under arrest?"

"No. We need you to make a statement."

"I can make a statement here."

Wong sighed. "Please don't be difficult."

"The law says I don't have to go with you to the station unless I'm under arrest. I can go there anytime. Which station?"

"Police Headquarters in town. You need to come with us now." He took a step closer. The other two stayed near the door, blocking her exit.

"So, you work for Chief Inspector Detective Mengzi?"

He eyed her, gauging if she was telling the truth. "He's my boss."

"I see. I'm still not going with you."

With a sigh, he said, "Enough. Either you accompany us voluntarily, or we arrest you for obstructing an investigation."

She tensed. This would only end one way, so she prepared her move. "You can't arrest me."

"Why not?"

"You're not cops. Chief Inspector Detective Mengzi doesn't exist."

Once she disclosed their failed ruse, Wong lunged forward while the other two reached for the masers resting in their holsters. But when Wong attempted to apprehend her, he grabbed thin air. She had dived sideways, bringing out her pistol at the same instant, firing two shots before she hit the floor, into the heads of each uniform. They fell in slow motion.

Wong grabbed his maser. But Chooli fired, hitting his hand and sending the maser flying across the room. He yelped in pain as he grabbed at his hand, blood gushing from the wound. She scrambled to her feet, kicked the firearm beyond Wong's reach, and booted him in the groin, her gun aimed at his head. He folded over in agony.

"Who do you work for?"

"No one."

"Wrong answer." She shot into his kneecap, shattering the bone, blood oozing from the hole.

He yelled in pain as he reached to hold his injured leg. Perspiration flowed from his face. "Riva. Vito Riva."

"Why does he want to kill me?"

"He doesn't. He sent us to collect you."

"Why?"

"I don't know. That's above my pay grade."

Chooli changed her aim to his other knee.

Wong saw and panicked. "I'm not lying. He didn't tell us why. Just said to bring you to him."

He was telling the truth. She considered her next move. "Why send bounty hunters last night, then?"

The question confused him. "I don't know about any bounty hunters. Vito doesn't work that way."

They must have been overenthusiastic mobsters who overheard Vito's wish and wanted to impress him. They had their reward. "Where can I find Travis?"

"I don't know any Travis."

Chooli re-aimed the gun again and cocked the trigger.

"Stop. If you mean Travis the drug trafficker, he works out of a warehouse in the light-industry district."

"How can I find him?"

"The Old Shanghai Emporium."

"That doesn't help."

"That's its name. There's only one of them."

She had run out of questions. She targeted Wong's head and fired two shots, staring at the dead body for a long time afterward, shocked with herself. The distinction between an undercover cop protecting herself and a ruthless assassin was muddy sometimes, and she wondered how far she had slipped toward the wrong end of the pendulum swing. What terrified her the most was her premonition that she had found her destiny.

Waking from her trance, Chooli realized she could no longer stay there. She was disappointed. It was an excellent base for her, but it now held too much risk. Cramming her meager belongings into her bag, she stood at the doorway, staring into her room, wondering if she should wipe the place clean. She had insufficient time to sanitize it thoroughly, so she left it, complete with cadavers.

She closed the door and glanced along the corridor toward Agate's room. After a moment's consideration, she headed there and knocked on her door. There was no answer. She might have gone to her cafe job. But then Chooli realized Agate's condition prevented her from working in her physical state. She tapped again. When Agate still didn't respond, she tried the door. It was unlocked. She opened it and peered inside the room.

"Please don't hurt me," Agate begged in between sobs from where she hid.

"It's me. Siren."

After several seconds, Agate's head poked up from behind the sofa along the rear wall. Her crying subsided as she stared at Chooli and wiped her eyes with her sleeved forearm. "How did you escape?"

"I didn't. I shot them."

Agate's jaw dropped. "You shot police officers?"

"They weren't police officers."

Agate tried to take in the information. "How? Where did you get a gun? When did you learn to shoot? How—"

"Slow down." Chooli entered the room for the first time and gave it a cursory scan. It was a mess with food containers and clothing strewn everywhere. She didn't need to hide behind the sofa, Chooli thought. She could have just hidden herself under the junk. "I got the gun last night. But it's not important now. We've got to leave before the real police get here, though I'm more concerned about the assassin from last night coming to finish the job. He'll kill you, too, if you get in the way. Get packed."

"What assassin?"

"Just move, Agate. I'll explain it all later."

Agate remained seated on the floor, still staring and gaping. She slumped there like a distorted statue and didn't seem to absorb Chooli's words.

"Sometime within the next half hour would be nice."

Rousing herself from her shocked state, Agate stood. She appeared exhausted and hung over. "Why would an assassin be after me?"

Chooli shrugged. "Tidy up loose ends. Do you want to chance it?"

"No," Agate mumbled to herself as she perused the rooms, wondering where to start. "I can't take everything."

She disappeared into the bed alcove. Chooli heard banging and scraping, and soon afterward Agate reappeared and headed to the kitchen space, packing more items into the bag she carried until it overflowed with her belongings. She stared at her bag and the rest of the room with forlorn disappointment. "That's it, I suppose."

"You can return once things settle."

"You reckon?"

"Maybe."

"Where're we going?"

"I've got to meet a friend. Come with me. We'll find a place to stay afterward."

Agate sighed. "Let's go then."

Chooli nodded and led her from her abode. Agate locked it behind her, but Chooli sensed they would never return.

Chooli was aware of appearing too calm, too blase. It covered the turmoil churning inside her. But it also reflected a new steely attitude in her that had arisen during the gunfight.

They descended the stairs.

When they reached reception, another homicide awaited them. The manager sat in his usual chair behind the desk, his head flopped back and sightless eyes staring at the ceiling. A cauterized maser hole blemished his forehead. Agate screamed.

"Let's go." Chooli almost pushed her out the door.

47

CAFÉ RENDEZVOUS

Chooli and Agate arrived at the rendezvous to meet Vapdog almost an hour late. With the excitement at the hotel, the difficulty in carrying their belongings, and frustration at transport availability, they turned up tired and ill-tempered. Chooli would have contacted him, but the possibility of someone tapping her comm concerned her. She did not want anyone to detect where they were. To their relief, Vapdog was still waiting.

Vapdog sat in the diner's rear, sipping coffee and with his eyes on the door. He started when they walked in the door, instantly waving to catch Chooli's attention. His eyes widened when he saw Agate walking in behind her. He glanced back at Chooli and raised a questioning eyebrow.

She returned his glare as they struggled with their luggage, weaving between the tables to reach him. They dropped their bags, and Chooli gestured for Agate to sit. She did likewise.

"Who's your friend?" he asked.

"Agate. Someone I met where I was staying." Chooli made the introductions. "Agate, Vapdog."

Agate nodded but slumped in her chair, her shoulders sagging and her head hanging with a vacant expression.

"She looks worse for wear."

"We drank too much last night. Then, I received a visit this morning from three fake cops. That's why we're late."

He raised his eyebrows. "How do you know they're fake?"

"Were."

"What?"

"Were. They're dead. They didn't know the correct police procedure, amongst other things. Besides, I pumped one for information, and he admitted they'd been sent by Vito Riva to take me to him. I refused to go, which upset them."

"So, one's still alive?"

Chooli shook her head. "Not anymore."

Vapdog raised his eyebrows again.

"We couldn't stay there after that, could we? Hence the bags."

"Why bring her?" Vapdog's eyes gestured to Agate and back.

"Given her relationship to the late Lingo, she may be in as much danger as I am — and I've taken a liking to her."

"Fair enough." He sipped his coffee as he stared over the cup rim at them.

"Can we get a coffee?" Agate asked, becoming interested in participating in the discussion. "And food. I'm starving."

With a wry smile, Vapdog said, "Be my guest." He glanced at Chooli. "You're paying."

Chooli rolled her eyes in reply. "Let's order then." Her stomach rumbled. She gazed back at him. "All this killing makes a girl hungry."

He stared at her. "I disapprove of this transformation of yours. I preferred it when you looked more defenseless."

"What's he talking about?" Agate asked.

"Nothing," Chooli replied as she glared at him. "Let's order."

They perused the menu and placed their orders for a meal, burger, and chips for Chooli, chow mien for Agate, and coffee. They only engaged in sporadic conversation while Chooli and Agate waited for the meals. When they came, Agate devoured hers. Chooli ate at a more leisurely pace, starting with the chips.

"Anyway," she said in between bites. "Apart from admitting they worked for Vito, the guy talked about this Travis—"

Agate's eyes bulged. "A-is," she got out, her speech garbled because of munching a mouthful of food.

The others looked at her.

She gulped down the food. "What do you want with Travis? He's bad news."

"What do you mean?" Vapdog asked. "What do you know about him?"

"He comes to the brothel with Lingo and talks to the people up front. I think they talk about drugs, but I'm not sure. Whenever I wander up there, they shut up and tell me to run away. He gives me bad vibes, an evil stare."

Chooli took up where she left off. "I found out he works from a place called the Old Shanghai Emporium. We need to go there next."

Vapdog held up his hands. "Whoa! We can't just walk into this place and introduce ourselves."

Chooli stared at him. "Why not?"

"If he's as bad as Agate says he is, he'll have security, that's why not."

"I'll go say hello. They want me anyway."

"Then what?"

"I'll ask him where to find Alex."

He roared with laughter.

Agate frowned. "Who's Alex?"

Chooli leaned back, puzzled, wondering what she'd said that Vapdog found so funny.

After he recovered from his fit, he studied her before saying anything. "You're serious, aren't you?"

Chooli shrugged. "Yes. I'm not going in there unarmed." She picked her bag up and unzipped a side pocket. Exposing its contents, she showed him the three masers and kinetic pistol she had collected so far and zipped the pocket back up before anyone else saw them.

"You opening an armory business or something?"

With a grin, Chooli replied. "Maybe. When I've finished this assignment."

A silence settled between them while he considered what Chooli had said to him. She used the time to eat her burger, sipping coffee between bites.

He sighed. "We need to research it first. Get an idea of the layout."

"No time," Chooli replied. "We have a day to find him."

"Who's Alex?" Agate asked again.

"We can't go in there blind," Vapdog insisted.

Chooli stared at him. She couldn't ask him to help her do what she intended. "I can do this on my own."

"You bloody well are not. You'll get yourself killed, and that won't help Alex."

"Who is Alex!" Agate almost shouted, exasperated over their ignoring her.

Chooli and Vapdog turned to stare at her.

"What?" Chooli snapped.

"Who's Alex?" Agate asked for the fourth time, calming her voice.

"He's my husband. Vito Riva kidnapped him and is holding him to ransom. He means to chop him up tomorrow unless his victim meets his demands."

"Thank You!" Agate folded her arms, satisfied they had acknowledged her presence at last.

A moment of silence passed between them.

"You could use my help," Agate said.

"I can't involve you more than you already are," Chooli said. "You're in danger just by knowing me."

"Then it doesn't matter if I get in deeper, does it?"

After studying her, Chooli asked, "What can you do?"

"Travis knows me. It'll put him off his guard if someone he knows rocks up. He might think I've come from the brothel with a message."

Chooli glanced at Vapdog.

He shrugged. "She has a point. Better than a stranger fronting up. Or worse still, he recognizes you and acts first."

Chooli looked at him and then Agate while she considered her options. "It might work," she said. "Let's make plans."

They spent the next hour discussing and closing the holes in a course of action to infiltrate Travis' premises, including working out several contingencies. By the time they finished, they were bursting with coffee and pleased with the scheme they had worked out. But first, they had to find the Old Shanghai Emporium, and for that, they needed to visit Vapdog's workplace, much to his displeasure.

48

THE OLD SHANGHAI EMPORIUM

With her stomach gurgling with tension, Chooli stood at a distance from the Old Shanghai Emporium building, studying its layout and entrance. Agate stood beside her, fidgety with worry. Chooli glanced across at her. "You don't have to do this, you know."

"Yes, I do," Agate replied. "It might give me a chance for freedom at last."

Chooli turned to Vapdog. "You ready?"

"I can't stop you, so, yes."

After Chooli checked her kinetic pistol and maser for the tenth time, she returned them to their hiding spots on her body, places she hoped a cursory search would overlook. "Let's go." She started pacing toward the building's entrance with Agate at her side, leaving Vapdog to adopt a more defensive role if her scheme unraveled. She adjusted her posture and lengthened her stride to ooze confidence and determination.

They made it to the doorway before two burly guards stationed at the entrance blocked their path.

The right-hand guard, his long black hair tied in a ponytail, stood a head taller than Chooli. His face was as round as a ball. The left one, taller still, had a long, thin face. Ball Face spoke first, a smirk appearing as he ogled them both. "You lost?"

Chooli smiled sweetly at him. "No, sir. We have come to talk with Mr. Travis." She figured starting off politely might throw them a little.

"You don't have an appointment. Does he know you?"

Agate spoke up, her voice thin but remarkably steady, "My name's Agate. Mr. Travis knows me from Madame Bengsei's."

Ball Face kept his smile, but she saw his façade falter. He glanced at Thin Face before returning his attention to Agate. "What business do you have with Travis that he can't handle at Madame Bengsei's?"

Chooli interrupted, "It's a private matter. Mr. Travis might not like it if you prevented him from hearing something he needs to hear. I'm sure you don't want to annoy him and endanger your manhood." She kept her tone sweet and her face deadpan but had to control rising irritation.

Thin Face roared with laughter. "She's got you there."

Ball Face's features soured.

"We wish to speak with Mr. Travis," Chooli repeated firmly.

Less cocksure, he asked, "And who are you?"

"Siren."

He glanced at his colleague, who gave a small shrug.

"Tell the boss a whore called Agate from Madame Bengsei's, and a chick called Siren, want to see him. I'll watch them."

Thin Face nodded and stepped away to speak into his comm device while Ball Face kept a wary eye on the two women, especially Siren.

Thin Face stepped back a minute later. "Says to frisk them for weapons and let them in."

Ball Face's expression threatened to turn into a smile halfway between menace and delight when he heard they had to frisk the two, but it was short-lived when he detected something glint in Siren's eyes. Choosing to adopt a professional manner, he said to the women,

"Arms out, legs spread. And no sudden moves, or we'll do it the hard way."

Chooli had no intention of becoming aggressive, even if his hands wandered. She wanted to arouse as little suspicion as possible and not be flung out before they even got inside. Travis was likely already suspicious. She spreadeagled, and Agate did likewise. This was one of the most dangerous parts of her plan, but she maintained a businesslike composure. Ball Face behaved himself, patting her lightly without discovering her hidden weapons. Thin Face did the same to Agate, although she had no secreted guns to worry about. She had refused to have them.

After obtaining clearance to go ahead, Ball Face said, "Follow me." He turned and started walking. Chooli sighed inwardly. *So far so good.*

Chooli and Agate followed in step behind him, leaving Thin Face as the solitary sentry at the door. Ball Face led them through a narrow corridor, past several closed doors. Chooli noticed several CCHV cameras along the way. No doubt, Travis was taking a long, hard look at them before they met.

They strode to the far end, where a door stood wide open. Ball Face stopped outside the doorway and ushered Chooli and Agate inside. Chooli paused and checked Ball Face before entering. He looked tame enough still.

She peered into the room. It was monstrous, much larger than it needed to be for an office. A converted warehouse came to mind. The walls had a red and gold Chinese pattern. Paper lanterns hung from the ceiling, glowing with warm-white illumination. The warehouse was dark, offering easy places to hide, but the lighting concentrated above a desk to the left of the doorway where a man sat studying a screen, apparently oblivious of their presence. Chooli was sure he sensed them but was ignoring them until he was ready to greet them. It felt like they were entering a lion's den.

Not wanting Travis to detect her uncertainty, she didn't even take a large breath to boost her courage but stepped boldly into the room with Agate behind her. At once, she noticed two more guards beside the doorway, hidden from view when she had surveyed the room. Ignoring them, she strode forward and fronted the desk where Travis sat.

A few moments later, he stood clutching a maser pointed at them. Agate yelped, but Chooli didn't flinch. She glared at him instead. "Is this how you treat your visitors?" she asked.

"At present, you're a threat and will stay so until I'm satisfied with your true purpose here." He looked over at Agate. "You're out of your neighborhood, aren't you?"

"I'm helping Siren with her business," she said in a shaky voice.

"You should stick to what you know and satisfy Lingo."

"Difficult now, don't you think?" Chooli interrupted.

He grinned with menace. "And why is that?"

"He's dead."

The news shook him. He covered his reaction well but not well enough to fool her. She added, "It wasn't me, by the way — in case you had any thoughts of revenge."

After several seconds, he lowered the maser. "How can I help you, Siren?"

"I wish to conduct business with you."

Travis laughed. "You think I do business with a stranger?"

"Everyone's a stranger until you get to know them."

"How did you find me?"

"Lingo told me," she lied.

He shook his head. "Good thing he's dead. I'd have killed him myself otherwise."

Chooli folded her arms. "Are we going to talk business? Or will we play fifty questions?" She had two reasons for folding her arms. One was her intensifying frustration with Travis, and the other was it gave her easy access to her weapons.

"OK then," he said as he sat, placing his maser within reach on the desk. "What business are you proposing?"

"I intend to increase my distribution network in this world, so I need a ready supply of the product. You sell the product. Hence, I want to conduct business with you."

He roared with laughter again. "This just gets better and better. I'm sorry, Siren, but this world's covered. Go someplace else."

Chooli rubbed her chin. "That could be a problem. Still, you can get rid of them. I'll give you a better deal."

"You don't understand. My associates run the supply and distribution business. They won't want to give half their livelihood to an unknown upstart."

"I'll give them an offer they can't refuse."

"Run away, Siren, or whoever you are. You're wasting my time." He sneered at Agate, "And you run away, too, little girl. I've already got a courier at Madame Bengsei's. I don't need you."

He glanced sideways at someone hidden from her, who had just entered. The person walked to him and whispered in his ear. Travis kept glancing at her and nodding as he did so.

The ruse was up, and it was time for direct action.

The man withdrew two paces from Travis and waited.

"Well, Siren — or is it Chooli?"

Without hesitation, she pushed a button on her jacket cuff, which opened a compartment on each boot. She bent and grabbed her maser and pistol from them while diving sideways and rolling to an attack position. "Down!" she shouted at Agate, who obeyed on cue. She glanced at the two door guards, shooting both with the maser. The other man started moving, which drew her attention. She shot him with the firearm.

The events happened so fast that Travis only made it halfway to grabbing his maser before she had her pistol and maser trained on him. "I wouldn't do that," she advised.

He stopped his action mid-movement and retracted his hand, sitting back instead. "Well done."

"Grab his maser," she told Agate as she moved to one side, so Agate didn't get in her line of sight.

Agate obeyed her but then stood staring at the weapon.

Chooli glanced at her. "Just hold it." She crept further around to view the doorway in case other guards came to help, although her biggest problem was that she didn't know how many more thugs he had on the site apart from Ball Face and Thin Face.

Travis stood relaxed, in control, as if he knew things she didn't. She had to improvise now.

"What do you really want?" he asked.

Despite the danger and tension, Chooli's relaxation and alertness surprised her. She expected her heart to be racing, but it beat barely above her resting pulse. *What's happening to me?* But now was no time to analyze herself. She just needed to use her unexpected strength to maximum advantage.

"Where is Alex Warner?"

"I don't know who you're talking about." His tone implied he was telling the truth, but his eyes told Chooli he was lying.

She changed her aim and blasted a maser pulse at the desktop. A hole appeared on Travis' righthand side next to his hand. He flinched before regaining control of his emotions.

"Do I need to ask again?"

"I don't know where Alex Warner is," Travis said, his voice now with an inflection of anxiety.

"Where would Vito Riva hide him?"

"You don't mess with Vito."

Chooli fired again, taking a chunk of the desk from his lefthand side. "You don't mess with me either. Stand up," she said in a calm, soft voice but with a menacing undertone.

He obeyed, raising his hands as he stood.

"Walk around your desk and stand three paces in front of it."

He walked to the position.

"Again, where would Riva be likely to take Alex?"

"How do you even know he's on Xi Boötis?"

"He's here. People saw him here, and there's no reason for Riva to remove him. This is his home base where he can watch over him."

Travis shrugged. "I'd keep him in a warehouse. You can hide him there with little risk of someone finding him by accident. Vito has several warehouses scattered around the capital."

Travis' advice was in line with what she thought. "Tell me where they are."

He shook his head. "I don't concern myself with such details. But they shouldn't be difficult to find on the property owner database."

Chooli considered his words and mulled over the information he had given her. "How does Ramira Lopez fit into this?"

Raising his eyebrows, Travis said, "You should fret if Ramira is involved. She's Vito's number one assassin: her and The Reaper, although he's more of a mercenary for hire."

A chill ran up Chooli's spine as she recalled her experiences with The Reaper. "I've met The Reaper."

"And you're still alive?"

"He amused himself in other ways. He deployed his artistic talents on my body."

"Well, if Ramira's involved with Alex, you have cause for concern. Few people she tangles with survive the encounter." He frowned. "Although I heard she had retired. Vito must have convinced her to change her mind."

Chooli had no more questions for him. Considering him more of an asset alive than dead, she prepared to leave. But then, voices emanated from the corridor. Guards were walking toward the office, oblivious to the drama unfolding within it. She held her forefinger to her lips, but as they approached the door, Travis yelled, "Arm yourselves!"

The speaking stopped.

Chooli gritted her teeth in anger. Her finger hovered over the maser's trigger as she aimed it at Travis, but she relented, directing her attention to the doorway instead. She motioned for Agate to hide behind the desk, and Agate scampered to its relative safety, needing no second invitation.

Moments later, Thin Face's head appeared past the doorframe. Chooli fired her pistol and put a bullet hole through his head. Travis still stood his ground. She moved to place him between her and the door, hoping Ball Face would hesitate, not risking killing his boss in the crossfire. This agitated Travis, making him more concerned with his predicament. Before he could speak, Ball Face burst through the doorway, his kinetic gun firing. But the only result he achieved was killing his boss. She let off a shot of her maser and disposed of him.

But that left her in a quandary. If they had come from guarding the entrance, were others protecting it now? She had no way of knowing. She had a room full of dead bodies she preferred to stay undiscovered. Others would arrive seeking Travis for their business and find the carnage if nothing else. There was only one thing to do.

With Agate's help, she heaped the corpses in a pile and used her maser to disintegrate them into ash.

They both crept from the room toward the entrance. After listening for evidence of enemies outside the door and finding none, Chooli poked her head out to confirm it.

"Let's go."

49

A NEW LOCATION

Alex woke sore and with a throbbing headache. He had no recollection of events from when the thugs bashed him after his attempted escape, but when he opened his eyes, as far as their bruises permitted, he saw they had moved him. He now sat in a chair in the middle of a large space, surrounded by crates and hand tools used to open them. A gantry crane spanned the width of the building, the hook suspended halfway to the floor. A motorized trailer stood to the side, dust and rubbish littering the tray.

Ramira was nowhere in sight. He wondered if they were interrogating her. Overhead lighting glared down at him, the brightness hurting his eyes. His whole body ached when he tried to move. He sat secured on the chair with shackles on his wrists and around his ankles, the latter binding him to its legs. He had no choice but to wait for someone to arrive and inform him what would happen next.

His cracked lips and dry mouth yearned for water. His tongue barely moistened his lips when he licked them. He could still taste the metallic flavor of blood. *Did Vito covet the mine this much? Was it worth this much to him?* If he were confident Vito would release him once Ahiga surrendered the asset, Alex might urge Ahiga to do so, but he understood Vito's breed well from his days in the GIA. Once Vito possessed the mine, Alex became disposable. He would disappear forever. His extortion value was all that kept him alive for now.

But how did Ramira fit into this? Her part in the entire ordeal stumped Alex. Her role seemed to be to lure him somewhere to kidnap him. But it didn't need Ramira to do that. Why Ramira? With any luck, he would discover the truth before he died.

50

FINDING A DRUG MULE

Agate and Chooli collected Vapdog and fled the Old Shanghai Emporium before anyone came looking for Travis, crashing at Vapdog's workplace until they could find more suitable accommodation. Vapdog was insistent they weren't staying at his residence. So Chooli went off to buy food and returned to fill grumbling stomachs while she considered her options. She couldn't afford the time to find lodgings. By the next night, she would have either found Alex or not. If the latter, he would likely be dead. And she dared not contemplate what she might do if that were the case.

Travis had mentioned he did business with a courier at Madame Bengsei's but had not said who it was. Agate said he joined the manager and the security personnel out back. Now that she knew Agate better, she marveled at her working in such an establishment. It was inconsistent with her behavior around Chooli. She glanced over at her as she considered her next move.

"Who did Travis see when he visited the brothel?" Chooli asked her.

Agate shook her head and gazed up as if thinking. "I saw him talk to one of the security guards once. But I didn't hear what they said."

"Would you recognize him?" A twinge of optimism sparked in Chooli.

"I think so. He seldom works there ... but he's there whenever Travis comes."

Chooli looked at Vapdog. "We're going back to the brothel."

"Is that wise?" he asked. "You wrecked the place last time."

She shrugged. "They'll treat me with more respect this time."

"Or bring out bigger guns."

"I have big guns too." She stared at him with defiance.

He sighed. "I won't talk you out of it. OK. Let me finish eating, at least. It might be my last meal."

She grinned. "Not if I can help it."

They finished their food and quenched their thirst. Once they talked through their plan, Chooli checked her pistols. She handed one to Vapdog and another to Agate while she kept the kinetic weapon and maser.

After traveling via taxi to a nearby location, they approached the entrance of Madame Bengsei's. Chooli's tenseness increased as her heart quickened, her palms damp.

"Ready?" she asked Agate.

Agate gave a non-convincing nod but stepped forward anyway.

This time when she entered, the manager-cum-receptionist glanced up at once and gave Chooli a hostile glare mixed with fear.

"What do you want?" she said. She turned her attention to Agate. "You're late. Get ready and head to your room."

Agate didn't move, although her dread was palpable when Chooli glanced at her. Chooli wondered how often they had threatened her in the past and the kinds of punishments they dished out to her and the other working girls for supposed misdemeanors.

"I'm looking for someone," Chooli told the manager.

After directing dagger eyes at Agate, the manager replied to

Chooli. "You said that last time. We cleaned up all day before we opened for business again."

Two security guards suddenly appeared from behind the curtain and stood with menacing intent. The manager must have sent an alert to security.

"So, be more polite and helpful," Chooli advised.

She glanced at the silent guards and turned to Agate. "Either of them?"

Agate shook her head. "No."

"We'll head to the office and introduce ourselves if you don't mind." Chooli threw a defiant stare at the manager.

"I do mind. Get out before they evict you."

"Them? You need better protection than that." Chooli grinned as she moved toward the wall presented by the two thugs blocking her way.

They tensed for a confrontation. She could have fought them, maybe should have fought them, but time was precious. She pulled her maser out and shot both in the chest before they realized they needed to defend themselves. Their bodies remained standing for a second or two before crumbling to the floor, a wisp of smoke and the smell of cauterized flesh highlighting their cause of death.

Both Agate and the manager stared at her in shock at her actions. She shrugged. "The quickest way of getting past them." She moved forward, stepping over the bodies as she breached the curtain into the inner enclave of the business.

The corridor remained empty and silent, a low hum of voices coming from beyond a doorway at the far end.

"In the back room," Agate, who had followed her, whispered as she pointed toward the sound.

The other doors stayed closed — the ones that still had doors. They hadn't yet fixed the ones Chooli had smashed. She turned to her. "No need for secrecy. Speed is essential now. We're running out of time to rescue Alex." She strode toward the noise source, simulating an indifference she didn't fully feel.

When Chooli reached the doorway and peered inside, she saw three men and one woman sitting around a table talking. The two men were obviously guards. Their biceps bulged. The woman was a worker. The last man, his back toward her, was slim and didn't belong.

One guard facing the door noticed her approach and glanced up at her.

"What do you want?"

"I'm searching for someone," she said with a deadpan face.

"You can search me," he replied and laughed as the others swiveled to see who he was talking to.

"I doubt that." She turned to Agate, who entered their field of view. "Any of these?"

Agate studied the men intensely before pointing with certainty at the slender man. "Him," she said.

"Sure?"

Agate glared at her.

"Fair enough." Chooli raised her maser and shot the two guards.

The woman screamed and rose to escape the psychopath confronting her, which Chooli allowed by stepping aside and letting her pass.

The remaining man stared at the dead guards on the floor before studying her. "What do you want from me?"

"Information."

He shrugged. "I know nothing."

"On that point, we disagree. You knew Travis."

The man's expression became wary. "Knew?"

"He had an accident." She gave a grim smile. "Which might befall you if you don't cooperate."

"I can't help you. I'm just a courier."

"Ha! Just a courier. A courier takes delivery of goods and delivers them. You took delivery from Travis. Who do you transport the goods to?"

He gulped. "Can't tell you that."

"I'm afraid you must."

"He'll kill me if I do."

"I'll kill you if you don't. Better still, you'll take me to him."

Terror flashed across the man's face. "You don't just walk in on him unannounced."

She shrugged. "Tell him we're coming or don't. It makes no difference to me."

Speechless, he sat undecided, staring into space. He studied the dead men before returning his attention to her and sighed. "OK. I don't have a choice. He might spare my life, given the circumstances."

"Wise decision. What's your name?"

"Belvedere."

"Let's go, Belvedere."

He stood and stepped toward her gingerly, careful not to get too near her. When he was a pace from her, he stopped, glanced at the open doorway, and back at Chooli, who allowed him to pass. With space made for him, the man walked past her and toward the rear exit of the brothel. She and Agate followed him.

He might be leading them into a trap for all she knew, but she was prepared and didn't care.

51

ONE LESS TRAFFICKER

C hooli's scooter, parked at the brothel, was big enough for the three of them to ride together across town to their destination: a dilapidated repair shop for air vehicles. Either the trafficker's business was doing poorly, or it was a front for his covert activities, Chooli thought.

She checked out the property as she disembarked from the vehicle. No one stood guard at the street entrance, but she spotted several surveillance cameras mounted under the eaves. No doubt, the rear had a similar security setup. She turned to their guide. "He's in there?"

"Yes." He fidgeted with his hands, his eyes darting to the doorway and the surrounding buildings.

Unprepared for her adversary and unaware of the internal layout, Chooli was reluctant to storm the premises. "Where's his office?"

"In the right back corner. It has windows overlooking the workshop. Impossible to sneak up to it without him noticing."

What he said rang true to her, although she hadn't expected to catch him by surprise, anyway. "What about those surveillance cameras? Do they link to his office, or does he have a dedicated room and security personnel studying the feeds?"

"There's a separate room with the feeds displayed, but Conrad can select any feed to study on his screen in his office."

Chooli raised her eyebrows. "So, it's Conrad? You said you didn't know his name."

Belvedere blushed and grimaced as he realized his slip.

"How many other people work there?"

"Two mechanics and a receptionist at the front counter. But he acts as a parts manager as well. He runs the rear warehouse and maintains the stock inventory."

Chooli studied him, examining the truthfulness of his words. They seemed genuine, but she doubted she would get any further useful information before entering Conrad's lair. One last question came to mind before she had to act. "What is your procedure when you visit him?"

The man averted his eyes. "That's the point. I never see him uninvited. He'll suspect something awry just by my being here."

"Let me handle that."

His eyes darted to her before returning to a spot on the ground he found fascinating. "I stop at the front counter and tell the guy I'm there to pick up a special delivery from Conrad. He comms the boss to check I'm legit and then tells me to go to Conrad's office. I go to his office, pick up the parcel, and leave — unless Conrad has any errands for me."

"And the workers — are they armed?"

"The clerk has one under the counter. The surveillance guards have weapons, but the mechanics don't carry any. They might have them nearby, but I've never seen them."

Chooli nodded. With that information, she felt prepared to implement her plan.

She looked at Agate, conscience-stricken at putting her in danger again. "It might be better if you wait here."

"You're not leaving me behind," Agate said, showing a spark of anger. "I'm as invested in this now as you are."

Admiring her spunk, Chooli relented. "OK. Let's go."

She gestured for Belvedere to lead them into the shop. She and Agate followed him. The light level dropped as they crossed the threshold, but spots of local illumination helped the mechanics with their work. The service counter lay to their left. No one stood behind it.

"Hey, Tzu. You there?"

A noise emanated from beyond a row of shelves stacked with parts before a short Asian man appeared. He smiled. "Belvedere, what are you doing here?"

"Came to see the boss. Can you tell him I'm here?"

Tzu frowned. "You're not scheduled for a delivery." He glanced behind Belvedere at Chooli and Agate. "Who are they?"

"Associates. They want to talk business with the boss."

Tzu shrugged. "Not sure he will like that. But it's your head, not mine." He went to the comm unit on the counter and pressed a button that gave him a direct link to Conrad, talking in whispers to him. After a brief conversation, he hung up, glancing at Belvedere and the women suspiciously. "He's waiting."

Chooli breathed easier, having passed through the first hurdle of her plan. She stared at Tzu as they strode through the workshop to the back office. Several scooters lay on the floor, mechanics working on two of them. They hid their activity from her, but they seemed busy with their legitimate work, so she concentrated her attention ahead of her. She had no way of knowing Conrad's reaction to their presence, but she would soon find out. And their defense capabilities.

The door was closed when they arrived, but the paneled window showed Conrad gazing at the screen of his tablet, his fingers dancing over the keypad as he studied whatever information was on it. Belvedere knocked on the door and opened it. He entered and gestured for Chooli and Agate to do likewise.

Chooli tensed as the danger of entering the confines of Conrad's office bore into her. They were now at their most vulnerable — his defenses before them and an unknown level of firepower behind them. It was too late to turn back, however, so she assumed a confidence she didn't feel and stared at Conrad, her hand near the maser she had hidden in her jacket.

"What do you want?" he asked, his attention still focused on Belvedere.

Belvedere fidgeted; his eyes were unable to meet Conrad's. Mumbling, he said, "These women wish to make a proposition to you."

Conrad grinned, a grin that said, 'What proposition from them could interest me?'

"Really? This I've got to hear." His eyes veered from Belvedere, first to Agate and then to Chooli. "Which one's talking?"

Chooli stared at him, putting as much steely focus as she could muster into her voice. "I have a business proposition. You give me information, and I let you live."

Belvedere jerked in disbelief.

Conrad burst into laughter. "You will let me live? You are a lively one. What information do you want? Directions to the nearest brothel? Ask your friend here. She knows, don't you, Agate?"

Agate stared at him in horror at his knowing her name.

"Of course I recognize you," he mocked. "Your mother will be very disappointed in you when I tell her the arrangement is forfeit."

"No," she said, her fear palpable. "You can't. Please. I'll go back. And I won't be any trouble, just don't hurt my mother."

"Too late for that." Conrad's eyes settled on Chooli again. "And I know who you are. So, let's cut the crap. You won't escape here except in a box."

Extreme calm flowed through Chooli. Her senses focused on Conrad yet extended beyond the office in a three-dimensional array. Any noise or movement flicked a switch in her mental awareness as she prepared for battle. "I'm sorry you've taken that position, Conrad. Seems our negotiations won't end amicably."

His hand started moving to below the desk.

Chooli's senses expanded outward and inward. Her heart began to beat faster, her adrenaline flowing steadily as her hand gripped the handle of her maser. She whipped it out and fired at the desktop where his hand moved underneath it. The top of the desk and several of his fingers disappeared.

Mayhem erupted at once.

Shouts and yells started from outside the office as men came running. Agate screamed and slumped to the floor. Conrad yelped and stared at his mutilated hand in disbelief. Belvedere jerked his head back and forth, searching for a haven but finding none.

Guards sprinted from the surveillance room, guns ready, as did the front desk clerk. Chooli couldn't see the two mechanics, but they had disappeared from their working spots. To even the odds, she shot the two guards through the window. They both dropped to the floor. She fired again, and the clerk met the same fate.

"Get out of the way," she said to Belvedere as she shoved him aside. After another glance at Conrad, ensuring his hands were nowhere near his desk, which they weren't — his good hand was holding the injured one — she took a quick look outside the office to find the mechanics. Wherever they were, they were out of her field of view. They had either fled or lay in wait for an opportunity to attack her. That would not happen. She strode to Conrad and grabbed him by the collar, lifting him from his seat and slamming him against the wall. "You've got five seconds to tell me what I need to know. Where's Alex Warner?"

He stared at her. She smelled his fear as the reek of urine filled the office. "I don't know. Believe me. I'd tell you if I did."

"Wrong answer." She moved to raise her maser.

"Please. Vito has been busy in his warehouse near the spaceport. I thought it was a consignment of chimera stardust, but it's not. It's something else, but no one knows what. That's all I know, I swear."

Chooli continued staring into his eyes, wondering how much truth was in his words and if he had disclosed all his intelligence. It would be easy to give her a red herring to save his life, but the fear in those eyes convinced her he was telling the truth. "Where are your two mechanics?"

"They probably ran away. They are just mechanics."

Even before he finished, Chooli saw he was lying. As punishment, she turned him toward the door, releasing a moan of disgust at the dribble of urine that now contaminated her clothes. She shoved the maser in his back and directed him to the door, making him stop when he revealed himself to the workshop. "Tell your mechanics to surrender and put their hands where I can see them."

Conrad tried turning his head to her, but she thrust the maser barrel harder into his spine. "Don't fire!" he called. "Give yourselves up, or she will kill me."

A sense of satisfaction crossed Chooli's face as her assumption proved correct. Time elapsed, but the mechanics didn't materialize. "You have ten seconds before I shoot him," she called. "And your friends lying on the floor would tell you I'll do just that."

Just as Chooli was starting to think they had either deserted or were too frightened to surrender, the two men stood up and fired their kinetic weapons, but the only thing they hit was their boss, doing her job for her. She poked her gun out from behind Conrad and fired two shots, blowing a hole in each mechanic's chest. She sighed, regretting the carnage she had wrought and yet at the same time feeling satisfied about ridding the galaxy of six more criminals. It was a new sensation, and she was uncertain whether she liked herself for relishing it.

"Let's go," she said as she moved to leave, taking it for granted that Agate would follow her. Belvedere could do whatever he wanted for all she cared.

52

MORE PLANS

"What was that about your mother?" Chooli asked Agate as they sped on their scooter across the city to Vapdog's workplace.

Agate's face reddened. "Mama borrowed money from Vito and couldn't pay it back. Ramira was her handler. She said if Mama couldn't pay off the debt, I should go to the brothel to work it off. I went to the brothel."

Chooli stared at her in disbelief. "Your mother let you do that?"

"It wasn't as simple as that. She didn't want me to go. But I figured the alternative was worse. They would have killed her, and maybe me too."

"So, what happens now? I doubt they'll welcome you back at the brothel, and I presume your mother will never pay off the debt."

Agate stared into her lap, clenching her hands together. "I don't know." She glanced up at Chooli. "I'm scared."

Chooli considered Agate's problem for a moment and then said, "By the time I'm finished, her troubles might have disappeared."

They sat in silence for the rest of the trip. After they landed, Chooli led Agate into Vapdog's office.

Vapdog sat at his massive screen display, his hands flying across several keypads at once. After a few seconds, he stopped and glanced up at them. "You got something?"

"Vito has a warehouse near the spaceport. We need to check that out. I'm sure they're holding Alex there."

"And how much did that information cost?"

"Let's just say the world has one less drug trafficker."

He shook his head. "You're worrying me."

She held up her hands. "I didn't kill him. He can thank his goons for that."

"And what happened to his goons?"

Chooli grinned. "I had to protect myself and Agate."

Vapdog sighed and returned his concentration to the screens. "We're looking for a warehouse, then." His hands sped across the keyboards again as he conducted a real estate ownership search for warehouses around the spaceport. His computer pinged moments later. "Found it. It's near the far end. Come look."

Chooli rounded the desk and studied the screen, showing a layout of the city surrounding the spaceport. It highlighted Vito's property in red. "That's it. But I can't go there unprepared. He'll have a load of security around there. We need more firepower than we have."

"Where will we get that?"

"I have a source. A favor I can call in."

He rolled his eyes. "Of course you do."

"Is it just an open-space warehouse? Can you find plans for the building internals to give us a better idea of where they might be holding Alex?"

"Let's see." Vapdog started another search. Before long, he displayed a blueprint of the warehouse layout. It had several smaller internal buildings, offices, or bond stores, judging by the size, but it was impossible to tell for sure from the drawing. He showed it to her, and they discussed their options in their plan of attack for the building. After half an hour, their scheme satisfied her, but they needed far more firepower to ensure success.

"What should I do?" Agate asked from the corner where she sat while Chooli and Vapdog discussed their plans.

Chooli had forgotten about her. "You? You don't have to do anything."

"But I want to help."

"This is dangerous. You could get yourself killed."

"It's a bit late for that now. They'll kill me anyway if they catch me." Agate's lips trembled. "Or kill my mother."

Chooli stared at her. She glanced at Vapdog and returned her attention to her. "OK. You can help."

"I need a gun, too."

Chooli grinned. "And a gun."

Vapdog shook his head.

"You ready?" she asked as she peered at them.

"Lead the way," he replied.

Chooli hired an air scooter. They first headed into the city center and the GIA office. She told Agate and Vapdog to stay in the vehicle while she arranged weapons.

After twenty minutes, she returned and took them to another part of the city where single-story self-storage garages lined an alleyway. Chooli took control of the scooter and coasted along the alley until she found the lock-up she sought and stopped. She eased herself from the vehicle. The others followed her to the garage. She punched in the code and authorization biometrics to open the door. A motor whirred, and the door slowly raised. When she glanced at the others, they both stood and stared openmouthed at the arsenal of firepower inside the building.

She chuckled. "Makes working for the GIA worthwhile."

"They aren't toys," Vapdog noted.

"No, they're not, and we need to return them once we're finished with them."

"Can't I keep just one?" he asked.

"No. They hold me responsible, and I don't want to end up on patrol duty or suspension for a month because you stole one."

He sighed but said nothing more.

Chooli entered the garage and fossicked through the armory until she found weapons for Vapdog and Agate. She continued searching and selected a maser pistol, a kinetic pistol, and a maser pulse rifle. After checking the two small handguns secreted in the concealed compartments in her boots, she grabbed several extra magazines, complete with a bandolier to hold them. Just as she was about to leave, she spotted several flashbangs and other grenades. She collected a couple of each and a bazooka for good measure.

"You got enough?" Vapdog asked, cracking a smile.

"Never too much firepower. That's it." Chooli led them back to the scooter as she juggled her weapons and ammunition into the storage space.

With a sigh, she said, "Here goes nothing. Let's go get Alex."

I hope I'm not too late, she thought as she jumped onto the vehicle and sped off, heading for the spaceport.

53

A DYING MAN'S LAST WISH

Vito stood to the side watching his enforcer as he pounded his fists into Alex's face and torso. Alex, tied to a chair, responded to the violence like a senseless dummy.

The universe had no beginning or end for Alex anymore; his only world was the pain each punch delivered. He barely remained conscious as he endured the brutality. He now sympathized with a cut of meat when the butcher tenderized it. Why Vito though such violence necessary, Alex couldn't fathom. It made little sense to him. Didn't Vito want him coherent enough to talk with Ahiga rationally? But he had given up trying to follow Vito's logic. His entire focus was now on lasting through the next blow.

"Enough," Vito said.

The enforcer ceased his exercise and returned to a stand that contained neatly positioned implements for easy access. He grabbed a towel and wiped Alex's blood from his hands, after which he gulped water from his refreshment bottle.

Alex gathered the energy to lift his head and glare at Vito through the slits his eyes had become. "Why are you doing this?" he rasped after spitting a ball of blood-infused saliva from his mouth.

"You must look the part," Vito explained reasonably. "Ahiga must know I'm serious when he sees you. He needs to believe we are prepared to mutilate you if he still insists on denying me my mine."

"He will never give in to you. You overestimate my value to him."

"Then he will watch you die."

"But even if Ahiga agrees and gives you the mine, what's to stop him from showing the authorities the recordings you've sent him? They will charge you with blackmail and murder and confiscate your assets, including the mine."

"That won't happen. Believe me, I have powerful friends who owe me favors."

Alex realized then that Vito's narcissism and greed had sent him insane, and there was no point in trying to reason with him.

This is it then, he thought. His biggest regret was not seeing his beautiful Chooli again. He would never again stroke the smoothness of her face, never luxuriate in her joyful laugh. The time spent with her had been the best of his life, and he wouldn't change one second of it. He flopped his head back down and waited with resignation for whatever came next.

Then, with a fresh burst of spirit, he raised his head and said to Vito, "Isn't it traditional for a dying man to be granted a last wish? If I'm going to be dead soon, what harm is there in filling me in on a few details of your plan?"

Vito laughed, but the idea of bragging appealed to him. "Fire away. This could be fun."

"How did you find out that Ahiga was mining crystal boramide on Sirius? Only three of us knew: Ahiga, Kansas, and me. And I take it you were behind the explosion at the mine — what did you hope to achieve by it?"

"You can't work those out for yourself? No one leaked. Ahiga's man, Kansas Salter, was a fool. He was indiscreet on his visits to the city. The explosion was to get Ahiga to send you to Sirius to start an investigation that would lure you to Procyon. It worked beautifully."

"I assume you enticed away Salter's explosives expert and put in one of your own?"

"Of course. It was a piece of cake to offer Salter's guy more pay elsewhere and put in someone who would blow the place up. It was necessary, you see, to separate you and Ahiga. Surely you can understand that?"

"But how did you get Dravo Chinko to recommend your expert?"

"All we had to do was send Salter a written message purporting to be from Dravo Chinko saying his buddy had recommended someone. What a gullible fool Salter was! Anything else?"

"But when I met Chinko, he confirmed he'd recommended the explosives expert based on Milan Asterov's say-so. Is Chinko in your pay too — like Milan?"

Vito chuckled. "Oh, that was one of my masterly strokes. The Dravo Chinko you met was not the real Dravo Chinko. The real one proved difficult to manipulate, so we got him out of the way — don't worry, he's not dead, just a trifle under the weather — and put in one of our own to meet you. His young daughter acted as his secretary. They did a great job, don't you think? Although I heard our guy almost blew it when he was too friendly to you — he didn't know you'd never met before, you see. Fortunately, you were too stupid to pick up on that. Then we sent him and another of my top operatives to Sirius to take over the mine and dispose of Salter." His face clouded momentarily. "Unfortunately, your meddling wife turned up, and we lost two very good operatives. One dead and the other — well, her injuries rule her out for operational work any time soon. What a waste."

Alex almost leaped from his constraints at the mention of Chooli. Sinking back into his chair, he ground out, "How did you stop the other people at the mine from reporting to Ahiga when a stranger turned up claiming to be Salter?"

"Alex, Alex, you really do lack imagination, don't you?" Vito taunted. "Our guy only pretended to be Salter during Chooli's visit. For the rest of the time, he was simply Salter's replacement after

Salter 'went missing.' Everyone believed Ahiga had appointed him. Why would they not? These things are not difficult to arrange, Alex, when you know how."

Alex tried one more question. "Why was there a dead body in Asterov's pool? I thought it was Asterov. Who was it? And what was the point of it?"

"Well, to be honest, that wasn't planned. Our explosives expert, who should have had the decency to blow himself up, got greedy, didn't he? He ran away after the explosion and tried to blackmail Milan, so Milan had to deal with him. He didn't do a very good job of it, in my opinion, but hey, it's hard getting good help."

"But the police? Milan called them fake. How could they be fake? I called them myself."

"Yes, it was unfortunate that you turned up before Milan could get rid of the body and were community-minded enough to call the police. But he got just enough warning that you were coming to divert your call to a couple of corrupt cops in my pay — so no great harm done. Milan is good with technology. I'll give him that."

"Who warned him?"

"Come on, Alex, can't you guess? Who knew you were going there?"

"Dravo Chinko."

"Exactly. All your questions answered now, are they?"

"Not quite. What is Ramira's role in all this?"

Annoyance passed across Vito's face. "I'm tired of this game. You need to start using your brains while you still have them." He turned to the guards. "Return him to the warehouse until we're ready."

The enforcer nodded and opened the door to the torture chamber, gesturing for help to do Riva's bidding.

As Alex was being led away, the thought occurred to him that Vito's readiness to satisfy his curiosity on so many points did not bode well for his immediate future. *Will there be time for Chooli to rescue me?*

54

TRICKED

Alex regained consciousness. Once his thoughts cleared, he realized he must've passed out somewhere between his interrogation room and where they now held him. His head remained muddled as if he was zoning between various phases of awareness.

"You sure she's coming?" a familiar female voice asked, one he should have known but couldn't quite place.

"She's coming," a male answered. "Our informant at Madame Bengsei's confirmed it."

"Good. At last, I will have my revenge. Vito has made me wait a long time."

The intonation should be familiar, but the person's identity escaped him. He tried focusing, but whenever his thoughts headed toward clarity, a cloud floated over them again. *Come on, think!* He still failed to place the voices and sensed himself falling into the pit of unconsciousness again.

When he woke up next, his mind felt stronger, and he opened his eyes to check his surroundings. He hadn't moved, and Ramira was sitting there staring at him. He remembered something, but it stayed uncrystallized, and the notion vanished.

"You OK?" she asked.

He was thirsty, his mouth parched dry. "Water."

She stood and went to the table where their captors had placed bottles of water. She grabbed one, unscrewed the cap, and brought it over to him, helping him drink in short gulps.

A wave of relief washed over Alex as the cool liquid refreshed him. He could barely see through his blackened eyes. "Do I look OK?"

Ramira chuckled. "No."

A wall of silence rose between them.

Another spark of clarity developed in Alex's mind. "Who is *she*?"

"What?"

"I woke up before. Only for a moment. And you were talking to someone. One of the guards. You asked him if 'she' was coming. Who? Who is *she*?"

Ramira stood and paced before him as if considering her options. She stopped, ambled over, and leaned over him, dropping her mask of concern for him. "*She* is Chooli."

55

PAYBACK

hat!" Alex's world spun out of control as his brain tried to process Ramira's revelation. Nothing made sense. "Why is she coming? Why would you want her here?"

Ramira laughed. "You fool! Why do you think you're here?"

Alex was confused. Even though it hurt to raise his head to look at her, he did it anyway. "To give Vito leverage over Ahiga so Ahiga will give the Sirius mine to him. Isn't it?"

"Oh, Alex, you're even more foolish and gullible than last time. Sure, Vito needed you for his negotiations with Ahiga, and he hired me to lure you to him. But why do you think I agreed to help him? I don't care about any mine or Vito's ambitions. Vito's goal was never my motivation. I agreed to help him for payback."

"What payback?"

She glared at him, her face portraying extreme bitterness. "You can ask that? You caused me insurmountable grief when you turned me in to the police, leaving me to rot in jail while you got a slap on the wrist."

"You manipulated me and nagged me until I provided the information you wanted."

"You didn't have to tell me."

"I was in love with you. I was willing to do anything you asked."

She sighed. "Oh, how very romantic of you. Does she manipulate you just as easily?" She paced off toward a stack of crates and then returned. "You say you loved me. And yet you turned me in. I thought you'd arrest me yourself. But you didn't even do that. I've had ages since then to consider how to pay you back." She gave Alex a menacing smile. "So, imagine my surprise when I received word you had married this Chooli bitch. And she is so attractive. I understand The Reaper enhanced her attractiveness on Franconia."

Ramira's needling was raising his temper. He struggled to escape his bonds with no success.

"Yes, I know about The Reaper. He's a good friend of mine. He often does little jobs for me out of friendship — like getting rid of an upstart informant recently who was telling your wife a bit too much. You should have killed The Reaper when you had the chance."

His mind raced as he digested her words. He glared at her. "So, this whole thing was a sham? You don't have a child, do you? You used that, so I would pity you and help you. But you were luring me into trap after trap after trap."

"Well done!" Ramira sneered, clapping her hands slowly. "Your brain still functions. I'm impressed. I wondered how long I'd have to lead you along before you twigged. Did you really think for a moment that I would have a kid?" She laughed at the thought.

Alex lowered his head in despair at his foolishness. This fiasco, at least as far as Ramira was concerned, was to punish him. He raised his head. "But why all the escape attempts and recaptures? Once you got me, why didn't you just take me to Vito like he asked?"

Ramira sighed. "And where would the fun be in that? I've enjoyed leading you along, prolonging the final encounter. It's driven Milan mad too, which is a bonus. And irked Vito. He always thought he was in control, including in control of *me*. He's almost as big a fool as you are." She laughed at the thought of the merry dance she'd led them all.

He stared at her, realizing she was insane. "Why do you want Chooli here?"

"Oh, use your brain, Alex — so you can watch me kill her, of course. I want you to suffer like I suffered in prison."

"She has nothing to do with the differences between you and me."

"But she has. You are devoted to her. I once had real feelings for you, Alex, but you rejected me. You turned me in and left me to rot. I want to see you watch your life partner bleed to death as I bled inside that jail, knowing I had lost you. Now it's your turn to have that experience."

Alex couldn't believe what he was hearing. "You are a psychopath! You're sick!"

Ramira shrugged. "If I am, it's your fault."

There was no getting through to her. She wouldn't listen to reason. She was too far gone. But she didn't know about Chooli's resourcefulness and determination.

"Once Chooli knows what you've done, she will tear you to shreds."

"Oh, I doubt that. We have plenty of protection where we are. They'll capture and restrain her long before she gets anywhere near us."

"You should hope you're right." Alex tried to say with confidence, but deep inside, he feared for Chooli with a despair he had never experienced before.

An explosion reverberated through the building. Ramira glanced toward the noise and grinned. "And so, the show begins." She strode to a table and punched in a code. A drawer in the table opened, revealing a hypodermic pad attached to a syringe. She extracted it in full view of Alex.

"What is that?" he asked.

She looked at him and smiled. "A little concoction developed by

The Reaper. It has no long-term effects." She strolled his way. "You will still see and hear everything, but you won't be able to move or speak. We don't want you to warn Chooli now, do we?"

Alex struggled, but it was hopeless. Ramira pressed the pad to his neck and triggered the drug's administration. The effect started instantly as his muscles stiffened toward stasis. He tried to yell, but no sound came from his mouth.

Chooli was walking into a trap, and he sat helpless, unable to warn her.

56

STORMING THE FORTRESS

hooli, Agate, and Vapdog arrived at the warehouse. They approached cautiously, landing the scooter a block from its frontage so they could conduct a reconnaissance of the place before committing themselves to an attack. Even though they knew the warehouse layout, they didn't know how many guards there were or where they were, so they needed time to collect that information instead of storming in blind.

Vapdog had brought an infrared scanner with him. He set himself up in a safe spot and activated the unit. Chooli looked over his shoulder as the device displayed a simulated heat image of the warehouse.

He glanced back at her. "Quite a few in there."

"I wouldn't have expected anything else," Chooli said with a grim, determined face. "Can we work out their location in the warehouse?"

He shook his head. "Not from this angle." After a quick search of the surroundings, Vapdog gestured to another building. "If I could access that roof, we'd have a better chance."

She peered at where he pointed. It was a three-story office

building with a flat rooftop. She surmised it was possible to gain admittance to the roof, although they might have locked the entrance. Despite the building being new, it looked abandoned, and several windows were smashed. "Let's break into it." She started walking but then stopped and turned to Agate. "Stay here and alert us to any danger from outside."

Agate made to protest, but after an indecisive, pregnant pause, she nodded and turned toward the warehouse to begin her surveillance.

Chooli and Vapdog continued to the office building, with Vapdog carrying the scanner.

"Is she going to be alright?" he asked.

"I trust her."

"That's not what I asked."

Chooli glanced at him. "She'll keep out of sight and let us know of any trouble. She's a survivor."

When they reached the site, they searched for an entry point and discovered an emergency exit door half off its hinges.

"Looks like we're not the first people interested in gaining rapid access to the building," Chooli observed.

"Looks more like a trap to me," Vapdog responded. "They must know we're coming."

Chooli chewed her lip.

They entered anyway and rushed up the stairwell to the top floor. On the topmost landing, a ladder attached to the wall rose to the ceiling, where a trapdoor blocked access to whatever was above.

"Looks like we go up there," Vapdog said.

Chooli nodded and stepped onto the bottom ladder rung before scaling up the ladder and testing the trapdoor. It was unlocked. She swung it open to access the antechamber above it. The space was windowless and dark except for a slit of light streaming under a doorway. She scrambled up the rest of the rungs. From the illumination available, she fathomed the compartment's sole purpose was a shelter from the weather when accessing the roof.

She tested the door, but it stood firm, locked. Instead of taking the time to pick the lock, she drew her maser and blasted it, making opening the door so much easier. A stream of light entered as she pulled the door open. Stepping onto the roof, she first made sure she couldn't see the warehouse from their vantage point to prevent discovery. She returned to the antechamber, leaned over the trapdoor hole, and waved for Vapdog to join her.

They crept to a suitable spot at the edge of the roof to gather necessary information while staying hidden. Vapdog set up the scanner and started monitoring the warehouse from their position. The number and location of people within the warehouse became obvious within seconds. Thirty or forty people occupied the building, spread across various locations. The major group congregated in a space at the rear of the warehouse, possibly an improvised barracks.

"Seems like an entire battalion in there. They must be expecting trouble with that many guards," he said as he glanced meaningfully at Chooli.

"We must pose a larger threat to them than we thought," she replied, frowning, her attention on the screen, trying desperately to plan an attack that wouldn't get them killed. "It's essential we incapacitate the ones inside there first. That will halve our problem."

"And how do you propose doing that? There are no outside windows. The only entry is through the warehouse."

"I don't know yet. There must be a way." She slumped in disappointment. Their attack had ended before it even started. It was suicide to fight so many. She couldn't ask the others to engage in such a dangerous assignment, but she knew she had to forge ahead or die trying.

She risked peering over the roof parapet above the warehouse, hoping it might offer a solution to her dilemma. "What are those things on the rooftop?"

Vapdog had a quick peek at where she pointed and lowered his head again. "Vents."

"So, one's positioned on top of that room?"

"I presume so."

"That gives me an idea."

They scrambled from the roof and back to Agate, still waiting beside the scooter.

"Everything OK?" Agate asked them.

"A few more guards than we expected, but I have a plan." She turned to Vapdog. "You got the EM scramblers?"

"Sure."

"I need you to activate them, and I want you, Agate, to fly me above the warehouse. I'll jump down, and you return here and guard the front of the building. Shoot anyone who comes out unless it's one of us. Can you do that?"

Agate looked squeamish. "Do I have to shoot them?"

"They'll kill you if you don't."

Agate gulped and nodded.

"Good. Let's do this before they discover us."

She watched Vapdog creep closer to the warehouse as she stepped onto the scooter with Agate. After several minutes, he returned and gave the thumbs up.

Agate gunned the scooter and flew to the warehouse roof, stone-faced as she hovered over the position Chooli wanted.

Chooli jumped onto the roof, breaking her landing with a roll. Without pause, she dashed to the vent, pulled out the flashbang pin, waited until just before it detonated, and tossed it into the opening. A satisfying thump resounded upward as it exploded. *Just in time*, she thought.

Shouts and screams of confusion rang out from the men below her.

Straight after the flashbang, she grabbed an ordinary grenade, pulled the pin, and pushed it through the vent.

The roof shook and buckled as the grenade detonated, but she was already dashing to the roof's edge. With one leap and without regard for safety, she jumped to the ground and landed with a roll, still running, at the front of the warehouse, her heart thumping and her veins rushing with adrenaline. What surprised her was the clarity of her mind. She noticed every feature and every movement in her surroundings in meticulous detail.

Vapdog rushed to join her, out of breath. She saw his fear, but he looked ready to follow her into the jaws of hell.

She pulled out her maser. "No point in waiting."

He nodded.

They dashed toward the door, but gunshots rang out before they got there. Bullets whistled through the doorway. She cursed to herself. She had hoped they would be too shocked to react immediately but adjusted her plan to suit. Pulling another flashbang and grenade from her belt, she passed the grenade to Vapdog. "Pull the pin and toss it into the warehouse as soon as I throw the flashbang."

He nodded.

She prepared the flashbang and threw it through the door; the grenade followed in quick succession. Within moments, a flash emanated from the doorway, followed by an explosion. Chooli didn't wait. She dashed through the doorway, aiming her maser and searching for targets to shoot.

The outlines of figures started appearing through the smoke. Once she confirmed they weren't friendly, she had no hesitation in eliminating them with a quick maser blast. She heard Vapdog fire his weapon likewise.

A stack of crates appeared a few steps away, so she sidestepped to give herself cover to continue her attack. Vapdog stepped to a similar position on the opposite side of the doorway.

She gestured to him that she was going to check the room to her right. It was quiet, but she didn't want a surprise from her rear from simple carelessness. He gave the thumbs up and a few rounds of covering fire as she dashed to the door.

With a blast from her maser, she destroyed the door. Then she grabbed a grenade, pulled the pin, and tossed it into the room. The grenade detonated, the remains of the door blew out, and shouts of pain came from inside as several men staggered out, dazed and injured, their kinetic guns firing at nothing in particular.

Chooli put them out of their misery.

Once the noise in the room ceased — something difficult to tell with all the commotion occurring elsewhere in the warehouse — she crouched and took a quick peek inside. No one appeared to be moving. She dashed inside, took her pistol from its holster, and fired a bullet into each man's head, making sure they were dead. She wondered why Vito didn't recruit women for his security but shrugged the thought away as soon as it occurred — she was too busy to think about his DEI policies. She counted five here. The three she had killed escaping the room, together with the five dead here, meant they had eliminated a significant number already, not counting the carnage she must have inflicted in the room where she dropped the grenade from the roof.

After checking for the enemy outside the doorway, she dashed back to the crates and searched for Vapdog. Gunfire from three assailants was keeping him cornered behind a warehouse transport trolley. They stood in a fan around him. Either they didn't realize she was there or were relying on others to take care of her because none noticed her approach behind them. With the three in her sights, she fired three short bursts of maser particles to drop them all before any reacted. Vapdog poked his head out and nodded his gratitude before creeping further into the warehouse, searching for his next target.

Chooli did likewise, but in a separate section to prevent any chance of crossfire. She came to the next cross-aisle, poking her head out and back. A chunk of crate sprayed over her as gunfire hit the barrier. She counted two more. After a momentary hesitation, she stepped backward and launched herself forward near the floor, sliding head-first as she entered the aisle. With her maser ready, she lined up both while she passed across and shot them before reaching safety behind more crates.

More gunfire came from Vapdog's direction before stopping. She hoped he was still alive. Another burst resounded, and she smiled. He was.

Chooli glanced around another stack of crates and saw her goal in sight. Just as she prepared to step across the aisle, she heard a burst of gunfire behind her, sending her heart into her throat, ready for the death shot that never eventuated. When she turned, two gunmen lay on the floor, and Vapdog stood in the doorway, his gun still smoking.

Then she looked down at the floor and saw that one of the gunmen was a woman, a red spot slowly appearing on her clothing at her chest.

"You've killed Agate!" she screamed at Vapdog over the noise.

"She was about to capture you," Vapdog screamed back.

With no time to take in the import of his words, but conscious that the battle would be over if not for Vapdog, a surge of determination made her run forward to the next cross-aisle, closer to her goal. As she ducked back under cover, an intense bout of fire washed past her position, narrowly missing her. The barrage continued relentlessly. Vapdog appeared ten meters away. *We must be near their last line of defense*, Chooli thought.

He singled to her to cover him as he prepared to move across the aisle closer to her. She nodded and grabbed her kinetic pistol. On the count, she exposed her gun around the corner and started firing in the general direction of the resistance. He lunged toward her but grunted halfway across, holding his shoulder when he reached her, blood soaking past his hand.

"No!" Chooli gaped in disbelief as she watched him fall to the floor, his eyes gazing at her in sorrow as if letting her down. She crouched, knowing she had no time to deflect her concentration from the action.

"It's all up to you now," he breathed, spraying a drop of blood on her cheek.

"Hold on, Vapdog. I'll be back for you."

A granite-like hardness entered her heart. She would return for Vapdog just as soon as she'd rescued Alex.

57

REVENGE

Chooli's mind returned to her plight as the gunfire ceased. They were moving toward her. She stilled her emotions because she knew they would kill her if she didn't control them. She prepared for her ultimate assault.

She grabbed her maser and stepped from her cover, the maser blasting ahead of her, destroying everything in its path, the power pack warming her hand as the lengthy release of energy heated the grip. Shouts and yells of agony emanated from the dying bodies in front of her.

She stopped and rolled across the floor before searching for her next targets, but silence met her as she listened intently for movement.

"Enough!" a familiar male voice resounded.

Vito Riva! Chooli wasn't expecting him to be here.

"Leave before my men kill you."

"Hand me Alex, and I'll leave."

"A battalion is coming. Leave now."

Although she had expected him to call in the cavalry, she hadn't expected so many. "A lot of men to kill one person."

"You're hard to exterminate."

This had to end immediately. There was only one solution in Chooli's mind. She crept toward Vito's voice. It made no sense he'd place himself in danger. He must be projecting himself from a protected location. *Where?* She hadn't touched two of the rooms left in the warehouse. He was either hiding in one of them or viewing the action through holo-vision cameras off-site. If he had located himself off-site, he had her beaten, but if he were here ... Once she reached the last stack of crates, she prepared to expose herself to peril, hoping he was foolish enough to stand there.

She lunged into the open. Four guards stood in front of her with masers ready. She fired two shots before her universe blanked.

Chooli woke groggy and disoriented. She should be dead. Why wasn't she?

"Have a nice nap?" Vito asked in a conversational tone.

Hatred filled her as she lurched her body at the voice, only to recoil backward. Restraints around her wrists and ankles tied her to a chair. *Alex!* She searched her prison cell for him but saw only the two guards and Vito, the real Vito.

"Sorry to disappoint you," he said. "I couldn't let you kill me. Besides, we can share the fun of seeing your beloved dismembered."

Chooli barely contained her fury. She took a deep breath, knowing anger was detrimental to clear thinking. They had disarmed her, which she expected, but she still had her boots. A plan coalesced from the fog, but first, she needed to reach her boots.

"I need to relieve myself."

Vito laughed. "You should have gone beforehand."

"I thought you were a gentleman."

"Who told you that?" He stared at her, assessing her. "Very well." He turned to the guards. "Untie her and take her to the bathroom.

But keep her in sight. Zap her again if she causes you any trouble. Let her piss herself for punishment."

The guards obeyed him.

Chooli couldn't believe Vito had fallen for such an old trick. He must have decided he had her covered, with her being unarmed and two guards training their weapons on her.

They pulled her to a standing position and shoved her toward the door. She showed her annoyance at the rough treatment by pulling her arm away from the one grabbing it. The other opened the door, holding it open until they passed through it.

She was pleased the bathroom was some distance away, out of Vito's earshot. Chooli entered it, followed by the guards. She stopped and turned. "Do you mind?"

In reply, a guard shoved her further into the room.

Yes, they do, apparently.

Another lucky break: there was a private stall. She stepped into one, tapped her boots, and retrieved the concealed weapons. To keep up appearances, she took her time and relieved herself. *You never know when there'll be another opportunity.*

Glancing under the stall door to check where the guards stood, she readied her guns and smashed the door open, firing both guns at once before they could respond. They slumped to the floor. *Teach you to check me properly next time.* She stepped over them and returned to finish her business with Vito.

Vito had his back to the door when she opened it, terminating a comm call.

"I'm back," she said, waiting for him to turn and spot her.

When he finally turned toward her, she saw a frown of irritation on his face as though the call had not pleased him.

"Tie her ..." he began. "Ah, I see you have disposed of my guards."

"Hope you don't mind if I grab the rest of my weapons." Confident that, without his guards, Vito was unarmed, Chooli strode to the benchtop where her maser and pistol sat. She pushed her guns back into her boots and grabbed the pistol and maser, shoving her pistol into its holster. Left with the maser, she pointed it at Vito. "Now, where were we before I had to use the bathroom?"

"We were discussing the immediate future. Yours."

"I seem to remember something about my watching you dismember Alex."

"That was the original plan, yes. Circumstances have changed since then," Vito's voice was as urbane as ever, but there was an undercurrent of tension. "My partner thinks it would be better to reverse the order — you go first and then Alex. A shame because it means you will miss out on quite a show, but there you go. There's just no reasoning with some women, is there?"

Chooli glared at him with hawkish eyes. She had a shrewd idea who this partner was but was not sure what Vito had up his sleeve. "Where's Alex? In the next room?"

"That's the only one you haven't searched yet, isn't it?"

"Yes. But is he there? And is this partner you mention with him?"

"That's up to you to find out, Chooli. Get on with it. I have places to be."

She plastered a fake smile on her face. "You should cancel your appointments, Vito. You'll be late." She pressed the trigger, and a beam of muons blasted a hole through Vito's chest.

"That's from Alex as well as me."

He gaped at the orifice and then at Chooli in disbelief before collapsing, dead.

She stared at him with no remorse. The galaxy was better off without him. The sensation shocked her. She had never considered assassination one of her job skills, yet she performed it as effortlessly as sending a message over her comm. Horror at her evolution froze her into inaction for an immeasurable time before her trance evaporated.

She needed to rescue Alex and end his torment. But she checked Vito first.

58

CHOOLI'S RETRIBUTION

Chooli returned to the warehouse and crept to the only room she hadn't inspected, her heart barely above resting pulse. The scan had shown it contained two humans, but she was aware others might have taken shelter in it since she started her attack. Once she stood before the door, she paused, undecided about her best approach. She could storm the room and hope she killed whoever was inside before they killed her — but now she had come this far, she was reluctant to throw everything away on a rash move. Alex, if he was there, could get killed in the crossfire. A weird thought crossed her mind: and she'd look silly. With a shake of her head, she concentrated on the door and whatever lay behind it.

She stepped to the side and tried the handle. It was unlocked. With her maser in one hand and her pistol in the other, she nudged it ajar with her knuckles and pushed it fully open with her foot. Everything was silent. Not even a fly buzzed.

She took a deep breath and exhaled before peeking around the door frame. What she saw burned an image in her mind. Alex sat in a chair, and a woman lay prone on the floor, dead or unconscious. Chooli closed her eyes to clarify the impression further. No one else was visible. A couple of crates lay scattered throughout the room. People might be hiding behind them, but they could conceal only two bodies at most, by Chooli's estimate. Good. The odds weren't terrible; she could live with that.

Memorizing the room layout calmed her, enabling her to focus on the task she came to complete. She stepped into the doorway, alert and ready to fire her weapons, as she scanned it for threats. With a step to her left, she checked behind one set of crates — no one. Once she inspected the others, she confirmed no one else occupied the place — just her, Alex, and the unconscious woman. With that knowledge, she relaxed and lowered her guns. The woman, whom she assumed was Ramira, posed no immediate threat.

Alex sat with his forehead strapped to the top bar of the high-back chair, his alert eyes the only evidence of consciousness. She saw begging in them, but his meaning escaped her.

"Hi, sweetheart," she said. She holstered her weapons and stepped toward him.

His pleading intensity increased, but Chooli didn't know what he was trying to communicate or why he remained silent and motionless. In the end, she assumed he wanted his restraints removed.

She detoured around Ramira and closed in on him. Reaching to undo Alex's restraints, she heard only the slightest of sounds behind her before something collided with her like a freight hauler. Before she realized her predicament, her pistols were snatched from her holsters, and she lay prone on the floor staring up at a very conscious and gloating Ramira. She groaned at herself for being so stupid.

Ramira was not aiming any firearms at her. She was just standing over her, a superior smile plastered on her face as if she were super-human and considered Chooli helpless.

"Who are you?" Chooli asked. She knew who she was but wanted to unbalance her.

"I'm Ramira Lopez. And you're the famous Chooli Richards. I must admit, my opinion of you has risen since you fought past Vito's guards to get in here. Never mind. Vito will send for more."

"That might be difficult," Chooli said, her courage returning to her.

Ramira straightened her stance and placed her fists on her hips. "Why?"

"He's dead. I killed him."

Ramira took a step backward in shock. She blinked and froze as if needing time to digest the information. "You shouldn't have done that."

"Why not?"

"It leaves a vacuum others will kill to fill."

"Not my problem."

"Where's your little shadow, Agate?" Ramira asked like an afterthought. "She should be here to witness my triumph, too."

"So, you were Agate's handler, were you? I admit she had me fooled, Ramira, but the last laugh is on you. Agate's dead."

Chooli saw her surprise and used it to wrangle herself from her predicament. Rolling sideways, she tangled her legs in Ramira's, knocking her off balance and making her tumble to the floor. The gun slid from her hand across the surface. But Ramira recovered quicker than she expected.

With one fluid motion, Ramira leaped to her feet and stepped back out of Chooli's reach.

Chooli stood, too. She watched Ramira's body language carefully, wondering how she might attack her. "This can end now," she said. "Just let me leave with Alex, and we can call this quits."

"Uh, uh. This moment's been too long coming."

"What moment?" Chooli frowned, puzzled by her words.

"The moment I get my revenge on Alex for leaving me. He let me rot in jail while he got a slap on the wrist. He threw me away like I meant nothing to him. I loved him ... in my own way. If I can't have him, no one will. What better vengeance but him watching his beloved die before his eyes and he helpless to save you?"

Chooli blinked. Vito had planned to dismember Alex, and

Ramira wanted to murder her in front of Alex. These people were insane.

She risked a glance at Alex, who remained statue-like with no expression. Except for his eyes, which registered fear and hatred as they darted to Ramira and back to Chooli. Her concentration returned to Ramira as she blinked, ready to pounce. "What makes you think you're a better fighter than me?"

"You're restrained by the police code and your sense of duty and honor. I'm not."

"I'm here on my own. No GIA protection is behind me. I don't have to play by their rules. And my sense of duty and honor has become more flexible of late."

"Even better."

Ramira lunged at her.

Side-stepping, she used Ramira's momentum to push her off balance, making her stumble again to the floor.

Ramira yelled, furious.

Perfect! Chooli thought. *You'll act out of passion and make mistakes now.*

With the fury of a bull at a bullfight, Ramira charged.

Chooli prepared to step away again, but Ramira was ready for her. She veered in the same direction and smashed into her, propelling her to the ground. Ramira landed on top of her, winding her. She struggled for breath as Ramira pinned her and arched her back backward, with her left hand pinning her right shoulder. Ramira lifted her right hand and pummeled it into Chooli's face, bringing stars to her eyes as she screamed in agony.

Apart from the pounding of her face, her ribcage seared in pain. She had a broken rib. Her breathing became ragged as she struggled to inhale air into her lungs. She knew she had to end this before she suffered a fatal injury.

"You're weak, just like your lover," Ramira yelled with glee as she landed another punch.

I've got to get to my boot, Chooli thought, weathering the inflicted pain while lying helpless on the floor. She didn't need her guns. She just had to retrieve the knife secured inside the scabbard of her left boot. With the dexterity of an acrobat, she bent her leg and brought her foot closer to her hand, but it was out of reach in her current position.

With her last scrap of energy, she channeled everything into her muscles, heaved her chest up, and yelled with pain as the rib sent sparks of agony through her, dislodging Ramira just long enough to give herself extra movement. Grabbing her ankle, she bent her leg further as she started feeling light-headed, struggling to stay conscious. She fumbled for the pummel but couldn't find it. *Where is it?* A spark of understanding flooded her. She was searching on the wrong side of her foot. Her hand crept to the inside.

Ramira's sole focus, in a manic psychosis, was on destroying Chooli's face as she continued pounding it while she cackled with glee.

Chooli found it. With her fingers, she inched the knife out until her hand wrapped around the handle. With one steady swing, using her last reserves of strength, she plunged the blade into Ramira's back and through her ribcage.

Ramira jerked to a standstill, surprise masking her face as she realized she had been outplayed. Blood seeped from the wound. Chooli swiveled the knife several times before extracting it. She brought the blade to her chest and sent the point up behind Ramira's chin, through her windpipe, and into her brainstem. Her body became limp and fell on top of Chooli, choking noises coming from her mangled trachea as she tried getting air into her lungs. Paralyzed, she was now as helpless as Alex as Chooli rolled Ramira off her.

Chooli struggled to a standing position. She leaned over and retrieved the knife from Ramira's throat as she stared into the crazed woman's eyes. She had a mind to let her drown in her own blood. But finding an ounce of compassion somewhere within her, she staggered to her maser, stood in front of Ramira, and pulled the trigger, blasting half her head off and ending her misery.

A profound sadness overcame her as she continued staring at the corpse. It was over, but satisfaction escaped her. She had inflicted the retribution she had intended, but it felt hollow. Something had changed inside of her, broken forever, and she wondered how she would continue her life, knowing every relationship had altered forever because of the chain of events along the path she had traveled.

Exiting her trance, Chooli redirected her concentration to Alex, who still had no mobility. His eyes emanated a sadness, too, as she cut the restraints from his wrists, ankles, and head. She supported him before he flopped from the chair and helped him to the nearest crate, where she rested him on the floor. As she sat beside him, she flopped her head against his. "What have I become?" she whispered.

59

PUNISHMENT FOR MY SINS

Chooli heard fast-approaching police and ambulance sirens as she and Alex continued sitting in silence, Alex because he couldn't talk and Chooli because she had nothing to say. She was numb, her mind on a surreal plane.

Ten minutes later, police stormed the warehouse. Detective Chiang intermingled with the officers as they searched the place. It wasn't long before the police found them. Ramira's corpse lay nearby, a pool of blood congealing on the floor in ever-increasing circles radiating from her stab wounds.

The officers retreated and whispered to someone out of view before Detective Chiang approached Chooli.

"Quite a body count," he remarked.

Chooli nodded.

"Your doing?"

She nodded again.

"How are you doing, Alex?"

"He's paralyzed," she answered for him. "Ramira drugged him."

"Oh." Chiang scanned the room before finding an officer and gestured to him. "Get the medics in here."

"Yes, sir." The officer rushed outside to alert the medics.

Chiang returned his attention to her. He studied her intensely before he said, "I have to take you in for questioning."

Chooli nodded.

"You need to be attended to first. You look like someone's used you as a punching bag."

"I'm alright. But I have two friends out there. One died saving my life. The other fought bravely and may still be alive."

"Well, while we're getting you checked out, we'll look for your friends."

It took another hour before the medics had conducted on-site treatment of Alex and Chooli and searched the array of bodies for any signs of life. The survivors, including Vapdog, were loaded onto gurneys for transport to the Xi Boötis capital hospital, where Chiang placed police guards outside Chooli's and Alex's rooms while they recovered.

He interviewed Chooli in her bed, where she gave him a summary of the course of events, including her suspicions about Milan Asterov. He told her that Alex, whose power of speech had returned, confirmed that Asterov was in league with Riva, and an arrest warrant had been issued for him on multiple charges, including murder.

The only thing Chooli kept hazy were the circumstances behind Vito's death. She just said she killed him and left it at that. Chiang could fill in the blanks.

Her broken rib took a long time to heal since the medics couldn't effectively place healing wraps around her chest to speed up the rebinding. As a result, a spasm of pain shot from her rib to her brain with almost every breath she took, making sleeping a challenge.

After three days, the doctor allowed her to leave her bed to visit Alex.

Despite the indignity of the hospital gown, she strolled down the corridor and into his room, where he lay with several tubes still protruding from his arms and patches on his chest. He had his eyes closed, and his head slumped away from her. She stood in the doorway staring at him, shy for the first time in ages, not wanting to speak for fear of what Alex might say to her, fear he might reject her for her murderous spree. She stayed that way until she became self-conscious and felt foolish. "Hi," she said.

He turned his head and opened his eyelids. He smiled. "Hi." He stared at her with gentle, loving eyes. "Come here."

Reluctantly, Chooli closed the distance to the bedside, her heart pumping with fear.

"I love you."

Tears welled in Chooli's eyes until her emotions overcame her, and she sobbed, the tears overflowing and cascading down her cheeks. "I'm sorry."

Alex looked confused. "For what?"

"What I did. You must hate me. I'm not the same person you met."

"Shh. You haven't changed. Believe me, you haven't changed. Come closer." He extended his closest arm to her and reached behind her head, pulling her to him and kissing her before resting his head against hers. "I love you. You did what was necessary. As you always do."

"Why do I feel so terrible, then?"

"Because of your conscience and your heart. And they are good things to have."

Chooli felt uncomfortable. She wasn't sure if she believed Alex's assessment but left the issue for now. She had plenty of time to contemplate it in the future. "The drug has worn off?"

"Yeah. But they found a secondary problem. I was teetering on the brink of irreversible addiction to chimera stardust. They're flushing it from my system. It takes a while."

"Oh." Words escaped her as she stood in front of him.

Worry lines creased Alex's forehead. "Are you alright? Do you need to talk to someone?"

Chooli shook her head. "I just need to try to understand my actions."

"Time's up, Ms. Richards," the door guard said to her.

She nodded at him and turned back to Alex to kiss him again. "See you soon."

He grabbed her hand and squeezed it. "Soon." He continued to hold her hand as she walked off until the distance became too far, and his hand dropped to the bed.

Chooli returned to her room and flopped onto her bed. Her mind wandered as she recalled the carnage she had inflicted over the past few days. *Had there been another way? What will my parents think when they hear of it?* Her heart went cold; dread engulfed her. She had brought disgrace to her family with her reckless actions. *All I wanted to do was save Alex. Was that so unacceptable?* She sighed. It didn't matter now. *What's done is done, and I must accept the punishment for my sins.*

She closed her eyes and thought sadly of Agate as she dozed off. She bore her no malice. Agate's short, sad life had been corrupted by Ramira and Vito. On Chooli's request, Detective Chiang had found Agate's mother, Bai, and let her know her long-suffering under those two villains was over. Chooli had also told Chiang to be sure he told her that Agate saved her life. She wanted Bai to think her daughter died a hero. *Not any harm in that, is there?* Alex and her father had said never to tell a lie, even for a good reason, but Chooli felt there were always exceptions. And she knew Vapdog would not welcome the attention that having his bravery formally acknowledged would bring.

Chiang had told her that Vapdog was making a steady recovery in a different hospital and would not face charges for his involvement in the slaughter.

———

Voices roused her. For a second, she lay confused over where she was, but the hospital room reminded her of her injuries and confinement. The words became intelligible, and Chooli turned over to see who was speaking. Detective Chiang and Li Meng stood in the doorway. Chiang looked furious, but Meng wore a blank expression.

Chooli blinked the sleep from her eyes. "What's going on?"

"You're being moved," Chiang said, grumpy. "How the GIA can expect us to maintain law and order on the planet when one of their operatives goes berserk and then demand we release you, I don't understand. Nor do I agree with the edict. I intend lodging an official protest."

"You may protest as much as you like."

Chooli sensed the tension in Meng's voice hidden behind a note of authority. Meng clearly considered her demand legitimate, and she was prepared to enforce its compliance. "Authorities at a higher level consider the action necessary for her safety."

"What? You think we can't protect her on Xi Boötis?"

"We have better systems for the task."

The argument between the two of them confused Chooli. What were they talking about, and why were they ignoring her? The more they ignored her, the more irritated she became. She tolerated the conflict no longer. "Will someone explain what is happening?"

They stopped their debate and stared at her as if noticing her for the first time.

"We're moving you to a safe location until you're fit enough to travel," Meng explained.

Chooli tried to fathom what her words meant. "Why?"

Meng glanced at Chiang and turned back to her. "We have credible evidence several gangs on Xi Boötis are planning to execute you and believe your safety is better assured in our hands than the local authorities."

Chiang glared at her. "You're just trying to remove one of your stuff-ups before it becomes an embarrassment."

Exasperated, Meng said, "I'm sick of debating this with you. We both have orders from our superiors. So, let's just do it."

Chiang raised his arms in defeat. "Do what you want." He stormed from the room, calling off the guards as he left.

Chooli studied Meng, trying to figure out what was happening. It made no sense. Why would the GIA care about a rogue agent gone off the reservation? Something else was happening here.

"Why are you doing this?"

"I told you."

"No. I wasn't working for the GIA."

Meng stared at her as if she had gained a new level of respect. "We have orders to transport you to Earth."

"I'm not going anywhere without Alex."

"You and Alex."

60

TO EARTH

"Why?" Chooli asked.

"That isn't for me to say. All I can say is that I have strict orders," Meng said.

"But you can't move Alex yet. He still has toxins being removed."

"He is already on board a GIA transport yacht with a full complement of medical staff and equipment. You will join him."

"What? When were you going to tell me?"

"I wasn't. But, since you asked, I decided I should." She smiled and became less formal. "I wanted to avoid your wrath — I've seen your work."

"Oh." Chooli was unsure whether she felt grateful or resentful. "I didn't mean to do what I did. I just wanted Alex back."

"As I said, I don't want to upset you. Now, pack your belongings, and let's go before people change their minds. Medics will attend to your injuries as we travel."

She jumped from the bed and checked the closet. Her clothes hung there. She dressed and packed her meager possessions into a refuse bag. "Lead the way."

Meng didn't move. She just stared at her for so long it made Chooli uncomfortable.

"What?"

Meng uncovered Chooli's pistol and maser. "You might want these."

"I don't think I need them — but thanks." She grabbed them and strapped the holsters to her legs.

The weapons exchanged, Meng said, "Come," and walked out. The medical staff stared after them as they traversed the corridors to the elevator and the waiting scooter.

Alex tugged at Chooli's GIA dress uniform to remove any creases or misalignments from its presentation. Somehow, agents had delivered her outfit from Caerus. Chooli fidgeted as she allowed him to fuss over her.

"What do you think he wants?"

"I don't know. But if Commissioner Harris orders a confidential meeting, you give him no reason to reprimand you." He completed the preening. "There." He stepped back and inspected her. "Perfect."

"Are you coming?" Chooli asked. She could feel her heart racing.

Alex smiled to himself. His wife faced murderers in open battle without raising a sweat but fronting up to the Commissioner of the GIA was turning her into a bundle of nerves.

"I'm not invited." He gave a supportive smile. "Relax. He probably just wants to see how you're doing."

Chooli threw him an 'Are you for real?' look.

"Yeah, maybe." He checked the chronometer. "You better get moving. You don't want to be late."

"No." She sighed and took a deep breath as she smiled tremulously. "Wish me luck."

Alex kissed her, brushing her lips with his. "You don't need luck. You make your own."

She nodded and left.

An air car waited for her at the hotel entrance. She hopped into it for the brief trip through the Sydney, Australia, skyway to the GIA Headquarters in The Rocks precinct.

Once she approached reception, the clerk contacted the Commissioner's office. After authorization, she gave Chooli a pass to use the restricted elevator to his office level.

She stepped from the elevator, her heart in her throat and stomach nauseous. It was taking all her energy to stop her aureole from revealing just how nervous she was. She straightened her uniform, took a deep breath, and fronted the Commissioner's personal assistant at his desk, standing at attention until the man acknowledged her.

"Agent Chooli Richards here to see Commissioner Harris," she intoned.

"One moment," the assistant said indifferently. He used his comm and spoke into it before breaking the connection and glancing at her. "This way."

He stood. He was slim and a head taller than her. His uniform needed mending. He escorted her to the office door with the Commissioner's name emblazoned and opened it, gesturing for her to enter.

Chooli obeyed and marched in, halting within two meters of Commissioner Harris' desk. The door closed behind her. She stood at attention and waited.

Commissioner Harris stared out the wall-length window behind his desk with his back to her, gazing at the edifice of the Sydney Harbor Bridge.

Beads of sweat developed on her forehead, and she sensed her aureole was ashen, but she had no control over either in her state of mind.

After several minutes, he turned. Whenever Chooli had seen his face in the past, it wore a jovial expression, but today it displayed severe authority, making her heart race more and her trepidation skyrocket.

Without inviting her to sit, he said, "I've read the report detailing the incident on Xi Boötis." He paused to scowl at her as though expecting a reply. But she continued staring straight ahead. From experience, she knew better than to speak without an explicit invitation. It would only make matters worse. "It makes unpleasant reading," he continued. "From one perspective, we could construe these deaths attributed to you as self-defense, except for one." He eyed her. "What do you say to that?"

She took a deep breath. "I was only giving Ramira Lopez a merciful death instead of the alternative, sir."

"I'm not talking about her!"

Chooli blinked as tears misted her eyes while she tried to understand his words. *All my victims were shooting at me, weren't they?*

"Vito Riva!"

Her intestines contorted into a convoluted Gordian knot that threatened to strangle her. "He ... he was about to call for reinforcements."

"He was unarmed!" Toning down his tirade, he continued in a calmer voice. "If it wasn't for that blemish, this might have been a simple matter, but we can't have GIA agents running around shooting defenseless civilians." He sighed. "You leave me no choice."

Dread washed over her, and a wave of light-headedness threatened to make her stumble, but her resolve kept her at attention. Doomed, as predicted. And she had tarnished her name forever. Her family disgraced because of her. Never gaining her father's pride and respect again. She could not bear the humiliation. Despite her strict control, a wayward tear trickled down her cheek.

Pulling herself together and standing erect before him, she said in a steady voice, "Commissioner, I wish to tender my resignation from the GIA, effective immediately."

"I hereby accept your resignation, Agent Richards, and discharge you from the regular GIA service."

Chooli's lower lip quivered. The punishment fit the crime, but that made no difference to her distress. Her life in law enforcement was over forever, almost before it had begun.

"At ease, Ms. Richards," Harris said in a friendlier tone, stepping away and returning to his chair behind his desk.

Chooli obeyed but was not motivated to relax, preferring the statue her body had frozen into, hoping her emotions would similarly harden.

He fidgeted with his stylus for a moment as if contemplating a weighty decision and then gave her his full attention again. "There are other ways you can serve."

"Huh? I mean — what do you mean, sir?"

"We have another division. Covert. Above top secret. Your actions have proven your suitability for it. You have raw talent, so to speak. With proper training and discipline, you could be useful. Should you be interested."

The offer thawed her. She took a step forward. "My desire was always law enforcement, sir. But my deeds prove I'm unworthy."

Harris chuckled. "Sit down, Chooli."

She obeyed, unsure what was coming next.

"You're not suited to normal GIA activities, that's for sure. I'm talking about black ops. Unsanctioned. We can never acknowledge your successes. As for your failures ... if you survive, we will disavow you."

Chooli's heart started beating fast for a different reason now. *Is this for real?* "Who else is in this section?"

"That I can't disclose for security reasons. To be honest, I don't even have a list of everyone in it. And you can tell no one you belong to this organization if you accept my offer. Not your friends, your family, not even Alex."

She worried about the secrecy. "Alex and I don't keep secrets from each other."

Harris raised an eyebrow. "Really?"

"No, not really." She gave him a sheepish grin. "What would my role be in between operations?"

He shrugged. "Train. Develop new weapons and techniques. Whatever keeps you fit and gives you an edge. Your bravery with Vito's men shows you have a natural talent for it. It will make me proud if you accept."

"Pay?"

"Ha! Through an untraceable account. Comparable to the danger we pit you against."

Chooli nodded. She ran the facts through her mind. They sounded unbelievable, but they were true. The risk was the only downside, but she had thrived on it when she faced Vito's attackers.

"Can you give me a cover story so that my family isn't ashamed of me?"

"We'll think of something."

She gazed at him. "I'll do it."

He burst into a beaming smile. "Good. One of our operatives will contact you soon with all the details, including how we will send your assignments to you." Commissioner Harris rose from his chair and rounded the desk, extending his hand when he fronted her.

She stood and shook it. After they released, she was unsure whether to salute and stand at attention. Technically, she wasn't an officer anymore. She saluted anyway.

He reciprocated, still grinning. "Get out of here."

Chooli obeyed and started for the door. Just before she reached for the open button, she turned and said, "He deserved it."

Surprised, Harris stared at her. "Who?"

"Vito. He deserved it."

He smiled. "I know."

Confused but resolute, she continued out of the office and back to the hotel.

61

LET'S GO HOME

Alex tried to keep himself busy while he waited restlessly for Chooli's return. He sensed she was in real trouble and wanted to be there to support her and protect her from the Commissioner's razor-sharp tongue. But he was stuck in the hotel, waiting for her.

Finally, he heard the door open. She rushed to him and wrapped her arms around him, crushing the wind out of him. He caressed her hair. "It's alright." He gently pried themselves apart so he could see her eyes. "What happened?"

She sighed and looked at the floor. "He said my behavior in killing a civilian — Vito Riva — in cold blood was unacceptable for a GIA agent. He could dishonorably discharge me, or I could choose to resign. I resigned."

Her calmness surprised Alex. "And you're OK with that? I thought you would be beside yourself."

"I thought I would be too. But I saw it coming. I accept that to stay in my existing position after Vito would be inappropriate."

"I suppose. What are you going to do?"

Chooli shrugged. "Might start a private investigation firm. Want a job?"

Alex laughed. "No, thank you. Not with you as my boss."

"Hey!"

He shook his head. "What about collateral?"

She released him and went to the bedroom, returning moments later clutching a key.

"What's that?"

"Vito's repository key. I found it on him. Decided I may as well grab it instead of handing his accounts to whoever steps up to take his place."

"But you can't access it."

Chooli grinned. "I opened it with his biometrics and changed the passkey to mine while he was still warm. His funds are mine if I choose to use them."

Her confession shocked Alex. "You conniving rascal! I'd run you in if I weren't married to you." He studied her and marveled at her beauty even though the severe bruises inflicted by Ramira were still visible. He loved her more than ever. "Let's go home."

Chooli glanced up as if to consider his suggestion. "Maybe tomorrow."

"Why? What should we do until then?"

"I have an idea." She grabbed his shirt and pulled him into the bedroom. Once next to the bed, she pushed him backward onto it and jumped on top of him, leaning over to kiss him while fidgeting with his clothes.

Before Alex relaxed and enjoyed the experience, a thought flashed through his mind: *I don't believe a word she just said.*

The End

Subscribe to my Newsletters and receive three free episodes of The Chronicles of Gatacus Todd as well as a (mostly) monthly newsletter from me.

Head to your browser and type
subscribepage.io/g4r4f8
P.S. You can unsubscribe at any time.

ALSO BY JOHN WEGENER

Books

Reach For The Stars Trilogy

FTL

Centauri

Ceti

Reach For The Stars Box Set (Books 1-3)

Loki's Fall

Zodiac Series

Scorpius

Libra

Taurus

Halwende's Legacy Series

Halwende's Redemption

Halwende's Resurrection

Halwende's Reincarnation

Halwende's Legacy Box Set (Books 1-3)

Solar Dawn Series

Lunar Rift

Other Stories

The Dark Ages

SAGI

Short Stories

The Love Particle

ABOUT THE AUTHOR

John Wegener grew up in the Adelaide Hills of South Australia. He now expresses his imaginative dreams by engaging in writing after a 34-year career as a Chemical Engineer in the steel industry, which has taken him to many countries and allowed him to experience many cultures. John currently lives in Wollongong, Australia with his wife and children.

Click on johnwegener.com to find more of my books or read his blogs. Type subscribepage.io/g4r4f8 to subscribe to my emails for more stories and information.

www.ingramcontent.com/pod-product-compliance
Lightning Source LLC
Chambersburg PA
CBHW072104020726
47501CB00003B/702